I0760895

TWILIGHT HORN

BOOK FOUR OF AURA HEALERS HALL

THOMAS K. CARPENTER

Twilight Horn
Book Four of Aura Healers Hall

Hardback Version

by Thomas K. Carpenter

Published by Black Moon Books

Cover design by
G&S Cover Designs

Opening Chapter Image by Grand Failure
Chapter Heading by AnimaPins

Discover other titles by this author on:
www.thomaskcarpenter.com

ISBN-13: 978-1-958498-26-2

TWILIGHT HORN

The Hundred Halls Universe

<u>Season One</u>

THE HUNDRED HALLS
Trials of Magic
Web of Lies
Alchemy of Souls
Gathering of Shadows
City of Sorcery

THE RELUCTANT ASSASSIN
The Reluctant Assassin
The Sorcerous Spy
The Veiled Diplomat
Agent Unraveled
The Webs That Bind

GAMEMAKERS ONLINE
The Warped Forest
Gladiators of Warsong
Citadel of Broken Dreams
Enter the Daemonpits
Plane of Twilight

ANIMALIANS HALL
Wild Magic
Bane of the Hunter
Mark of the Phoenix
Arcane Mutations
Untamed Destiny

STONE SINGERS HALL
Song of Siren and Blood
House of Snake and Tome
Storm of Dragon and Stone
Sonata of Shadow and Thorn
Well of Demon and Bone

THE ORDER OF MERLIN
The Order of Merlin
Infernal Alliances
Tower of Horn and Blood

The Hundred Halls Universe

Season Two

THE CRYSTAL HALLS
Shadows in Amber
The Emerald Eclipse
The Sapphire Strategem
Chains of Obsidian
The Bloodstone Rebellion

AURA HEALERS HALL
Half-Pint Hex
Full Moon Demon
Blood Witch Curse
Twilight Horn
Deathless King

Other Works

ALEXANDRIAN SAGA
Fires of Alexandria
Heirs of Alexandria
Legacy of Alexandria
Warmachines of Alexandria
Empire of Alexandria
Voyage of Alexandria
Goddess of Alexandria

KINGMAKERS SAGA
The Stone Tree
The Crystal Bard
The Ghost Tower
The Champion's Prophecy
The Shadow Labyrinth
The Autumn Empire

OTHER SERIES
The Dashkova Memoirs
Gamers
Mirror Shards

Arcanium loves books
Coterie adores power
Assassins will kill you
Stone Singers has a stone flower

Animalians is a zoo
Alchemists, you'll devour
Tinkers loves gadgets
Protectors makes you cower

Aura Healers wants to fix you
Blue Flame has a tower
Dramatics loves the spectacle
Oculus has grown sour

One Hundred Halls
Each with their own magic
The Patrons protect
Because faez madness is tragic

In the city of sorcery
Invictus is the Head
His students are many
But the foolish end up dead

- A Children's Rhyme

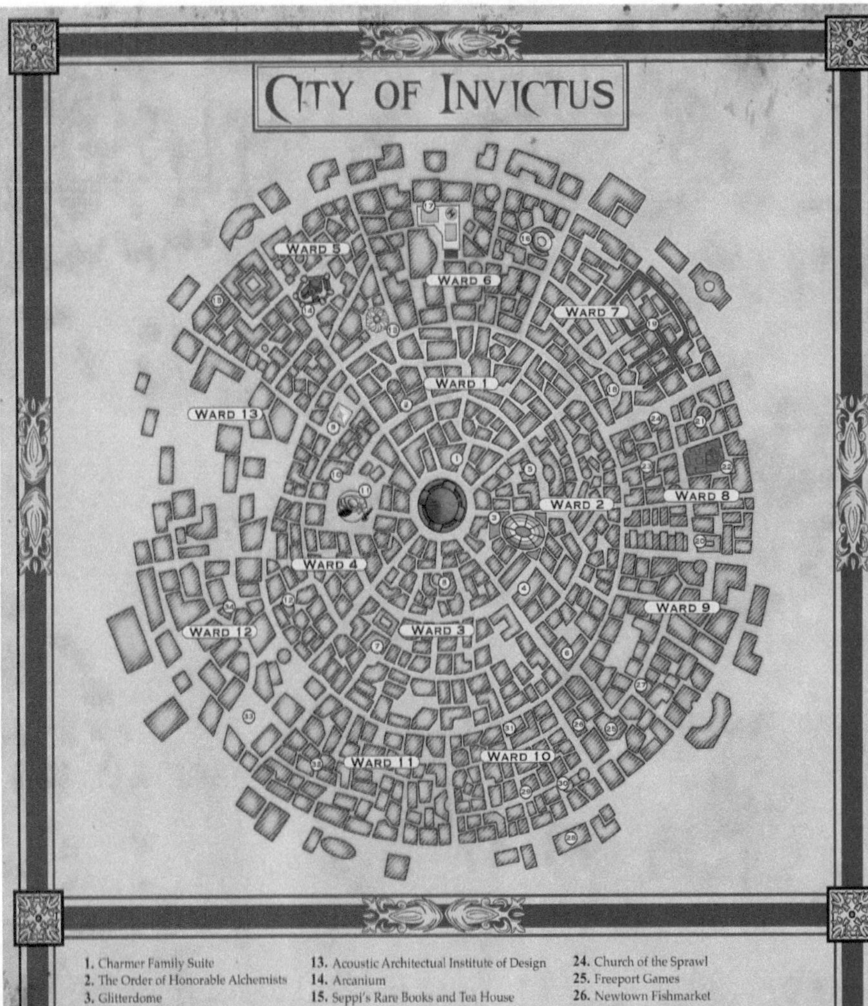

1. Charmer Family Suite
2. The Order of Honorable Alchemists
3. Glitterdome
4. Ashnod's Theater
5. Mystic Chord
6. Herald of the Halls
7. Left Tower Books
8. Protectors
9. Coterie of Mages
10. City Library
11. Statue of Invictus
12. Amber & Smoke
13. Acoustic Architectual Institute of Design
14. Arcanium
15. Seppi's Rare Books and Tea House
16. Museum of Magical Artifacts
17. The Holistic Institute
18. Glass Cabaret
19. The Canal District
20. Oestomancium
21. Animalians
22. Invictus Menagerie and Cryptozoo
23. Goblin's Romp
24. Church of the Sprawl
25. Freeport Games
26. Newtown Fishmarket
27. Uncle Larice's Bodega
28. Royal Society of Illustrius Artificers
29. Wizard's Wax Museum
30. Metallium Nocturn
31. Howling Madwoman's Fortunes and Spells
32. Enoichian District
33. Oba's Autumnal Garden
34. Gamemakers Hall

ONE

The ritual words droned from Remi's lips like the buzzing of cicadas, ebbing and waning with a slight vibrato. Dr. Morsdux circled the patient, lighting candles with a golden burner that flickered in unseen winds.

The cold grasp of the Veil lay at her back. She could feel the emptiness, and sometimes when she glanced down, greenish mist curled around her feet like fingers. Remi maintained the spell as the patient, Elvi Sohkki, was on her last breaths. Wisps of still-blonde hair stuck to her forehead. The wrinkled woman's short heaves were painful to watch, even though Remi knew she'd been given a potent elixir to help ease her to the other side.

The scratching of claws on the window nearly broke Remi's concentration, especially when she noticed an owl on the ledge, peering into the room. Even Dr. Morsdux seemed startled by the appearance of the creature, but he made a motion for Remi to continue.

In uncertain moments, Remi focused on the craft, whether it was picking a lock or enunciating the words of a Veil ritual. The candles flickered in unison, bending towards Remi, which brought a knot to her chest. The bowl of reindeer blood next to the old woman trembled as if there was an earthquake but Remi could feel no vibration in her feet.

Remi glanced to Dr. Morsdux, indicating concern with her eyes, but the skeletal doctor in his white coat merely gestured to continue.

A gurgle formed in Miss Sohkki's throat, the precursor to choking. Dr. Morsdux knelt by her side, casting a relaxation spell on her neck which eased the convulsions, but they would continue until the woman's death.

Focusing on the words helped Remi manage her anxiety. This was the first time she was shepherding a Veil-touched to the beyond. The woman had been an instructor for Alchemists decades ago, but had left the profession when she contracted a ghastly curse while traveling in Danir that had made her susceptible to beings from beyond the Veil. Her final years had been a torment, with constant visits from those that refused to let go. She'd come to them a month ago, having seen her death in a vision, and had asked specifically for Remi to perform the rites which had been a shock to her, but not to Dr. Morsdux.

"The dying see more clearly than the living," he'd said.

The owl remained on the ledge. Remi stared into its wide, all-knowing eyes. Dr. Morsdux had warned her that psychopomps—escorts for the recently dead—sometimes visited the Hospice Ward, but she wasn't expecting to see one on her first ritual.

She stared, transfixed by the stillness of the creature, focusing on the little feathers and tufts of down around its eyes. The cool air from the Veil wrapped around Remi's body like snuggling into bed in winter.

The drift came without warning. Dr. Morsdux said there would be more signs if it happened to her, but she either she wasn't paying attention, or things were different. She didn't have time to ward against it.

One blink.

Remi found herself on a featureless plain wrapped in pale, greenish mist that swirled lifelike along the ground. Scant, skeletal trees stuck out from the bleached soil.

Fear ratcheted up her spine, so she checked to her left. She could still see into the hospital room, which was a good sign, but the fact that she'd Veil shifted was problem enough.

"Stay calm. Stay present. If anything happens, I will protect you," Dr. Morsdux had told her before the ritual.

But now that it was happening, she couldn't help the tremor in her voice. Nor would her gaze stop bouncing from rock to tree, expecting the hounds of the Veil to appear and drag her permanently into their realm.

At first it started with a blotch of darkness on the horizon and then slowly, inexorably, the smear became a figure which gained features until she could see him standing on the ridge opposite.

He was a man.

Or at least looked like a man. Dark hair, the brooding arrogance of a being that has existed for countless lives.

Remi had seen such power in Lady Nimueh, or the Patrons of the Halls, but this being gave her both fear and comfort. She could sense his awful knowledge, the truth of living in a place between the living and the dead, and yet, she could also sense a kernel of familiarity.

Humanity, even.

She would have liked to have seen his face, but he stayed just at the edges, leaving his features hidden by shadow. When his gaze fell upon Miss Sohkki, the old woman's chest heaved upward in a final gasp.

The dark figure continued watching Remi as she kept up the ritual words, determined to help this woman reach her final peace. Sohkki's biggest fear had been that she would get trapped in the Veil, destined to haunt her family until the end of their days.

But rather than slip into the Veil, the old woman's form collapsed into permanent stillness, the last exhale wheezing out like an empty balloon.

As Remi felt herself getting pulled back into the hospital room, the dark figure raised his arm, pointing his index finger at her. He spoke but she couldn't hear the words.

The mists folded around Remi until she was once more standing in the hospital room.

Dr. Morsdux stood opposite, staring at the lifeless body at the center of the ritual candles.

"It is done. You can stop now."

Remi didn't realize she was still chanting. She let the words dribble off her lips as she stared at the flesh that had once been Elvi Sohkki.

Dr. Morsdux led her out of the room. Two ward nurses were waiting. They hurried inside to prepare the body while Remi followed her teacher down to his office, which could have easily been confused for a museum. Numerous ritual items, like a desiccated hand or a glowing ball of orange goo, were contained within glass boxes.

He pulled a bottle of whiskey out of a drawer and poured two glasses, handing one over to Remi.

"It helps with the chill."

"Does it get any easier?" she blurted out.

Dr. Morsdux stared into his glass of amber liquid.

"Once it does, then it's time to retire. It's the second most important moment in a person's life."

He raised his glass.

"But you did admirably. Even with the distractions. I wasn't expecting those difficulties."

Remi took a sip, letting the liquid warm her throat.

"I saw someone in the Veil."

Dr. Morsdux's bushy white eyebrows wagged upward.

"I couldn't see his face, but he seemed like he belonged there. As if he'd come for Miss Sohkki's end."

Remi had only been with Dr. Morsdux for a month, but she was learning his moods and tendencies. His expressions were generally unreadable, as he kept his emotions deep within, but she saw a world of thoughts passing across his eyes and in the squeezing of his lips.

"That's the Stranger."

"The Stranger?"

Dr. Morsdux stared out the window.

"I've only seen him a few times. That he would appear on your first is grim tidings."

"Who or what is he?"

"No one knows, but I'm almost certain he wasn't there for Miss Sohkki."

"Me?"

"I'm afraid so. But this might explain your other gifts."

"Am I Veil touched?"

The doctor's lips flattened.

"It doesn't appear so. But it's something like it. A point to explore during your time here."

"Something like it?"

Dr. Morsdux thought for a second and then poured more whiskey for both of them.

"Every few generations someone is born with special gifts. Maybe they had a near-death experience as a child, or bore witness to a mass casualty event. Or perhaps they were just born in a place near the Veil, but whatever the reason, they have a connection to the land between the living and the dead."

Remi thought about a passage she'd read in the tomes that he'd given her.

"An Ossarii?"

"Yes. An odd name to be sure. The Latin translation is the places where the bones are kept. But Ossariis are known for summoning beings from the Veil as easily as one might bring a mage light into existence. But like I said, there hasn't been an Ossarii for generations. I wouldn't think too much about it. It's unlikely you are since you haven't had any of those experiences."

Remi looked inward for a moment.

"Should I fear the Stranger?"

Dr. Morsdux tapped on his lower lip with a long finger.

"I do not think so, though I would not let your guard down. He seems to appear during fraught moments, or with patients who are particularly troublesome, as if he's hoping for problems. Just do not let him touch you."

"I remember the rule."

"More so in his case."

Remi raised an eyebrow.

"Is there a reason?"

Dr. Morsdux leaned back and smoothed his hand across the front of his desk.

"Call it intuition." He checked the clock on the wall. "You should hurry on. You don't want to keep your instructor waiting."

"Shit," muttered Remi as she saw the time. She downed the whiskey before she sprinted out of the office.

TWO

A woman in a white lab coat carried a box of alchemy supplies past Damon as she headed into the construction area. Damon stuck his head through the hanging plastic to see a small alchemical laboratory in what had once been a waiting room. A half dozen workers were busily setting up the space. The equipment was all brand new. Damon spotted the newest and most expensive titration machine on the market in the corner.

"Jeb getting a satellite lab?" he asked the nearest worker.

The guy looked up with a frown.

"Who's Jeb?"

"The head Alchemist," said Damon, confused.

"We don't work for him."

"And?"

A woman brushed past Damon carrying a box full of plants, which she set on the table.

"You don't work for Marcus."

"Marcus? As in Dr. Marcus Broomfield?" asked Damon.

"This is his private research lab. He explicitly does not allow visitors."

"What are you researching?"

The woman's forehead knotted.

"That's up to him to tell you. Please remove yourself from the room."

"I have to get to a meeting with him anyway. Thanks for nothing."

The entire class was already waiting in their common area, except all the couches and other comfortable spaces had been removed and replaced with hard plastic chairs the color of vomit.

A stern-looking doctor with skin the color of bruised onyx stood behind a table covered in medical tomes. His hands remained clasped behind his back as if he were contemplating punishments for an unknown crime. He was more youthful than Damon would have guessed, but age was difficult to determine in a world of sorcery and enchantment.

"Are you waiting for an invitation?" asked Dr. Broomfield.

"Oh? Sorry."

Damon had the brief urge to introduce himself but something in the doctor's eyes told him that it wouldn't be welcomed. So he found a seat with the others, checking to Lily when he saw that Remi wasn't present yet.

As the second hand hit the top of the round clock, Dr. Broomfield stepped to the door and turned the lock.

"Good morning, Aura Healer fourth-year students. I'm Dr. Marcus Broomfield, your new lead instructor and head of the Cursed Ward. I would—"

His speech was interrupted by the rattling of the door. Remi stood outside with a confused expression. She knocked, but when Sasha, who was closest, half stood to let her in, Dr. Broomfield waved her back.

"If you can't be on time, you can't be an effective healer," said Dr. Broomfield.

Remi spread her arms wide.

"I was with a patient," came her muffled voice through the window in the door.

Dr. Broomfield faced the class.

"Now where were we? I was saying—"

Remi stepped through the open door, deftly sliding her picks back in a fanny pack before taking the final empty seat next to Damon.

The glare from Dr. Broomfield could have started a forest fire. Remi spoke under her breath without moving her mouth.

"He's a fun one."

"Good morning again. Despite the inadequacies of your previous instructor, I'm here to put you on the right path to becoming a passable healer, and more importantly, a great supporting cast for the doctors of Golden Willow, or whatever facility would dare take a chance on you."

Dr. Broomfield reached under the table to produce a plastic bin, which he slammed onto the table.

"First things first, I want you to get rid of those childish divining rods. We're a serious hospital, not a playground for fake wizards."

"It's not a wand," muttered Lily.

"Yeah," said Remi. "I was skeptical at first, but Dr. Decker taught us a lot of ways to use them effectively."

Dr. Broomfield sizzled with barely contained anger.

"It wasn't a suggestion."

He snapped his fingers.

"Quickly now, get rid of that superstitious crap, or would you prefer me to tell Dr. Fairlight you all failed?"

The class hesitated, but eventually everyone climbed to their feet and dropped the rod into the bin. Damon followed the others, grabbing Remi's arm to pull her standing so she didn't get in more trouble.

"Now, that wasn't so hard. First, I know that your previous instructor encouraged a lot of risky behavior, especially from a small subset of this class. I am putting you on notice right now that freelancing will not be tolerated. Second, I've seen that your rigorous studies have been neglected, leaving you woefully underprepared."

He gestured towards the stacks.

"Each one of those is your reading material for the semester. There will be a new one in January. You'll be expected to master them each in order, and I will be testing for competence. There will be a daily meeting, plus weekly reviews with me where I will clearly explain your deficiencies so that you may improve. These reviews aren't a conversation, so I'll expect you to listen carefully and take notes. Next I want to talk about professional behavior."

He raised an eyebrow at Sasha's Union Jack undershirt.

"And dress. I know other doctors are lenient when it comes to the grabass and other chicanery that goes on with Aura Healer students, but let this be a warning now. If I catch word that any of you are sleeping with the staff, either on or off property, organizing your little games, or playing pranks on each other, I will fail you immediately. Is that understood?"

"No more funsies?" asked Boon, falling back into his chair with the back of his hand against his forehead like a damsel in distress.

"Healer Davis, will you please sit up straight as befitting your station and take those damn earrings out. You're a healer, not a high schooler at a gym rave."

"My earrings?" asked Boon.

"Was I not clear?"

Boon reluctantly removed his earrings and placed them in the front pocket of his scrubs.

Before he'd arrived, Damon had been excited to meet Dr. Broomfield. The doctor was a fellow therianthrope, a grizzly bear, and had contacts throughout the therianthrope community. In fact, he'd worked at the major research facility that Damon aspired to join after Aura Healers. It would give him a chance to help other young therianthropes who'd encountered issues during their pubescent years.

Even after the terse start, Damon had been trying to keep an open mind, but it was growing increasingly harder. The doctor seemed to want to run them like a military hospital.

"To show that I'm not all bad," said Dr. Broomfield, "I'm offering a reward for your help in my research. On top of your reading material is a pamphlet explaining the details, but the short version is we're looking for a unique mixture that could revolutionize medical elixirs by making them more effective and easier to ingest. If you're able to solve the alchemical problem, then I will help get you into the post-Aura Healers facility of your choice. I have many contacts within the industry, whether it's research or hands-on work. My word goes a long way. Any questions?"

No hands went up. After a few seconds, Dr. Broomfield nodded towards the piles.

"Class dismissed. I'll see you in an hour at the fourth wing nurses station for a review of your curse testing techniques. Don't be late."

Before he could make it out of the room, Damon surged to cut him off.

"Is there a problem?" asked Dr. Broomfield.

His eyes searched Damon, making him hesitate.

"I don't have all day."

"The Institute for Childhood Therianthropic Studies—"

"Yes. I served as a Fellow at the Institute."

"I would like, it's what I want to do, I'm a member of Zev clan. It happened when I was in the middle of my first change, I want to help others like me."

Dr. Broomfield faced him. The stiffness in his jaw softened.

"I am aware, but I must warn you that any recommendations will have to be earned. I don't do charity. Is that understood?"

"It is," said Damon, nodding vigorously.

"I don't think you do."

His gaze shot to Lily and Remi standing in the hallway waiting for him.

"Your background speaks to your promise and you have the right history for a role at the Institute, but they only take the best, and right now, I would only count you slightly above average in this middling pack."

The words cut deep, but Damon steeled himself from reacting.

"Finding the solution to my problem would go a long way to earning that recommendation. Good day, Mr. Wolfhard."

"Thank you, Dr. Broomfield."

Damon almost followed him out, but he walked over to the whiteboard that had been shoved into the corner. The doodles that usually filled the empty space had been erased. Damon was about to turn back towards the hallway when he caught the reflection on the closet window.

He shifted the board to the side to find a message written on the back. Damon recognized the handwriting, not that it wasn't clear who the author was immediately.

"Rule #10: All rules were once good ideas drained of life by well-meaning bureaucrats. Follow accordingly."

THREE

The Mists revealed itself to Lily without the spells she'd been forced to cast previously. Since her sister had started working for Lady Nimueh, Lily's visits had grown easier. The warm glow of gaslight mixed with the catcalls from the workers on the balcony made her smile despite herself.

"Hey gorgeous, you sure you don't want to come up and see me? I promise you the night of your life, Miss Lily."

The heavyset woman on the balcony was wearing a black teddy that highlighted her ochre skin and the corkscrew horns sticking from the loose curls of her dark hair.

"Good evening, Miss Divine. Your horns look lovely this evening."

"You'd be surprised what I can do with them, but you never gonna to find out unless you come up and see me. I do recall Lady Nimueh saying you can have one on the house. It would be my pleasure if you choose me."

Lily chuckled to herself.

"Have you seen my sister?"

She could have gone in to check, but since Neko was with her, she knew that Lady Nimueh would prefer she stay outside, and getting on the bad side of a powerful being like her was always a poor idea.

The double red doors split wide, revealing her younger sister Alice. While Lily had been regularly visiting Alice since she'd chosen to stay in the city of sorcery, she was always surprised how she'd transformed herself. Gone were the pastoral peasant dresses that Biddy would have approved of, replaced with black leather pants, a cream top that showed off her milky pale shoulders, and an updo that turned her auburn hair into a scorpion tail.

"Love the eyes," said Lily when she embraced her sister.

Alice pulled back, cheeks hinting crimson. She touched the corners where the stylized lines made her eyes catlike.

"They're functional as well. Helps me see anything that might be trying to hide its true nature, which happens more often than you'd think. Some people are going to be shite no matter what."

"You don't look like the same girl who came here last year," said Lily as she hooked her sister's arm. "I was thinking we might—"

"I have a place I'd like to take you," said Alice suddenly.

The intensity in her gaze, the nervousness hiding a tremble in her lower lip—these told Lily that her sister had something important to show her.

"Lead on."

As they strolled through the mists, exiting Lady Nimueh's protected area and entering the regular streets, Lily noticed that her sister was wearing powdered makeup to hide black lines snaking up her neck. They'd discussed the effects of the corruption previously, but Lily didn't want to ruin a good night with heavy talk.

Alice led her to a bright café tucked between a busy nightclub and a bakery. An older woman with a fire-tongued lizard on a leash was eating a bagel while her pet was shooting flame at a curious cat that kept hissing from a distance.

"Cryptid Café," said Lily, peering at the illusionary sign floating above the sidewalk.

"We like to come here."

"We?"

Alice's cheeks burned as her cheerful expression twisted with concern. "Be nice. Please."

Her sister pulled her into the café. The place was packed with people their age, fellow students or travelers to the city, sitting at round tables while humanoids the size of a small child covered in knotted hair moved between the people. The small beings had bright, golden eyes that peered out from their brown and sometimes whitish hair.

"Are those…?"

"Pucas. Yes."

To Lily's left, an older woman had a puca sitting across from her. The little creature was chattering in barely recognizable English. Half the words sounded made up while the other half matched the gibberish of children.

"I never thought I'd see the day when a whole gang of pucas were working in a café."

"Better than stealing from cupboards and closets to survive." Alice grabbed her hand and tugged her towards the back. "Mag is in the corner."

A handsome young hob with mottled skin was reading a book while enjoying a cup of coffee. His open-collared shirt was unbuttoned halfway down his hairy chest. He smiled and set down his reading when Alice arrived, pulling her in for a long kiss.

"Mag, this is my sister Lily. Dear sister, this is my boyfriend, Mag."

"Lovely to meet you, Mag."

"You as well," he replied in a Boston accent.

As Lily sat, she caught a whiff of brimstone and reflexively stiffened.

"Mag," said Lily, tasting the name.

"Short for Magninnin."

"That's a Fomorian name," said Lily.

"It is. My mother was full blooded." He raised an eyebrow. "It's not a problem, is it?"

A hundred replies shot through Lily's head, but every one of them sounded like something that Biddy would say.

"Of course not. If my sister likes you then I know you're a good soul. But should her judgement prove incorrect, know that I can bring the heavens down around your head. I love my sister more than anything."

The playful glint in Mag's gaze was followed by the inclination of his head.

"I wouldn't have it any other way."

A tugging on her sleeve had Lily looking down into the wide, golden eyes of a puca.

"No black wind the fable came?"

The lack of fear in the creature's eyes made Lily swallow any retort that was lurking on her tongue. The pucas in Ireland tended to nuisance in the best of times, and outright destruction when things were bad.

The puca left her side, wandering to more receptive tables.

"Strange..."

"It was for me at first too," said Alice with her hand in Mag's lap.

"What do you do?" asked Lily.

Mag cleared his throat and sat up straight.

"I'd like to get into finance, but it's hard to get my foot in the door."

Alice's expression turned fierce.

"He's aced all their entry tests. He'd be better than most of those idiots that they take only because it's their cousin's son, or some other nepo shite."

Lily almost missed the glance of absolute adoration from Mag as she defended him. He was clearly infatuated with Alice.

"I'm sorry. People can be right bastards, even in the city of sorcery," said Lily.

"Not all of it is, you know. Some of it's just hard to get through the family legacy bullshit. Half those places are filled with the same stupid families. Dupont. Lockwood. Bishop. Dreadmarsh. I throw up inside every time I hear one of those names," said Mag.

"Why finance?"

Mag wrinkled his nose, which revealed long canines.

"I'm good with numbers, and honestly, that they don't want me makes me want it more. I really thought things would be easier here than Boston."

"Was Boston bad?"

He pulled the sleeve of his shirt up, revealing a thick scar on the interior of his forearm.

"A bunch of kids threw me off a building when I was fourteen. Lured me up there with the promise of 'seeing a baby dragon salamander,' then they launched me over the side and I landed on a chain-link fence. Lucky my auntie was a shaman, or it would have been worse."

He moved his fingers, but only the first three shifted while the pinky was locked into place.

"Want me to drive to Boston and put a hex on those kids?" asked Lily.

Mag tilted his head.

"Part of me wants to say yes, but no, no thank you, it'd only make them worse."

Seeing the way the story was affecting them both, Lily wanted to shift the conversation to something less fraught.

"How did you two meet?"

The couple stared into each other's eyes, smiles growing on their lips.

"I was on my way back to my apartment after work when I heard a lovely singing voice."

The hob's cheeks burned crimson.

"I didn't know anyone was listening. Was waiting for the bus."

"It's quite lovely. Mag wanted to be in the school musical, but they'd only let him play the evil henchman, which didn't have a speaking or singing part."

"It's nothing, Alice. Really."

"It's more than nothing. They're a bunch of arseholes."

"Maybe I could hear you sing sometime," said Lily.

Mag hung his head.

"Maybe."

Alice put her hand flat on the table.

"Did you see the news last week?"

"I'm happy to see the inside of my eyelids. No time for the news," said Lily.

"The botany Hall is growing an Eó Ruis tree."

"What?"

Lily leaned against the table.

"They can't grow outside of Ireland. Or the Fae. Not a true one, anyway. Tell me this is just a bloody fake."

"Apparently, they can. Arcane Phytology is growing a lot of things that supposedly can't be grown outside of their home environments."

"I don't understand," said Mag. "Wouldn't being able to grow it be a good thing?"

Lily frowned, knowing she sounded more like Biddy than herself.

"It is, but—"

"My sister likes to believe that our home is a special place."

"It *is* a special place. The Eó Ruis trees in Ireland are like ley lines. They help hold the magic in the soil and air."

"I think it's a good thing, sister," said Alice. "They're growing them because of the corruption of the Fae. In case that realm is lost forever."

Lily squeezed her hands into fists.

"What does it matter if they can regrow the trees if I lose my family?"

Alice reached across the table and grabbed Lily's hands, forcibly unclenching them.

"We'll find a solution. I know you won't let us down."

As Lily looked into her sister's eyes, she saw the little squiggles of black in the whites. No amount of makeup could hide the fact that the kalkatai was slowly claiming Alice and the rest of her family. She'd long hoped that the end stage would be decades away, but now she could see that it was growing closer by the day.

The buzz of her phone on the table startled them to laughter.

"Bloody fucking ringer."

Lily grabbed it only to see a message from Dr. Broomfield calling her back to the hospital for an emergency meeting.

"Fucking wanker," she said.

"Problems?"

"I apologize, but I have to return to Golden Willow. But it was lovely meeting you, Mag. If you need anyone cursed to let you into the finance business, please let me know. It would be my pleasure."

"Thank you," he said earnestly.

Before Lily left the café, she checked back to her sister and her boyfriend. They looked happy as they stared into each other's eyes. A few years ago she couldn't have pictured one of her sisters with a Fomorian, but seeing how much Alice was in love made Lily want to tear a hole in the world to fix the corruption.

"I swear it, sister. I'll find a way to fix it. I swear it on my magic. All of it."

FOUR

The woman in the sequined red outfit burst into flames next to their table while the other customers applauded. Remi gulped from her nightshade-infused whiskey, hoping the energy boost would kick in quickly.

"Do you not like this place? We can go somewhere else," Damon said.

Remi forced a smile despite her exhaustion. She'd finished a double shift, but hadn't wanted to disappoint Damon by rescheduling their date.

"No, it's lovely," she said, gesturing towards the enormous illusion of a dragon swooping over the streets from their balcony. They had an amazing view of the second ward from the balcony of the restaurant. "I'm just tired is all. Broomfield keeps adding extra shifts on top of my hospice work."

"How is the old death ward?"

Remi jawed at the empty air, searching for words.

"It feels...right?"

Damon leaned back in his chair and smoothed the front of his jacket.

"That wasn't the word I was expecting you to use."

She looked across the city at the way the lights reflected on the massive Spire at the center. It felt like a dream meant for someone else.

"I know it doesn't seem like we do anything. We don't cure any diseases, or fix anyone. Not in this life. But it's important."

Damon reached across the table and set his hand over hers. It was warm.

"As long as it's important to you, it's important to me."

She could see the doubt in his eyes, but their conversation was interrupted by the waiter arriving to refill their water.

"How are the twins?" she asked afterwards.

"Taking the world by storm. I can't believe it's their second year already. Nat was the lead in the Dramatics season opener, The Five Halls, and Talia already earned her spot in the detective wing of the Hall for her final two years."

"Parents doing okay?"

Damon wrinkled his nose.

"They're taking ballroom dancing lessons. Don't know if I can see my father doing that, but supposedly they're enjoying it. Do you ever think you'll hear from your parents?"

Remi shot an angry retort of air from her lips.

"If they do, they'll show up wanting something. You know what, I don't want to be here. Can we grab some street food and just take in the sights?"

"You really want to walk around after a double shift?"

"I took one of Jeb's elixirs before I left. Along with the nightshade infusion, it's making me antsy."

Damon threw some bills on the table and they headed for the exit. The streets were busy on this late September evening. It was nice enough the tourists were out in force, gawking at the illusions or buying cheap trinkets from the sidewalk vendors. A leashed bonbour demon caused a stir at the corner near the Glitterdome, but they strolled past, not interested in the harmless creature that looked like a monkey jester.

"Check out that busker," said Remi as she ate her caramel chocolate ice cream cone.

"Huh?" asked Damon.

Remi gestured towards a woman in silvery tights making her fingers grow at an alarming rate for the gathered crowd. The noises of disgust were drowned out by the delight and laughter.

"Anything feel weird to you here?"

Remi checked over her shoulder.

"Now that you mention it, I feel like someone's watching us."

Damon started reaching to his front pocket to check his wallet, so Remi swatted his hand away.

"Thieves like to make people nervous so they give away the location of their valuables."

He held out a clawed hand.

"I think they'd rather find easier prey."

That was the moment Remi saw them.

She spotted Big Al first, since she was hard to miss, and once she knew the Scythe Sisters were lurking about, she checked the other parts of the crowd, finding Nina the Knife and Halley after the first scan.

"I figured out who's watching us..."

"Who?"

The three sisters approached once they'd been spotted. Adelaide, or Big Al, had wrestled in the heaviest categories in her high school until she broke a girl's neck for taunting her during the competition. She had small, beady eyes like a trapped rat, and most of the other inmates underestimated the big woman, but Remi knew how cunning she was.

On the other hand, Nina the Knife was exactly what she looked like. Her face was filled with too many angles, and in another life, maybe she could have been a model, but there was something dark and petty in her brown eyes. She'd held a girl down, cut off all her hair, and then made slices in her cheeks that never quite healed right—all for accidentally bumping into Nina in the chow line.

And the last time Remi had seen the youngest, Halley, it was when she was getting hauled away on a stretcher, head bleeding profusely from hitting the concrete after she'd pushed her. It was the reason she'd spent the last few weeks in solitary at Utica. But there was something different about Halley that made Remi's stomach turn queasy. Halley looked like she was barely paying attention, yet she stunk of supernatural awareness.

"I thought I smelled something rotten," said Remi.

Nina flashed a blade, but Big Al grabbed her arm and nodded towards the knot of police officers standing on the other corner.

"How did a slimy pap smear like yourself get into the Halls?" asked Big Al.

"Did they forget to change your diaper before they let you out of Utica? We smelled you long before we saw you," said Remi as she tried not to stare at Halley, who was standing like an automaton with a blank expression.

"Nice looking cherry," said Big Al, gesturing towards Damon. "Is this a badger game?"

"This is my boyfriend."

"He smells like death," said Halley without a trace of emotion.

"I'm glad to see Halley's okay. I never meant to hurt her. I just didn't want her hurting my friend," said Remi.

"She's not the same Halley you knew," said Big Al, flashing crooked teeth.

"I don't think it'd be a good idea to mess with us," said Damon, showing off his claws.

"Werewolf, huh?" asked Big Al. "Do you let him mount you when he's changed? You know the old saying, when you lie down with dogs, don't be surprised when you get fleas."

The urge to ask the Scythe Sisters to walk away from their feud was strong, but she knew that people like them couldn't be scared away with nice words.

"If you want to play, we can arrange a time. I'm not the same person you knew in Utica either," said Remi, coaxing a ball of flame in her palm.

Halley's hand twitched and a shroud of cold surrounded Remi, making her shudder and swallow the elemental magic until it puffed out. Damon stepped towards Halley, but Big Al moved into the way. The standoff fizzled when a police officer wandered past, giving them the side eye as he reached for a shock wand in his belt.

"It was lovely seeing you again, Miss Wilde," said Big Al, flourishing a graceful bow. "Come on, you two. We've made our point. We'll be seeing you both soon, I'm sure. Don't let your guard down."

The Scythe Sisters backed away before disappearing into the crowd.

"Shame we weren't somewhere more private," said Damon, flexing his clawed hands.

"Don't underestimate the Scythe Sisters, especially Big Al. I've seen her take down three big guards without breaking a sweat. I've always assumed they had supernatural blood, but now I'm almost certain."

"What was with the odd one?"

Remi shook her head.

"She wasn't like that before. She was the most normal of the three. I didn't want to fight her, but she tried to hurt my friend. That injury changed her. Whatever that was she did back there, it felt like the Veil."

"Sometimes injuries can wake latent abilities," said Damon.

"As if they weren't problem enough." She shook her head. "Sorry about my past ruining our night out. To think I thought that I could avoid it."

"It's okay," said Damon, pulling her against his chest. "Since it's probably not safe to wander around just the two of us, we could head back and spend the rest of the night in my room."

A smile bloomed to her lips.

"That sounds like an excellent idea."

FIVE

The line for tickets at Ashnod's Theater stretched around the block. Damon's foot bounced at the thought that he might be late for Nat's big play. He'd really wanted to take Remi, but since their last date a few weeks ago, she'd been too busy with Dr. Broomfield's extra work.

A presence at his back had him spinning around with his claws out only to find a smallish guy with glasses holding out a ticket.

"Are you Damon?"

"Yeah."

"Nat wanted me to give this to you. She would have been out here herself, but she's getting ready."

He accepted the ticket and the guy ran off, disappearing into the theater.

Damon found his way inside. The attendant pointed him towards the front of the theater on the right side. Better seats than he could have found himself. Nat must have cashed in a favor to get him this spot, since it was the hot show in the second ward.

The other guests around him were all wearing suits and dresses, making him feel out of place in his fresh scrubs. A change in schedules had freed him up for the evening, and he'd rushed out, texting his sister right away. He'd hoped that Talia could have joined him, but she was on a training trip in Krakatow.

An itchy feeling between his shoulder blades had him checking the people behind him. He didn't see any of the Scythe Sisters, but the uncomfortable sensation didn't dissipate, leaving him with the surety that someone was watching him.

After the Scythe Sisters had shown up at their date, Remi had made her friends promise not to wander off alone, which Damon realized he'd violated in his haste to support his sister. But the middle of a busy play was hardly the place for revenge. If they were the ones watching, he could expect them to make their move in the bathroom, or after the play on his way back to Golden Willow.

The lights went down not long afterwards, which set the hairs on the back of his neck standing.

"It's not like they're snipers or something," he muttered to himself.

Damon's concerns evaporated the moment the curtains went up and he caught a glimpse of a blonde woman sitting at a table in an old tavern. It took him a second look to realize it was Natasha in a wig. He checked the playbill to confirm she was a young Celesse D'Agastine. The play was about the early years of the Hundred Halls and how the first five Halls were formed.

The idea that it was his sister on stage fell by the wayside as he quickly became enraptured by the story. Damon was no judge of acting talent, but he saw how easily his younger sister embodied the famous patron as she sparred with the other four while they worked out the earlier details of how the university would function.

Damon knew little about the early history of the Halls, but he could easily see how hard it would have been to combat the superstitions about magic. Had it only been the five of them, they wouldn't have managed, but with the power of the former Head Patron Invictus, they overcame the political and societal resistance to the existence of magic.

When the end of the play came, Damon was on his feet along with the rest of the audience in rapturous applause. He couldn't have been prouder of his sister as she stood at the center of the group bowing and waving.

Then the spotlight shifted up to a balcony, revealing the real Celesse D'Agastine whistling loudly with her fingers between her teeth. The applause turned thunderous after that display and lasted for longer than Damon thought possible.

Damon headed backstage when the audience started filing out. The security had his name on the list, so he hurried past the crew in their black outfits until he found the actors' section.

To his surprise, he found his sister still in her wig talking to the real Celesse. Natasha broke away and threw herself into a big hug while the head of Alchemists Hall looked on with curiosity.

"Celesse, this is my big brother, Damon. He's a fourth year at Aura Healers."

Damon had been around older mages before, but the intensity of her presence had him stammering his greeting as he shook her hand.

"It's...to meet you."

Nat put her hand on his shoulder.

"You can see why he's a healer, not an actor."

Damon gave his sister a playful punch on the arm.

"Not only are you an actor, but you're amazing. I kept forgetting it was you under that wig. Especially during the battle scene. When did you learn those spells?"

"She's quite talented," said Celesse. "I've seen a lot of actors play me, but I've never felt more proud than Nat's portrayal. You have a bright future in front of you."

Nat gave the elder mage a quick curtsey.

"I have to go, but congratulations on your play and good luck in the future, though I don't think you'll need it." Celesse winked at Damon. "Keep your sister safe."

After Celesse was gone, Nat started bouncing on her feet like a pogo stick.

"Can you believe that? I'm so glad you were here or Talia would *never* believe me. I noticed her about halfway through the play and I almost flubbed my lines. I'm still jittery from the end."

Damon put his arm around her shoulders.

"I couldn't be prouder. I heard Mom and Dad might come out before the end of your run."

"Maybe we could all go out afterwards?"

"Maybe," said Damon. "The hospital has been crazy, especially with our new head instructor. But I'll try my best."

"Do you have time tonight? We're headed out to the Mummer's Delight to celebrate."

"I have to get back. My shift starts in five hours," he said, lifting his shoulders.

"They work you so hard."

"It's for a good reason."

"I know, I know. But I thought I'd see you more since we came to the Halls. Except for, you know, it hasn't been much."

"Speaking of," said Damon.

Nat glanced around.

"He's not back, is he?"

"No. But some people from Remi's past showed up in the city a few weeks ago. Three sisters. They're looking to get revenge for something that happened at Utica. I had a weird feeling earlier, as if someone was watching, so please be careful. I don't think they'd go after you or Talia, but Remi said they're capable of anything. Make sure you stay with a group."

"You don't have to worry about me," said Nat, adding a crisp salute.

"I'm serious. I know you and Talia can take care of yourselves, but they could really hurt you."

"You're the one that needs to be careful. You came all this way alone."

"I know, I'll take a cab home right away."

The other actors looked like they were gathering, so Damon pulled Nat in for a long hug.

"Have fun tonight and congratulations on getting those kinds of kudos from Celesse herself."

Nat lifted a single shoulder.

"Well, Celesse is the star of the show, so I can see why she would like this version."

"Stop deflecting. Go have fun."

Damon worked his way out from the busy backstage. The seats were empty except for cleaning staff. He made his way outside only to find the sidewalk empty with no taxis available.

After confirming no one was nearby, he turned up the street while on the lookout for a ride. He spotted a beat-up taxi with one dim headlight swing around the corner headed his way.

As he waved it down, a tall woman with pale blonde hair came shuffling out of a doorway after the same taxi. She had ice-blue eyes and was built like an athlete in a simple business dress.

"I already waved at it," he told her.

"I'm late for meeting," she said in a Scandinavian accent. "Please, all other taxis headed to Glitterdome for Garbage Kings concert."

The stadium was a few blocks away and he could hear the thumping of the bass as the building lit up with colorful illusions.

The taxi pulled up next to them.

"Who am I taking?" asked the driver through an open window.

"I was here first," said Damon, as that itchy feeling between his shoulder blades returned.

"Please," said the woman. "This city is very confusing. I thought I was staying at big hotel, but it is this shithole next to the theater. Could we share cab at least?"

"Where are you headed?"

"North side of first ward."

Damon sighed.

"That's on my way."

He reached towards the door handle with the intent of opening it for the woman when he looked through the window at the driver. He wasn't the usual that Damon expected. Tall, handsome, but wearing clothes that didn't match his looks. There was nothing that stuck out, but he remembered Remi's stories about the cons they'd pulled when she was younger.

"You know what," said Damon, "why don't you take it?"

"No, no, it is okay. I would feel terrible if I took your cab. Isn't sharing best?"

Damon backed away.

"I think I'll take the train. Not feeling like sitting in a stuffy car."

When the woman glanced into the taxi, Damon knew something was definitely wrong. He kept moving backwards until the woman finally climbed into the back of the vehicle and the two sped away, leaving Damon alone on the street.

The feeling of danger had passed, but he couldn't understand why those two had been after him. Maybe it'd been a random con? Or perhaps the Scythe Sisters had employed others to take him to them. Either way, he wasn't getting in any taxis. The train station was a few blocks away and he didn't feel entirely safe until he was sitting in a train car heading back towards the sixth ward.

SIX

The orangish-red chits on the door told Lily that the patient inside had a fire problem. She entered to find a middle-aged man sitting on a fireproof blanket with none of the normal equipment nearby and scorch marks on the insulated ceiling.

"Good morning, Mister Balakrishnan," said Lily, hearing the exhaustion in her own voice.

"Hello—"

His greeting was interrupted by a belch of flame that licked out his lips. He threw his hand over his mouth in apology.

"It's okay, Mister Balakrishnan, I've seen this problem before."

"You have? And you can call me Amir."

"I'm Healer Lily, and yes. It's not entirely unusual, though the volume of flame that you're emitting is. Can you tell me how it happened? Did you run afoul of a hag or another powerful hexer?"

The exasperation in his eyes was palpable.

"I wish. My Fatima told me not to order chalta from home anymore, that there were ramped curses affecting the supplies in the region, but I love them dearly. They're so sweet and tangy like nothing else."

Amir rested his fingertips on his lips with the memory of the flavor in his eyes.

"Chalta?"

"Elephant apples, but with cities encroaching on the swamps where they're grown, they're hard to come by anymore. I thought I found a reputable vendor, but—"

His explanation was interrupted by a gout of flame that scorched the end of the bed. Amir held his throat with a grimace.

"Oh, it's the worst heartburn ever."

"Cursed fruit," said Lily.

Even though it wasn't related, she couldn't help but think about the kalkatai. It was the kind of thing that was happening in the Summer Fae because of the corruption—a problem she still hadn't figured out a way to fix, despite long hours of research. There wasn't a library or bookstore in the city she hadn't visited looking for tomes on realm-wide curses.

"Healer Lily?"

"Hmmm, oh yes, apologies, I was thinking about the proper counter for the cursed fruit," she lied.

"You'll be able to fix it?"

"The cursed fruit?"

"My flame breath."

Lily put up a professional smile despite her flagging energy levels.

"Of course, Amir. Let me order you an elixir from the alchemy lab. I'll have it sent up right away. It should take care of the problem, but we'll have you stick around for a few hours to confirm its effectiveness."

Lily stepped into the hallway, resisting the urge to lean against the wall and catch a nap. She typed out an order and sent it to the lab, then after a moment of consideration, added an energy elixir for herself.

She swung by the nurses station to pick up the charts for the next group of patients while she waited for the elixir to arrive. Lost in reading, she didn't realize someone was standing next to her until she glanced up to see a young woman with a head full of messy brown curls and more freckles than the night sky.

"How long have you been bloody standing there?" asked Lily in surprise.

The girl, wearing scrubs, Lily realized, swallowed as she stared back at her.

"Do I have something on my face?" asked Lily, touching her skin.

"No," said the girl in a squeak.

"Daryna," said Lily, reading her name tag. "You're a first year, aren't you? I think I've seen you in the cafeteria."

"You have?" asked Daryna breathlessly.

"It's a big hospital, but it's not that big. Can I help you?"

Daryna swallowed and stared at her white shoes.

"I'm working for Jeb."

"And?"

"I have your potions."

"Where are they?"

Daryna let out a noise that sounded like a mouse had been stepped on.

"I'm such an idiot, I left them in the lab. I'll be right back."

The first year burst away, speeding towards the open elevator doors and narrowly throwing herself through the gap much to the horror of the family inside.

"First years..."

Lily heard a snort and glanced up to see Nurse Tishanti smirking.

"I wasn't that bad, was I?"

"No, not at all. You were never much like a first year. Most of your class, too. That's more like the usual that we have to deal with."

"I'm bloody sorry."

Daryna appeared a few minutes later covered in a sheen of sweat from the mad sprint to the basement and back. She had a protective elixir box in her hands.

"Did you really come to Aura Healers, even though you were a witch in Ireland?" asked Daryna the moment she arrived.

Nurse Tishanti let out a curt laugh and then excused herself as she rolled away from the station in the desk chair with a grin bursting from her lips.

"I did," said Lily, reaching for the plastic box.

"I heard you fixed an uncurable blood disease a few years ago. Like, no one thought it was remotely possible."

As Daryna spoke animatedly, she unconsciously moved the box out of reach.

"Nothing is impossible if you're willing to do the work," said Lily, gesturing for her to hand it over, but Daryna was too busy staring to notice.

"I want to be in Curses like you. I read everything I could find about the de Meath family. It's crazy that your sister, Evangel, is dating Zak Prophet. He's, like, the most famous thunderball player in the entire world."

Lily was only vaguely aware of her sister's dating habits, only having been updated by Alice during one of their text sessions. But it wasn't the first time Evangel had dated a global superstar and it likely wouldn't be the last.

"Can I have the elixirs?"

"And then there's your sister Nyx. Don't even get me started—"

"Please don't."

Daryna rambled for another minute while Lily tried to snatch the elixir box out of her hands. Frustrated by the first year's vomit conversion, Lily produced a tiny shock, which startled Daryna into attention.

"Daryna. The elixirs please."

The first year was staring at her arm where she'd been shocked with the excitement of a child receiving a puppy.

"Oh, yes. I'm sorry. It's just so lovely talking to you, I've been thinking about this moment since I entered the trials. It took me two tries, but I managed to make it and then, oh Merlin, I was so blessed to make it into Aura Healers."

Lily wrenched the box from her arms, which didn't keep her from continuing to spew every thought entering her head. The interior of the box had four unlabeled elixirs rather than the two Lily was expecting."

"Excuse me, Daryna. Which one is mine and which is my patient's potion? The counter for fire breath. There aren't any labels."

"Darn it," said Daryna, her accent shifting to a more rural one. "I forgot to put them on before I left. I was too excited because—"

"I know, I know. But which one? I have patients to get to and none of these look like Jeb's usual."

"He said he made a special one for you, knowing the others weren't working."

"And that was?"

Daryna closed her eyes for a moment.

"The purple one."

"Are you sure?"

"Totally. I wouldn't never mess this up. Not for you. Today totally started off, like, a total shit show, but this makes everything okay."

"And the fire counter?"

Daryna put her finger on the brown vial. Lily thought she saw hesitation, but it could have been her flagging attention.

"Thank you. Since you've made me late, could you drop off the fire counter with my patient in four eighty-eight? Thank you."

"I'd be honored," said Daryna, still standing in view.

"Go be honored as you deliver the potion."

"Right! Sorry!"

As Daryna scurried off, Lily sighed, catching Nurse Tishanti cracking up in the documents area.

"There are first years like her every year?"

"Maybe not like her, she's really taking it up a notch."

Lily unscrewed the top, giving the liquid a sniff. It didn't smell like the usual, more sticky sweet than the expected bitterness, though Jeb had made her a custom elixir.

"Down the hatch."

It tasted like liquified cotton candy. An airy belch came out immediately.

Then Daryna came running up with the sleeve of her undershirt scorched.

"I think I gave you the wrong one."

"What?"

"As soon as I gave the potion to the patient his eyes bulged and he blew a fireball across the room. I barely got out of the way. Then I remembered when I was picking up the potions, I like to use mnemonics to remember things, I thought 'encircle the purple' but what exactly does that mean, so then I tried 'down the brown for fire town' realizing that was the wrong one, but I think that sort of stuck in my head even though I...oh, Healer Lily, what's wrong?"

The bloat in her gut felt like she'd just chugged a dozen fountain sodas. Her skin, already pale from her heritage and the endless days indoors, turned even whiter. Vaguely, she heard Nurse Tishanti say, "Oh no, let me get you somewhere to sit."

Lily's stomach gurgled painfully and then a thick cloying feeling climbed up her throat. She leaned her head back as a bubble expanded out her lips until it was as big as a bowling ball and then burst upward until it landed on the ceiling.

"That was unpleasant—"

"Healer Lily, I'm so sorry. I screwed this up again. Merlin's hairy tits, Dr. Paddock is going to kill me."

As the nurse wheeled out the desk chair, she said, "You, first year, run down to Jeb and explain exactly what happened and ask him for counter-elixirs. Now!"

Daryna squeaked and sped off towards the elevators, once again throwing herself through the open doors with the same family from before.

"My belly," said Lily, holding her midsection as another bubble came out her lips.

This one was as big as a kid's bouncy ball and it was followed by two more smaller ones.

"Can you send someone to check on Amir?" Lily asked between bubbles.

The station was empty, so Tishanti hurried to his room. When she opened the door, flame came shooting out.

"Oh, hell no. I'm getting the moon suit on."

The moon suit was a flame-proof, stab-proof, and generally magic-proof outfit that was required when the patient couldn't control themselves. She ran into the back, while Lily's stomach continued to expand and more bubbles kept coming, but not fast enough to relieve the tension in her gut.

"I swear, if I explode—"

The words died on her tongue when she lifted off the chair. The sudden levitation had her flailing as her mind envisioned she was falling, but she only managed to rotate in midair and knock the rolling chair away from her.

"Help."

Within a few seconds, even as a new bubble formed on her lips, Lily's back impacted with the ceiling. The next bubble was almost as big as she was, but it didn't help with her levitation.

Nurse Tishanti ran by in her thick, marshmallow suit with protective headgear shouting, "We'll get you next! Don't float away!"

The painful bubble belches continued until the first year returned with two vials in her fists.

Lily pointed towards Amir's room.

"Bring that to Nurse Tishanti."

When she opened the door, flame came rolling out. Daryna ducked, then tossed in the vial with a squeak and slammed the door shut. Lily was in too much distress to roll her eyes.

Daryna appeared beneath her, holding up the vial.

"I can't reach that. Help me down."

She set the elixir on the nurse's desk and tried to jump up to grab Lily, but she was too short.

As another bubble expanded rapidly on her lips, and Daryna was jumping up and down without coming within two feet of Lily, a voice startled them from the hallway.

"Can you tell us where the—"

The same family that had been going up and down the elevator stopped in their tracks the moment that the other door burst open with Nurse Tishanti in her protective suit throwing herself into the hallway while flame blew out the opening.

"—never mind."

"Please can you help me!" Lily called after them, but the family was already gone.

Nurse Tishanti waddled over in the oversized outfit as she pulled off the helmet.

"If there was ever a reason to murder a first year, this is it."

"I'm so sorry," said Daryna, shrinking under the nurse's gaze.

"Climb on my shoulders, first year. Let's get her down."

As Daryna pulled Lily from the ceiling like a wayward balloon, she belched three more times. There were dozens of the weird bubbles floating around, bouncing into each other.

Once they had her down, Tishanti tied her to the rolling chair and grabbed the elixir.

"We'll get it down between bubbles."

At the appropriate window, the nurse handed Lily the potion, which she chugged as fast as she could before another bubble formed in her throat. Lily had a moment of worry that it was the wrong elixir again, until relief started setting in. Her strained and distended gut relaxed as smaller bubbles came shooting out like she was a kid's toy.

Within a few minutes, the pressure on her midsection had dissipated and she was no longer emitting bubbles. Lily set Daryna in her sights, which elicited a squeak from the first year.

"I'm so sorry..."

Nurse Tishanti put her hands on her hips.

"I'm gonna have to tell Dr. Paddock about this."

The fear in Daryna's eyes was palpable.

"Maybe we can keep this one to ourselves," said Lily, reluctantly.

"You serious?"

She looked at the first year, who looked ready to melt into the floor.

"No, but on the other hand, Dr. Paddock would blow this out of proportion."

"If those had been different elixirs, you two could be dead, or worse."

"Daryna. Did you learn a lesson?"

She answered with a squeak and a vigorous head nod.

"You can head back to Jeb. Tell him thank you for the quick fix."

"Thank you, Healer Lily and Nurse Tishanti."

"You're lucky she's nicer than I am," said Tishanti.

After Daryna left, Dr. Fairlight came strolling down the hallway with a couple of the hospital board members. Her eyes widened at the sight of dozens of bubbles floating around the ceiling.

"Birthday party," said Nurse Tishanti as she walked around the desk.

After the Chief of Staff and her charges were gone, Tishanti said, "You owe me one."

"I owe you a thousand."

SEVEN

Remi was on her way to the cafeteria when she ran into Boon. Her fellow fourth year was jogging the opposite direction with his forehead hunched.

"Problems?"

He slowed, and backed down the hallway.

"Weird case in the ER."

She was tired, hungry, and really wanted to crawl into her bed after ushering a young woman into the afterlife, but curiosity got the best of her.

"Weird?"

Boon shook his head.

"A couple came in complaining they were seeing ghosts and a hidden treasure. They were asking if we had a structural map of the hospital so they could prove that the ghost's information was real."

A cold chill went down her spine.

"Ghosts?"

"Yeah, I tried to explain that we have upgraded wards and that it would be really unusual for them to be able to see them in the hospital, but they were adamant."

Remi put a hand to her forehead.

"What's wrong? You seeing ghosts too?"

"By any chance, are they a moderately attractive middle-aged couple? The woman with a slight Norwegian accent and blue eyes, while the guy has a little scar on the left side of his chin?"

Boon stiffened.

"Yeah. How'd you know? Is this a trick?"

She shook her head.

"A con actually. Though the blueprints are unusual, unless—"

"What?"

"What name did they give you? Oh, never mind, I'll go deal with them. Where are they at?"

"In 3C."

On the way down to the ER, her stomach rumbled with hunger and the tension at her temples threatened a migraine. Remi had the urge to swing by the Curse Ward to see if Lily could join her, but she was probably too busy.

Remi stood outside the privacy curtain with her heart in her throat listening to the couple talk quietly. It was them. It was really them.

She threw the curtains wide, startling her parents.

"Remington!"

Her mother, Greta, stood up with her arms spread.

"What a beautiful surprise."

Remi allowed her mother to put her arms around her.

"Hello, Mother."

"Hey, kiddo," said her father, Archer, adding a wink for good measure.

"Hey..."

Remi pulled herself from her mother's arms and stood back with her arms crossed.

Her parents shared a look before her father shifted past her and closed the curtain.

"So...what's the game?" he asked in a hushed voice.

"What's the game? You guys forgot me when I left juvie. I thought you would be there. That's what you always said. That you would be there."

Remi hated how much emotion was collecting in her face. She'd always been able to separate herself from how her parents made her feel and focus on the job, but after three and a half years it was like her insides had been hollowed out and filled with tar.

"Oh honey, Remington darling, we would have but we ran into a little issue with Normal Bob. He really wanted that money and we didn't have it, so we had to skip town. We knew you would understand. You're such a professional," said Greta in that offhand diva way that drove Remi nuts.

"That was years ago. Couldn't you have a sent a message? Anything?"

"Well, it took us time to find you. It's not like we were expecting you to join the Halls. We're proud of course, just think of the things you can do now. We could really make a killing."

"We?"

"Of course, we. We've always been a team. Right, Arch?"

Her father cocked a grin.

"Your mother is right, Remington. We're a team. A damn good one. So tell us, what have you got cooking here? I bet this place is loaded with stuff no one would miss." He snapped his fingers. "I saw an alchemy lab earlier. I bet they have some rare and expensive stuff here we could easily sell on the black market. Warnock has the connects."

"You've already seen Warnock?"

"Yeah, last week. We made him promise not to tell you we were here. He's got quite the setup. Said you'd pulled some jobs when you first got here, but hasn't heard from you since."

Remi growled under her breath. She wanted to kick Warnock in the shins for not warning her that her parents were in town.

"I can't believe you saw him before you came to me."

"We didn't know where you were, only that you were in town. Trust us, it took a while to figure that out."

"How did you?"

Greta waved her hand dismissively.

"It's not important."

Her father approached and put a hand on her shoulder, which she flinched away.

"The important part is we're all together. The three of us. The best damn team in the country."

"I'm not on your team anymore."

"What?" they both exclaimed.

"I'm a healer now."

"Honey," said her mother, "you look miserable. Like you're in pain. Surely you're joking with us. We've been scouting the hospital for a few days. I don't understand why anyone does it. All that time and effort for what? The pay can't be that good, can it?"

"It's not about the pay," said Remi in a quiet voice.

"A long con?" asked her father.

She shook her head.

"It's not a con. People need me. There was a case today, a young woman, not much older than me. I...she..."

"You saved her? That's amazing, Remington. You see how good she is, Arch? She can do anything. I've never been more proud. Our daughter, the healer."

"We didn't save her. She died," said Remi.

"She died? Did you do something wrong, kiddo?"

Remi looked away, telling her eyes not to water, which wasn't helping.

"No. She died. But we made sure it was peaceful and that she wouldn't come back."

Greta recoiled.

"That's gruesome. You just let her die? What kind of hospital is this?"

"I work in the Hospice Ward, Mom. The people there aren't going to survive, so we try to make it peaceful. There are things with the Veil—"

Greta waved her off.

"I just ate, Remington. Let's not upset my stomach."

"Why are you two here?"

"To see you, kiddo," said her father.

"Bullshit. You're running the lost treasure con. If I hadn't run into Boon, I wouldn't even know you were here."

Greta rolled her eyes.

"You know we can't help it. We meant to see you first, but the con sort of slipped out my lips and before we knew it, that young handsome doctor was running upstairs."

The way her parents looked at her, as if they expected her to believe their lies, made her wonder about her entire childhood. She saw them for who they were, petty grifters looking for the easy way out. They were handsome and smart enough to get by, but lacked the perseverance to ever make anything of themselves.

"Why are you looking at us like that, Remington?" asked her mother.

"I'm tired. It's been a long day."

Archer snapped his fingers as if he'd just thought of something, but Remi knew that was a lie. It was a tell she'd discovered years ago. Whatever he had to say had been lurking behind his lips since she burst through the curtains.

"Hey, speaking of jobs, whatever happened to that necklace you stole?"

"You mean the one that got me thrown in Utica for a year?"

"Yeah, that one," he said with a forced casualness.

"I threw it in the river."

"What? You're joking, right?" asked Greta as she surged to her feet. "We put so much time into that job, and the—"

Archer waved her off.

"That's the Big One, kiddo. Did you really throw it in the river?"

Remi narrowed her gaze.

"It's not worth anything. I showed it to a couple of fences, but no one was interested, so I got rid of it. Would hate to have to go back as an adult for something my parents made me do."

"Made you?" Her mother laughed. "You begged us to do that job. Said you were the best one for it. We warned you that you weren't quite ready, and wow, were we right. I hate to say it, but that year in Utica was all on you."

The rebuke was like a two-by-four to the forehead. Remi stared back, stunned.

"I don't know why I never saw it before—"

"Saw what, kiddo?" asked her father. "And don't take what your mother said too harshly. It hasn't been a great couple of years for us. We owe people and they're expecting us to pull through for them. The pendant on that necklace would go a long way to making things right. If we could fix that, maybe we could move to the city here, and we'd get to see you again. Wouldn't you like that?"

"I think you'd like it more," said Remi under her breath. "I don't have it."

Her father narrowed his gaze.

"Are you sure? It's not like our Remington to just throw a valuable piece of loot into a river. You haven't hidden it in the hospital somewhere?"

She stiffened with realization.

"That's why you wanted the blueprints. You weren't even going to ask me. You're trying to figure out where I hid it."

"So you do have it," said Archer with a broad smile. "Just tell us, kiddo. I can see you're mad at us. And that's understandable, but it's been years and we're had some struggles. You might even say we're a little desperate. A little."

He added a wink to go along with his winning smile.

"Can you tell us where it's at, Remington?" asked her father.

"Did you really lose a bet to name me Remington?"

He lifted his shoulders.

"Does it matter? But, of course. Yes."

"I don't have the pendant. I swear. It was Fae-cursed, so I got rid of it."

Her parents stared at her, then looked to each other, before exhaling.

"We believe you," said her father.

She knew he was lying, but was too tired to call him out.

"You really should go. The ER needs the room."

Her mother grabbed her purse. They stood near her as if they were expecting a hug. Her father handed her a card from the Charming Hotel in the tenth ward.

"We're in Room 302 if you need to reach us, or change your mind. It's good to see you, Remington. We *did* miss you."

Her father tried to lean over to give a hug, but she made no motion to accept it, so he shifted to the side like he was stretching his back.

"Love you, Remington," said her mother, leaning over to give her a peck on the cheek. "I'm sure you think you're hurting us by taking this awful job, but you're only hurting yourself. Only suckers join the grind."

"Greta," said her father as he pulled his wife away. "See you around, Remington."

Once they were out of sight, Remi collapsed onto a chair. She felt like a marionette with her strings cut. Every decision she'd made since she came to the city of sorcery was called into question. She couldn't decide if she wanted to scream or cry more, but eventually a nurse stuck her head in and she knew she had to give up the space. No longer hungry, Remi headed straight for her room.

EIGHT

The elderberries squished beneath the pestle, forming a dark purple goo at the bottom of the ceramic mortar. Damon could have used a mixer, but he wanted to strain out the skin, leaving only the juice, so keeping them whole was important. He checked the tome he'd found at Left Tower Books for the next step, which required him to add faez to the mixture. Once the golden light sparkled on the surface, he poured the liquid through cheesecloth. The thick elderberry juice dripped into the lower vial. He'd have to wait for the elderberries to strain through the cloth before he could work on the next step.

While the mixture slowly trickled through the cloth, he checked the pamphlet Dr. Broomfield had given them at the beginning of the year. The goal was to produce an extract of vervain, or iron grass, an ancient alchemical reagent that went back to Roman times. The flower resisted the normal industrializations associated with modern alchemy. Any larger-scale reductions ruined the essence that made the extract work.

The secondary problem, one he'd worry about once he could reduce at scale, was to intensify the mixture to a one-hundred-to-one ratio. Damon wasn't a true alchemist by any means, but as Aura Healers they did enough work in the lab to have a solid handle on the craft.

With the beaker a quarter full, he placed a burner beneath it and turned the flame on low to help burn out excess liquid.

A knock on the door had him looking up to see Dr. Broomfield peering through the narrow window. Damon waved him in.

"I thought I smelled elderberries," said Dr. Broomfield as he glanced to the pamphlet. "Making any progress?"

"Not yet, but I'm learning a lot. I thought if I could intensify the elderberry juice, it would help me learn how I might be able to do the same for the vervain."

"Why would you think that would help?"

Damon swallowed.

"The two are associated in history, especially with the Fae."

"Those links are mere speculation."

"More than speculation. If you search for 'Tears of Isis,' as the Egyptians called it, there are more suggestions of linkage, including a whole piece written by Pliny the Elder that suggests the iron grass was modified somehow before it was mixed in larger quantities, though he never explains how."

"Suggestions aren't fact even if they come from a storied historian like Pliny."

"That's why I'm testing my theory," said Damon.

Dr. Broomfield raised an eyebrow.

"An unusual direction, but maybe that's what this little project needs, some unusual ideas."

Warm pride rose up in Damon's chest.

"I appreciate that you've taken on my challenge," said Dr. Broomfield. "I'm not aware anyone else from your class has chosen to do so."

Damon found it hard to meet Dr. Broomfield's gaze.

"I want that recommendation."

Dr. Broomfield tapped his fingernail on the glassware in contemplation.

"If you spent less time with those miscreants and more time in here, you might have a shot."

"Those are my friends, Dr. Broomfield. We've been through a ton together."

The head instructor arched an eyebrow.

"One day you'll have to learn that to truly be successful you have to shed those that are holding you back. While it might seem like your friends have your best interests at heart, they're interfering with your greatness. I can see it in the day-to-day operations. You could be celebrated, Damon Wolfhard, but you have to decide."

"I can't turn my back on them."

"I'm not asking you to, but if you join the Institute for Childhood Therianthropic Studies, you'll be too busy to see them and it would be highly unlikely that they'd even be in the same city. Friendships are great for surviving Aura Healers and Golden Willow, I know I had some myself when I was a student, but I didn't make them my whole life."

He put a hand on Damon's shoulder.

"Don't worry, you'll still see them at reunions, weddings, and funerals."

"Thank you, Dr. Broomfield."

"I don't think you understand how much I can help you, Damon. There are lots of very talented healers like yourself, and positions at the Institute are hard to come by."

"Understood."

"I don't think you do. Look. Your family has a troubled background, especially in the therianthropic community, which I should remind you, I'm well thought of in. My word goes a long way, and frankly, I'm not sure how you could get an invite to the Institute without it. And for good reason. I take those recommendations seriously. I would feel terrible if I helped elevate someone to that position that didn't deserve it, over other more worthy applicants. You understand, right?"

"I do, Dr. Broomfield. Thank you for your advice."

The doctor gave Damon a cautious glance. He was so worried about what Dr. Broomfield was thinking, he'd forgotten about the elderberry reduction until it started bubbling against the glass stopper.

"Shit," said Damon as he rushed over to turn down the burner, but it was too late, the juice was running over the side. He'd heated it up too fast, causing it to boil, which would ruin the mixture.

"See, Damon. Distractions can be disastrous. Sorry about your elderberries."

He paused before he left the room.

"Next time, if you use a double beaker, suspending the elderberry jar in water, it'll modulate the heat and make it harder to burn. Good luck, Mr. Wolfhard. I'm sure you'll have a perfectly normal life if you don't get into the Institute."

With the door closed, Damon sank against the table as he stared at the sticky mess that had bubbled onto the table. He turned the burner off and dumped the mixture into the industrial sink.

That was the last of his elderberries. He'd have to make another trip into the city to get more, but he wasn't even certain it was worth it.

Even if he managed to find the solution to the iron grass problem, he wasn't sure that Dr. Broomfield would even extend his recommendation due to his association with Lily and Remi.

There was no way he was going to go back on their friendship, not after everything they'd been through. His entire family wouldn't be alive without their help. Damon couldn't imagine not having them in his life. Some things were more important than a career.

NINE

The cold patter of rain tapped against the window, distracting Remi from her task. Dr. Morsdux cleared his throat, a reminder to focus on the runes she was drawing on the tile floor. They'd cleared out a storage room in the Hospice Ward to give her a place to practice the Veil magics required as Dr. Morsdux's assistant.

"A bit more curl to the Ohm rune, but you have the gist of it."

Remi flexed her wrist as she drew the ward between two parallel circular lines.

"Excellent," said Dr. Morsdux, clapping his bony hands. "I couldn't have done it better myself."

Remi sat back on her heels as thunder rumbled against the window. The sun had set while she was engrossed in her work. She stared out the glass into the dark city.

"Don't worry, Healer Wilde. The frightful land doesn't care about weather in this world. I dare say the hounds would likely be startled by it."

"I'm not worried about the storm."

He tapped his flat hand under his chin, indicating she should lift hers.

"We are the guardians at the gates of death. We do not shy from our task no matter how it makes us feel."

Remi cracked her knuckles and stepped into the ritual circle.

"Are you sure I'll be safe?"

"I'll be right here with you, Healer Wilde. But I won't interfere unless your life is in danger. You must learn to be comfortable at the edge of the Veil."

She nodded as she shifted her mouth to the side. "It was one thing to coax those ghosts into returning, but to put myself there...what if I see the Stranger again?"

"Then we'll get to learn more about him."

"I feel like I'm the idiot heading into the haunted mansion on a dare while everyone's screaming at the screen 'don't go in!'"

"I've never been a fan of scary movies. They fail to illuminate the real dangers in the world."

Remi thought back to her encounters with the White Worm, or Koschei the Deathless.

"Amen to that."

"Remember to approach this task with a calm heart. The beings of the Veil will not bother you at the barrier between our two realms unless you give them something to look for."

Remi wanted to make a snide quip that bringing it up would only make her feel more anxious, but he'd already explained last week when he first brought up the task that the only way to get more comfortable was repetition.

Dr. Morsdux took a step back until he was against the wall. He placed his hands behind his back.

"Shall we begin?"

The words came haltingly to Remi's lips. The spells common to the Hospice Ward came from ancient times and were born of languages no longer spoken in the modern world.

After a few minutes of chanting, wisps of chilled air swirled around her feet along with greenish mist. She kept up the ritual as the words settled into a rhythm.

The lights of the hospital room faded away as a dreary, endless landscape came into view. Misshapen leafless trees reached their skeletal arms towards the nonexistent sky.

Remi felt like she was dangling her feet in shark infested waters, waiting for a bite, but after a few moments of observation, she realized that she was relatively safe in her ritual circle on the edge of the Veil.

"Are you feeling comfortable?" asked Dr. Morsdux from somewhere nearby.

His voice sounded modulated as if it were being transported by a tube.

"No. Yes. I'm ready."

"Good. Now I want you to open your mind and release faez into the air."

"I thought you said we weren't supposed to use magic in the Veil?"

"You're not entirely inside the Veil, and exhaling faez is different from a structured spell. Call it putting chum in the water."

The analogy only reminded her of her first thoughts when she arrived at the edge of the Veil. She checked over her shoulder expecting to see the Stranger, or Dr. Morsdux, but only bore witness to the endless landscape.

Remi pulled faez from her mind, exhaling golden mist which sparkled and swirled in an unseen wind before disappearing.

"Now I want you to close your eyes and reach into the darkest corners of your mind where your fears exist. Not the imaginary ones, but the real ones. The Veil is a transient realm. Sometimes called a precursor realm. It is not anchored like ours, which is how the souls of the dead can exist. Some even think they are just imprints of the souls that pass through. You must master your fears in the safety of the ritual so you cannot be surprised when you need all your focus."

It sounded like a good idea to Remi when Dr. Morsdux was explaining it, but now that she was inside the Veil, getting ready to unleash her darkest fears against herself, she was questioning ever joining the Hospice Ward.

Darkest fears...darkest fears...

As Remi plumbed her thoughts, she heard a wailing howl followed by two identical voices.

"The hounds—"

"Do not worry, Healer Wilde, they're still far, far away. There is time still to find your center."

Remi tried to dive back into her thoughts, but her gaze was nailed to the horizon. The hounds were one of the guardians of the Veil, servants of the realm's mistress. When she heard no more howls, Remi let her thoughts settle into herself.

"Who am I? What am I afraid of?" she whispered as lingering thoughts of the day she left Utica took hold.

A condensed darkness like a hole being opened up in the world appeared a dozen steps from her location. The emptiness whistled as the opening grew, spewing out blackness until she could no longer see.

The lack of vision brought chills to her spine as she worried something lurked just beyond. The Veil was filled with beings that could easily annihilate her, but that wasn't what bothered her. It was the not knowing.

A second set of howls startled her. They were more distant, as if the hounds were moving away, but she couldn't help but think they were trying to trick her. Convince her to let her guard down so they could sneak up and catch her unawares.

"Breathe, Remi. Breathe," said Dr. Morsdux.

When she let her chest relax, she realized she hadn't taken a breath in a minute and now it came laboring to catch up with her lack of oxygen. The forced breaths made it hard to hear what was directly around her.

Then she heard the crackle of a footstep.

Or was it her imagination?

Remi strained against the noises of her own body. The hammering of her heart. Her breath leaking out her lips. The maelstrom of thoughts careering around her mind.

When she heard a second step, she knew that it wasn't her imagination.

"I hear someone."

Dr. Morsdux didn't answer right away, which only made her more fraught.

"Focus on yourself. The Veil is not like the land of nightmares or other dangerous realms. And on the edge, it's only the things we bring with us that are dangerous."

"And the hounds, and other things that will kill us."

"Only if you enter the Veil. You're safe at the border, as long as you remain calm."

She closed her eyes and focused on her surroundings. She couldn't tell if she sensed the presence anymore.

Remi...

The voice was like a whisper in her ear and then she felt a brush against her arm which made her cry out. Remi threw herself back into the hospital room. Vision returned instantly. She stood outside the ritual circle as thunder rumbled against the window.

The flicker of disappointment in Dr. Morsdux's gaunt face brought heat to her cheeks.

"Someone touched me and spoke my name."

He raised an eyebrow.

"Are you certain? Or was it your imagination? Your fears? You must learn to focus, Healer Remi."

They were interrupted by a heavy knock on the door. A ward nurse called out.

"There's a problem in the west wing."

Dr. Morsdux yanked the door open.

"Can it wait?"

The look on the nurse's face suggested that it was urgent.

"We'll be right there."

Remi dismissed the faez link to the Veil and hurried after Dr. Morsdux.

"I'm sorry I failed."

"You haven't failed yet."

"I don't know why I did that. I got startled, or something."

He turned his head slightly as he made long strides that required Remi to hurry to keep up.

"Were you expecting mastery on the first try?"

The warm, but mocking tone popped the bubble of her self-importance as she accepted the ridiculousness of her expectations. The response that she formulated died in her throat as she heard a familiar voice down the hall.

"Make 'em dance, Halley, or you'll give 'em the ghost," said Nina the Knife from the doorway.

"Get away from my patient!" yelled Dr. Morsdux in an angry tone that Remi had never heard before.

They stopped the moment Nina pulled a blade the length of her forearm from a sheath. From inside the room, Remi could hear the sobbing of Mr. Brown.

"Care to dance, old man?" asked Nina, tossing the weapon from hand to hand.

"Dr. Morsdux," Remi said when Big Al and the youngest, Halley, shifted into the hallway. "Careful."

"You know them?"

"I'm afraid so."

He turned to the sisters.

"What are you doing to my patient?"

Halley held out her palm and blew mist from it.

"Showing that bag of bones where he'll be going soon enough."

Nina turned her head towards Big Al.

"Can I give 'em a permanent smile?"

"Why are you here?" asked Remi with fists at her side.

She wanted to summon elemental magics, but didn't want to trigger a fight in the middle of the hospital. They still didn't know what Halley had done to Mr. Brown.

"All this wasted energy," said Halley with an off-kilter grin as she produced puffs of Veil smoke with the flick of her fingers. "I'd burn down this place with it."

The girl had been almost normal the last time Remi had seen her. It'd been her sisters' taunting that had gotten her to attack Remi's friend. They'd been calling her too soft and warned her that they wouldn't always be around to protect her.

"Halley, please. Leave Mr. Brown alone. Whatever you're doing to him. He's an old man who's going to die soon. He deserves better."

"You made *me* die," said Halley, tapping her finger on her chest.

"It wasn't deliberate. I just wanted you away from my friend."

Halley stared back with the blankness of death. The emptiness of it was unsettling.

"I'll *always* be there."

Halley raised her hands, producing threads between her fingers as if she were pulling black taffy from the air, then shoved them forward. The miasmic energy spun towards them before Remi could consider what to do.

"Nocte ballis!"

Dr. Morsdux thrust his hands forward, sending out a wave of baleful energy that crackled in the air. As it slammed into Halley's creation, the two burst into golden light, which quickly faded to crackles.

"Do not test me in my own home. I will not hesitate to remove you from this existence," said Dr. Morsdux in a deep, booming voice that startled Remi with its thrumming power.

Nina raised her big knife, but Big Al put a hand on her shoulder.

"Come on. We've had our fun. I think our old friend has gotten the message."

The Scythe Sisters, led by Big Al, headed past them. Remi stepped to the side to give them room.

When Nina passed, she lunged towards Remi, making her react, then quickly pulled back. Laughing, she extended a middle finger.

"Made you flinch."

After the sisters disappeared around the corner, Dr. Morsdux strode into Mr. Brown's room to find him staring into empty space with a look of horror on his face. Tears were rolling down his cheeks.

Dr. Morsdux cast a short and potent spell that erased the knot of blackness above the patient's head. Mr. Brown fell back into his pillow as if the strings holding him taut had been cut.

"Seven hells," he muttered as Dr. Morsdux put a hand on his arm in comfort.

"I'm sorry. It was my failure that allowed those women to assault you. I won't let it happen again, I swear," said Dr. Morsdux.

Mr. Brown clutched at the doctor's hand.

"Please...that was awful. I can't do it again."

"I'll send for one of the special elixirs. Will that help?"

Mr. Brown nodded profusely.

"Thank you."

After the order was sent down to the lab, Dr. Morsdux confronted Remi in the hallway.

"You knew those women?"

"From Utica. They were the scourge of the prison. I pushed Halley when she tried to hurt one of my friends, but she tripped and cracked her head open. She was in the prison hospital the entire time I was in solitary. I saw them a month ago in the city, but I didn't think they'd come here."

Dr. Morsdux nodded.

"I understand. Thank you for telling me the truth. What do you think they mean to do?"

"Kill me. Or worse." Remi bit her lower lip. "What was Halley doing to Mr. Brown? She seems very different from before."

"I'm afraid she's Veil-touched, or perhaps something more. Sometimes when people are on the edge of death for too long, they become infected by the Veil. What she did to Mr. Brown shouldn't have been possible, not that easily."

"Great," said Remi, shaking her head. "She's not an Ossarii, is she?"

The question seemed to pull the string in his back tight.

"The signs are certainly there, but it would be most odd to have two Ossariis in the same generation."

"If that's what I am..."

"That's true."

Dr. Morsdux put a bony hand on her shoulder.

"I'll contact hospital security and make sure they're not allowed to enter again. I can also post guards in the ward if you'd like."

"No. No guards. It would remind me too much of prison and I don't think it would help. Even the guards were afraid of Big Al. She has supernatural strength."

"I see," he said, removing his hand.

"Can you teach me that spell you countered her with?"

"Normally I wouldn't recommend it, but under the circumstances I will teach you. But it will mean more work on top of your Veil training and the needs of the ward."

"I never liked sleep anyway."

Dr. Morsdux gave her a wistful smile.

"I will send over a few tomes from my private collection with the suggested reading order. But I should warn you that they're not in the usual languages. The Veil is one of the oldest realms, and the magics that were gleaned from it require tongues no longer spoken in this world. You'll have to learn them first before you can begin."

"Thank you, Dr. Morsdux. I'll get on them right away."

He left to contact security, leaving her in the middle of the hallway. But it wasn't the Scythe Sisters that her thoughts trended towards, but whoever, or whatever touched her arm and spoke her name in the Veil.

TEN

The magic flowing through Lily's fingertips felt warm and tingly as she weaved a protective barrier over the unconscious patient. The golden threads hovered in place until she was finished tying them together. Once the last knot had been created, the threads flashed bright white before sinking into the body lying on the bed.

Lily turned towards Dr. Broomfield, who had been standing to the side observing. She steeled herself for the inevitable condemnation.

"Passable at best," said Dr. Broomfield as he scribbled notes in a little red book. He always had it with him, especially on rounds. Lily had dreamed about burning it, or launching it into the Veil.

The doctor looked up as she stared back, his lips snarling with disappointment.

"The angle of your wrist is all wrong. This is what happens when you come to the Halls with too much false knowledge."

"There's nothing false about my family, and the warding spell was unaffected by the difference in my wrist angle," said Lily sternly.

Dr. Broomfield scoffed.

"These little errors will add up until you bring great harm to one of your patients, and then how can I defend you from the review team when you defied my instructions this entire time?"

His gaze flickered to her hair, which she'd tamed with a few cords.

"When are you going to cut that hair? Or at least color it something less...bright. It's unprofessional. Whenever you lean over, your cursed hair practically tickles the patient's nose. Imagine yourself in their shoes. What would you think of a Healer with hair like that?"

"That they have great taste in hair style. None of my patients have complained, Dr. Broomfield."

"They're too afraid of you. I've watched you interact with the nurses and other doctors. You treat them like you've been here for decades. You're lucky none of *them* have complained."

"That's because my outcomes are in the highest percentile. I may be new to Aura Healers, but I've been fixing sicknesses and broken bones in Ireland since I was a wee lass."

"Mere superstitious country crap. Charlatan work meant to take your patient's hard-earned coin while you keep yourself safe from risk. Real healers, and doctors, put their lives on the line for their patients."

She knew he was baiting her. Probably wanted her to lash out in a way that he could use against her with Dr. Fairlight. Lily gave him a sweet smile.

Dr. Broomfield stared back for a long time before turning and walking out of the room, expecting her to follow. He entered a new patient's room. Outside the window, snowflakes were swirling around. Nothing was sticking but it gave the air a holiday feel.

"Please," said Dr. Broomfield, gesturing towards the patient with a smirk on his lips.

The young woman on the bed was watching frightfully with the covers pulled to her chest. She had big blue doe eyes and pink cheeks. She was the essence of the young maiden.

"Good afternoon, Miss Patience Moffat," said Lily after she read the chart. "It's my understanding you believe you fell through a portal into the Fae and were cursed by a goat man?"

Her blue eyes darted between them.

"I know, it sounds ridiculous, but I swear it's what happened. I woke up with a fistful of clover," said Patience, gesturing towards a tray of greens.

Lily quickly inspected them to find they were all of the four-leaf variety and in the bloom of health. While they could be found anywhere, to collect that many before they shriveled up would be difficult, especially in the dead of winter.

She felt Dr. Broomfield's judging gaze, but tried to push his presence out of her mind. He was trying to rattle her. To prove a point about her supposed inexperience, but she wasn't going to let him have the satisfaction.

"Can you tell me about the falling through a portal experience?"

"I work in the ninth at D'Agastine Industries. I like to take my lunch in the park near my building. It was a lovely day. For winter, anyway. I was sitting under a tree enjoying some homemade cottage cheese when I heard a voice call my name from nearby."

"A voice? What did it sound like?" asked Lily.

Patience paused as she jawed at the empty air in thought.

"Like my best friend whispering in my ear. I know it sounds crazy, but I trusted them as soon as I heard their voice."

Beings from the Fae sometimes had the power of suggestion, which made Lily think she *could* be telling the truth.

"What happened next?"

"I stepped around the tree and then I felt like I was falling. When I opened my eyes I was in a glade surrounded by trees with golden sunlight warming my skin. I'd been wearing a heavy coat, but it hadn't come with me."

"A glade?" asked Lily. "Can you describe it?"

"It was warm and wonderful. The grass felt like silk and the air was as sweet as syrup. I wandered out of the glade and found a spring where I dipped my toes in."

"Your toes? Did you lose your shoes when you came over?"

"I suppose I did," said Patience with a hand to her chest.

There was nothing false or obfuscating about the woman, but Lily couldn't understand how she had experienced this vision because of the corruption. If it'd been decades ago, it would have been a perfectly acceptable—though generic—description of the lands of the Summer Fae.

"Then what happened?"

"I remember looking at the plants and the flowers and thinking how perfect a place. I plucked a cluster of purple blooms. They smelled like lemons. I was enjoying the feel of the cool water on my feet when the goat man accosted me. He grabbed my arm and yanked me away from the spring and blamed me for destroying his lands."

The anguish on her face felt real, even as Lily thought it must be false.

"What did the goat man look like?"

"He had stubby horns and legs covered in brown velvet, ending in hooves. He was mean and cruel, calling me awful things. I never felt so terrified. He kept pushing me back to the glade and when I reached that place, I felt myself shift through the world and then I woke up in the park with an older man shaking my arm."

"And you said you were cursed?" asked Lily.

She nodded.

"I hear haunting pipes. They sound like a funeral dirge. Always in my head. Always, always, always. You can help me, right?"

"We will, but first we need to understand the nature of this curse. May I cast a spell on your ears?"

Patience nodded.

The spell would illuminate any adverse magics affecting her hearing. When Lily was finished, she saw no signs of a curse. She looked to Marcus, who was watching her keenly.

"Can you tell me more about the Fae lands? Did you see anything strange?"

"It was all strange," said Patience.

"Not that kind of strange. But did you notice any twisting of the trees? Dark places? Was it difficult to move towards the spring? Thick undergrowth. Anything like that?"

Patience shook her head.

"No. It was most lovely and serene. I would love to live there. Do you think I'd ever be allowed back? Assuming I can get rid of these awful pipes."

Lily shifted her mouth to the side.

"I'm afraid I don't think you were lured into the Fae. I believe you are hearing pipes, but this clearly has another cause."

Dr. Broomfield cleared his throat loudly.

"Yes, Doctor?" asked Lily, trying not to make a rude face at his interruption.

"Wouldn't a Harmane's Juxtaposition give you more information about her condition?"

Lily tilted her head in thought.

"I suppose, but it would be an unusual use of the spell and expose me to her condition unnecessarily."

"You just said it was nothing to worry about."

Lily faced him.

"I just said that I believed her, but that it wasn't the Fae."

The patient whimpered behind Lily, which made her back off from further confrontation.

"My apologies."

"Would that Jux spell help?" asked Patience softly.

Lily glanced between the woman and Dr. Broomfield.

"It might, but—"

"But what, Miss de Meath?" asked the doctor.

"Healer de Meath," replied Lily. "And I don't believe the spell is prudent. Yet. There are other things to try that would be less dangerous."

Dr. Broomfield shook his head as he wrote notes in his little red book.

"I'm sorry you believe that."

"Is that true? Would it help me?" asked Patience.

Flustered by the circumstances, Lily stammered out her response.

"It's not, well, it could, but I don't know..."

She'd never felt so impotent, as if she were a first year rather than on her fourth at Aura Healers. When she checked back to the doctor, his pen was poised above the paper. She hated how much his word mattered for her final two years at Golden Willow. While Dr. Decker was unorthodox, he had everyone's well-being at heart. Lily couldn't say the same thing about Dr. Broomfield, who wielded his power like a sledgehammer.

"If you think it'll help."

Lily faced the patient, who sat up straight and let her hands fall into her lap. The spell wasn't difficult, but if the cause of the haunting pipes and the belief that she'd been transported to the Summer Fae was something other than a delusion, then the evening might get much worse.

With one hand on Patience's ear, Lily cast the spell with her other hand, feeling like she was a backwater healer in a tent selling ineffective potions. As the spell began to take hold, a strange feeling trickled up her arm. Lily managed to shift her gaze towards Dr. Broomfield, who was watching earnestly, his pen no longer hovering over the paper.

Right before the spell's conclusion, Lily purposely fumbled the final gesture. She'd done it out of instinct rather than real thought, but as she pulled away, she saw the glint of anger in Dr. Broomfield's expression.

"Bloody hells," said Lily, pulling her hand away from Patience's ear. "I'm sorry. I had a cramp in my hand and the hook gesture went sideways."

She wasn't quite sure, but she felt profound relief at the spell's failure, even as Dr. Broomfield was gearing up to admonish her.

"Quite disappointing. Will you cast it again?"

Lily shook her hand, stretching it as if she had a cramp. Dr. Broomfield eyed the motion suspiciously.

"Maybe in a little bit. Can you do the spell? I'm sorry, Dr. Broomfield. I was practicing the level-eight finger gestures this morning and I think I might have overdone it."

He glanced to Patience with his lips squeezed flat.

"We'll come back to our patient later. Come with me, *Miss* de Meath."

Lily didn't bother correcting him this time as she followed him into the hallway. Dr. Broomfield spun on her once they were away from the room.

"Why have you defied me?"

Lily clutched her hand against her chest as she massaged it.

"Defied?"

"Don't give me that. I've seen you work. Your gestures are flawless. You purposefully screwed up that spell. Explain yourself."

"I thought you said my gestures were sloppy and going to get someone killed earlier?"

He opened his mouth but nothing came out.

"That's not what I said."

"It's exactly what you said."

"Are you refusing to cast the spell on the patient?" he said loud enough the two nurses at the station glanced up.

"Not refusing. Incapable," she said, holding up her hand. "But feel free to do it in my stead."

Dr. Broomfield blinked with thought before growling under his breath.

"You're dismissed for the day. Go back to your room and I'll decide what kind of punishment you'll be receiving for your insolence."

He marched away, leaving Lily by herself. She thought about returning to Patience's room to see if there was another way to fix the haunting pipes, but she knew Dr. Broomfield would throw a fit if he found out.

"What an utter bloody gobshite," she muttered under her breath.

As she headed to the cafeteria to get some dinner, she thought about the whole encounter. While Patience had seemed genuinely frightened by her condition, there was something off about the whole ordeal. For one, she couldn't have visited the Summer Fae, not as she described it, since it was overgrown with the corruption. And two, while sometimes the barrier between realms grew thin and people did fall through, it was never in the middle of a park. Those kinds of things happened at shimmering where there was a reason for the barrier to be thin. That no one else had reported odd sightings suggested that whatever had happened to Patience had been something else entirely, and though she found the idea ludicrous at first, Lily's gut told her that Dr. Broomfield had something to do with it.

ELEVEN

As Remi headed back to her room, she debated between stripping naked before crawling into her bed until the next shift, and heading to the shower to scrub the disappointing day from her memory. It'd been one of those days that Dr. Morsdux warned her about when everything seemed to go wrong, even the simplest things.

They'd been there at Mr. Jacob's death to help usher him into the void. He had a long history with ghosts. Remi suspected he might have been a serial killer when he was younger, but Dr. Morsdux had cautioned her against having those kinds of thoughts. They were there to help the patient, no matter the contents of their past. And even if he had been, it was important to ensure that none of those incorporeal beings caused problems for anyone else.

Remi checked her forearm which had been bandaged up after Mr. Jacob had passed. The air had been alive with scalpels and surgical scissors.

Remi felt lucky neither she nor Dr. Morsdux had lost an eye. He'd completed the banishing with a titration glass three inches deep in his shoulder. One that hadn't been in the room when they'd started the ritual.

As her hand brushed the handle to her room, she heard quiet muttering inside. Someone was riffling through her things.

Remi kicked the door open, startling her parents. The mattresses had been flipped and all the drawers were open.

"Remington," said her mother as she opened her arms, expecting a hug.

"Do you think me that stupid?"

Her parents glanced between themselves. Archer stepped forward with his hands clasped together.

"There's a perfectly good explanation."

"You're looking for the pendant," said Remi with her arms crossed.

"Of course, but the reasoning, Remi. That's what's important. We're trying to protect you from the people who want the pendant. You know how these things go. You take a job, and it turns out being much more important than you first thought."

"I always thought this job was something the both of you dreamed up. Or was that a lie too?"

"Ha ha," said Archer. "If you were in our shoes would you reveal the danger that we were all in? There was already so much pressure on you. Too much, it seems, since you got caught."

"I got caught 'cause you two pushed me to do it earlier than planned. I wasn't ready, because I hadn't found all the warding enchantments yet. Is that why I got caught? You two got spooked and pushed me even though you knew it wasn't safe?"

"The people who wanted the pendant were adamant about a schedule. Unfortunately, that schedule was more aggressive than what we were used to."

Remi threw her hands into the air.

"And then you two left me in Utica without visiting, or contacting me, or being there when I got out!"

A couple of orderlies in the hallway hurried past. In her anger, Remi slammed the door to keep others from overhearing, regretting it instantly.

"Look what you made me do."

"We've never made you do anything, darling," said Greta.

"You've always wanted to be a part of our jobs, kiddo," said Archer.

"Who *are* these people?"

"Who?" asked her father.

"The ones who want the pendant."

Archer swallowed.

"That's knowledge you'd be safer without. The less you know the better."

"I'm beginning to think it's the other way around. You want me to make a decision without all the facts. You're trying to con your only child. Your daughter. The one who went to jail for you. If I'd been in the mob or the yakuza, they'd be celebrating my return, not making me eat shit. You're not even *good* criminals."

Greta stepped forward and crossed her arms defiantly.

"Don't you dare say that to me. After everything that we went through to have you. We're the only ones that can protect you. We've been protecting you this whole time. You know I couldn't have kids after you. It was a difficult birth. I nearly died during the C-section."

It was a story she'd heard before, trotted out whenever they wanted to make her feel guilty.

"Maybe it would've been better if we'd both died."

"Remington! I can't believe you'd say that," said her mother.

Remi checked the scar on her forearm, wondering if that early near-death experience was the reason she had a connection to the Veil.

"You're shitty thieves, you know. Relying on your kid to bail you out again."

"Shitty thieves? Oh, child, you don't know the half of what we've done. Need I remind you of the time we snuck into the Fae and stole a valuable artifact?" said Greta.

"Far too many times. I'm beginning to wonder if you really did."

"Kiddo. I promise you we did."

"Then where's the riches from that artifact?"

Her parents shared a meaningful glance.

"They've gotten us this far. Unfortunately, it wasn't as valuable as we first thought. Some magics come with drawbacks," said a flat-lipped Archer.

"Remington," said her mother, "if you just give us the pendant, we can take care of some things. Once it's over, we'll bring back some treasures for you too. But if you don't, people are going to figure out you have it and come looking for it. I can't imagine you want more things weighing on your mind, what with the trials of the hospital, and I know those women from the prison are after you as well."

"How do you know about the Scythe Sisters?"

"We're your parents. We only want what's best for you," said her mother.

Remi opened the door and extended her arm.

"Get out. Now."

"Are you serious?"

"You were rummaging through my room to steal the pendant from me."

"Our pendant. We were a part of the job."

"And I was the one who spent a year in jail for it." She shook her arm. "And how fucking insulting you'd think I'd leave it in my room like some teenage girl hiding her diary. I assure you, it's nowhere near the hospital.

The city of sorcery is a big place covered in powerful magics. There are much better places to hide it than my dorm room."

Her mother exhaled and stormed past while her father walked slowly behind.

"I'm sorry, kiddo. We have a lot of pressure on us. Bad people want that pendant. If you can't give it to us, they might come looking for you, and they'll have ways of making you reveal it."

"Get out. Now. I don't care about your stupid pendant."

They disappeared around the corner, and Remi let out a scream of frustration. She sat on the bed and put her face in her hands. A part of her wanted to call them back and take them to the pendant, if only to get them out of her life. But she had spent a year in jail for it. While she didn't want to go after the item, she certainly didn't want them to either. The idiots would probably get themselves killed and then she'd be an orphan.

"Fuck this," she said, grabbing a coat and slamming the door behind her.

She knew it was risky leaving the hospital alone when the Scythe Sisters were lurking about, but she needed a drink. Or a jar of smoke. Some way to release the tension bottled in her chest.

As she strode across the cold sidewalk to the bar two blocks away, she couldn't help but think about Dr. Decker and the joke that everyone eventually went mad in Golden Willow. Remi just hadn't expected it to happen to her so soon.

TWELVE

The sidewalks were littered with discarded novelty wands and spark powder burns from a never-ending fireworks display a few days ago at the turn of the new year. Lily had been in the Curse Ward during the festivities, avoiding Dr. Broomfield. She couldn't even do a simple aura cleansing without him coming down on her about some minor error that she knew was one hundred percent grade-A bullshite.

"He's a fucking menace," she said, receiving a squeak of agreement from inside her hair.

A woman on the sidewalk gave her a wide berth, clearly thinking she'd gone mad. It kinda felt that way to Lily. She'd never felt incapable, but the constant nitpicking from Dr. Broomfield was making her feel like that first year Daryna.

Lily knew she shouldn't have headed into the city alone. The Scythe Sisters had been seen lurking about the hospital on numerous occasions, but she wanted to talk to her sister in person. And maybe she just wanted to get out of Golden Willow. It wasn't feeling like home anymore with Dr. Broomfield constantly breathing down her neck.

The train ride was uneventful. Not counting a couple of Oestomancer mages performing bone-breaking feats to the horror and amusement of the other riders. When a blonde woman unhooked her jaw like a python about to swallow a baby piglet whole, an older man in a suit and carrying a briefcase passed out.

Lily had messaged Alice that she was coming, but since she had Neko with her, they had to meet at the Cryptid Café. Alice already had a table with her boyfriend, Mag, who looked up from his financial textbook with a smile. He was wearing wire-rimmed glasses.

Three cups of tea were waiting for her arrival. Alice leaned over and breathed on them and suddenly they were steaming again as if they'd been freshly poured.

"Thanks, sis, for seeing me on such short notice."

Alice's forehead was hunched with concern as she cradled her teacup.

"You don't sound yourself."

"Aye, that's a fair assessment."

Lily settled into the seat, taking a sip of the black tea, which sent shivers of pleasure down her spine.

"Oh, I miss the days of sittin' around the cottage enjoying the mists rising on green hills."

"Feels like another time entirely," said Alice, staring out the window wistfully.

"How are things?"

Alice squeezed her lips tight.

"I have good days and bad days. Better than Evangel. Her hair is starting to fall out. She won't leave the house without a covering."

"I'm sorry, Alice. I'm trying. When I'm not in the hospital, I'm reading everything I can get my hands on, but nothing suggests a reason why an entire realm would become sick, or how to fix it. It's not like when the Fomorians ruined their own realm. Sorry, Mag."

He looked up from his reading with a faint smile.

"Since I wasn't the one who did it, I don't feel guilty."

"A perspective I wish I had," said Lily with a sigh. "But as for the kalkatai, I feel like I'm close, even with my hands as empty as they are."

"I know you'll find a solution, Lily. I've always believed that."

"I'm not sure I believe it anymore, but I'll keep trying. Right up until the bitter end."

"Is that what you came to talk about?"

"Yes and no. I don't know, honestly. It's the head of my department, Dr. Broomfield, I wanted to discuss."

"The asshole," said Alice right away.

"Aye, the asshole."

"Want me to put a curse on him?" asked Alice with a playful eyebrow raised. "Make his fingernails grow uncontrollably, or give him awful halitosis. Or maybe just make it so he sees ghosts all the time."

Lily chuckled.

"My sweet, sweet sister. The city has changed you."

"Dying has changed me," said Alice.

"Aye, I suppose it would. But no, I don't want you to put a curse on him, as good as that would make me feel. What I want you to do is to look into his past. Talk to people who know him. You've always been the best of us when it came to people. You kept Biddy and I from killing each other last year, and that was no small feat."

"What do you suspect?"

Lily shifted her mouth to the side.

"I wish I knew, but he strikes me false. He might just be a bloody jackeen, or he might have something cooking in that nasty pot of his."

"All fart and no shite?" asked Alice.

"No. He's got plenty of shite. A whole heaping of it. And he's been dumping it on me in buckets. Finds fault with everything I do, and a month ago, I swore he was trying to trick me into cursing myself."

"Cursing yourself?"

Lily spent the next twenty minutes explaining Patience Moffat and the story of her unlikely trip to the Fae.

"That doesn't make a bloody lick of sense," said Alice. "Her tale sounds like a story."

"But she believed it through and through."

"What happened to her?"

"I don't know and I didn't see her again. I assume he gave her something for the pipes she was hearing, if she was hearing 'em."

"Patience Moffat," said Mag, looking up from his textbook. "That sounds familiar."

"Familiar how?"

"I don't know, but if I think of it, I'll let you know," he said with a shrug.

"I'll do it, of course. I'll look into Dr. Broomfield, and Patience Moffat too. If I can find her."

Lily pulled a piece of paper out of her pocket and slid it over to Alice.

"I wrote everything I know about him on here. He stays at the hospital frequently, but he also has a place in the city."

Alice briefly reviewed the paper before folding it up and shoving it in her pocket.

"Maybe Lady Nimueh knows something about him."

"How is the Lady of the Mists?"

Alice tilted her head.

"Distracted, but thankfully she has me."

"Yeah, something's brewing in the city. I can feel it." Lily checked the time and sighed. "I need to get back. My next shift starts in a few hours. Would like a bite to eat before the hammer comes."

Alice stood and they exchanged hugs. Mag broke away from his textbook long enough to wave.

"Be safe."

Lily was two blocks away from the Cryptid Café, suspicions of Dr. Broomfield heavy on her mind, when she heard the crack of knuckles.

The Scythe Sisters were standing in her way and the sidewalk was suspiciously empty despite it being busy only moments before.

"Get out of my bloody way before I turn you bunch of eejits into wee bugs and then stomp on you."

"Wee bugs, eh?" asked Big Al.

Lily was reaching for Neko in her hair when Halley struck. The youngest Scythe extended her arm. Tendrils of greenish mist snaked around Lily's waist and slammed her against the brick building. The impact stunned her and erased the spell brewing on her lips.

"Shadows below..."

The cold was like having an icy hand wrapped around her heart. Lily found it hard to breathe and muster the energy to resist. It was like the girl had brought the Veil into the city. Halley's eyes were as dead as the realm she was channeling.

"Neko—"

The changeling leapt from her hair, but before he could transform, Nina threw two knives. The first one pinged off the concrete, nearly imbedding in Lily's leg, while the second caught Neko with a glancing blow. The white rat scurried away, squeaking in pain, then Halley made rising gestures and skeletal hands rose out of the concrete and grabbed Neko, trapping him against the sidewalk.

"You're full of surprises, just like your friend," said Big Al. "So tell me, Lilith de Meath, where does Remi keep her special valuables? If you're extra sweet and give us the location, we'll leave you alive enough that they can put you back together in that hospital of yours."

As Lily was being choked by the smoky tendrils, she saw the way the three sisters looked like they'd been turned up to eleven. They were on some kind of elixir that was making them stronger and faster than normal, which made resisting them even more fraught with danger.

"Go. Fuck. Yourself."

"Bad choice," said Big Al, gesturing towards Halley, who twisted her hand, squeezing Lily's windpipe harder.

Dots formed in her vision. Lily struggled against Halley's magic, but the strange girl was too strong. As her consciousness faded, Lily heard a shout and the crash of impact.

Moments later, she woke on the sidewalk. Lily looked up to see Alice sending crystalline vines undulating towards them that exploded into shards whenever Nina hit one with a knife. Big Al rumbled after Alice, but the glasses-wearing Mag slammed his backpack full of books into her head, spinning her into the street.

Lily couldn't see straight, but Neko was a few paces away, still trapped by skeletal hands. She crawled over and snapped the bones, turning them into dust and releasing Neko so he could transform. The changeling shimmered and morphed into a white tiger with fangs the size of daggers. When Neko charged Halley, Big Al stepped into the changeling's way, tackling the big cat onto the sidewalk.

As Lily regained her feet, she saw Nina lunging after Mag with her knife.

"Watch out!"

Mag spun around and the tip of the blade went into his backpack. He spun the pack over his head, and right against her skull, which sent the blade skidding across the concrete. Nina stumbled to her knees.

"Let's scram," said Big Al as she tossed Neko away.

The big woman had bloody scratches along her forearms but seemed unaffected by the wounds.

"Bloody hell you will," said Lily.

She prepared a defibrillator spell in hopes of knocking one of the sisters out, but before she could reach Nina, Halley exhaled an enormous cloud of greenish smoke that burned Lily's eyes. By the time she stumbled out of the mist, it was dissipating, revealing that the sisters had fled.

"Everyone okay?" asked Lily.

Mag held up his backpack which had a deep gouge from Nina's blade. He peeked into the interior.

"Never thought *The Halls and Financial Markets* would save my life."

"Never thought a Fomorian would save mine," she said. "Sorry. I'm still getting used to it."

Mag smiled and adjusted his wire-rimmed glasses.

"Are you okay?" asked Alice

Lily rubbed her neck. "That Halley is more powerful than I thought. I couldn't do anything against her."

"She's got the grave touch."

"Aye, fucking Veil."

Alice crossed her arms.

"No more going into the city alone."

"Aye. I was a bloody fool to think I could get away with it. I've learned my lesson, youngest sister." Lily smirked. "When did you become the wise one of the family? And what was with the crystalline vines? Medb giving you new gifts?"

"Not Medb. The city makes it hard to access her, but I've found other ways to be effective."

Lily checked her watch.

"Alright, I really need to get going. The station's only a block away. I should be fine now. Thanks, Alice."

She gave her sister a long hug and then after a moment of hesitation, threw her arms around Mag too.

THIRTEEN

Damon was kneeling in the corner of a hospital room investigating a fallen stuffed rabbit when he was attacked. A small body landed on his back with a fierce roar.

"Ack!" he cried with feigned horror. "I've been attacked!"

The young patient threw his arms around Damon's neck and made more roaring noises. Damon spun around, lifting Andrew off his shoulders and tossing him playfully onto the bed.

"No fair! You're bigger than I am," said Andrew, pouting.

Damon flexed his forearm, producing claws on his right hand, which brought coos of excitement.

"Meaner and tougher too."

"You're not mean," said Andrew, putting his hands on his hips.

The boy had hair coming out of everywhere, but he was grinning for the first time in a while.

"I can be. If the wrong people make me mad."

Andrew grabbed his arm.

"When will I get claws like that?"

"Later. A few years from now. But don't worry. It'll happen."

A knock on the frame had Damon turn. Dr. Lara was standing in the doorway with a wistful smile on her lips.

"Hey Andrew, can I borrow Healer Damon for a little bit?"

Andrew extended his hairy arms and growled fiercely before breaking into a warm smile.

"Only if he can come back. I wasn't done hunting him."

Damon mussed his hair and headed into the hallway with Dr. Lara. She tilted her head towards the open door.

"He seems to be accepting things better."

"He'll come around," said Damon. "I wish I could say the same for the parents."

Andrew had a recessive gene for therianthropy. When he was born they just thought he was unusually hairy, but eventually they realized he was showing signs of being a werewolf. At first they were horrified and sent him to therapy thinking that if he didn't believe he was a werewolf that he wouldn't change. It wasn't until he started having physical issues that they brought him to Golden Willow.

"Jeb's brewed up some new elixirs that might help his premature transformations, but honestly, the physical stuff we can deal with. You've been amazing with him on the emotional side. When they first brought him in and he was hiding in the corner and pissing on the equipment, I thought it would be a much longer road."

His cheeks warmed with pride. "Thank you, Dr. Lara. This is exactly why I joined Aura Healers. I know how hard the change can be."

"I have a favor to ask."

"Another therianthrope?"

"No, but I think it's a case that you're best suited to deal with."

Damon furrowed his forehead.

"I don't understand."

Dr. Lara made a random gesture with her hand.

"It's best that I let you figure it out on your own. I'm sorry to be so obtuse, but you'll understand the reason once you talk to the patient."

He headed towards the room with heavy thoughts on his mind. Why wouldn't she tell him? It was quite unusual, especially for Dr. Lara, who tended towards open communication.

Damon hesitated outside the door. He hadn't heard of any unusual cases entering the hospital, but maybe someone had been brought in while he was busy with Andrew or one of his other patients.

He took a deep breath and stepped through the door.

"Surprise!"

The cacophony of voices, both young and older, nearly had Damon dropping his clipboard. All the patients from the ward that he was working with, along with his fellow fourth years and his sisters, were crowded into the small room. A cake in the shape of a werewolf was resting on a rolling table with twenty-one unlit candles.

"Blood and bone, it's my birthday already?"

Remi threw her arms around him for a hug and then gave him a kiss, which brought laughing noises of disgust from the children.

"Gross!" said Andrew, who'd somehow gotten into the room before he'd arrived.

Damon mussed his hair again.

"You'll change your mind one day."

The kids started chanting, "Cake! Cake! Cake!"

Boon snapped his fingers and all the candles lit at once. Damon leaned over and blew them out to the cheers of the kids. After removing the candles, he served small pieces on paper plates.

"Only a half piece for you, Piper, otherwise you'll be floating on the ceiling from the sugar."

The little eight-year-old with pigtails tugged on her harness.

"I'll strap myself in. Please, Healer Damon. Everyone else is getting a full piece."

"Okay, fine," he said, grinning and adding the other half to her piece on the plate.

"Everyone back to their rooms," said Dr. Lara.

After the kids left, Boon shoved a perfectly wrapped box in his hands. It felt heavy like it was holding a bag full of sand.

"What's this?"

Boon smirked.

"No fun if I give it away."

Damon produced his claws and ripped right through the outer packaging. When he pulled out the light blue bag he was confused until he read the label.

"Luxurious Kitty? Really Boon, cat food?"

He winked.

"In case Regina comes back."

A squeak from Lily's hair had everyone laughing.

The next present was from the twins, who threw their arms around him before handing over a slim box. He opened it to find a silver bracelet.

"It's enchanted to protect against knives, you know, in case you stab yourself with a scalpel, fumble fingers," said Nat with a wink.

"Scalpel, huh?" he asked with a wry grin.

"Or swords," said Talia.

"This is pretty nice. How'd you afford that? Also, the silver is a nice touch."

"You don't think I'm lead in the play for free," said Talia.

When he linked the clasp on the bracelet around his wrist, Damon felt a tingling sensation across his skin that went away after a few seconds.

"Thanks, you two."

They gave him pecks on each cheek.

"We've got to get back to our Halls. We don't get all this free time like you Aura Healers," said Nat, winking to the others.

Boon stuck out his tongue.

After the twins left, the others gave him small presents: a jar of his favorite peanut butter, an elixir to strengthen his claws, and some other knick knacks.

When it was only the three of them, Lily brought him an exquisitely made leather sheath with runes etched into the outer covering.

"Is this for…?"

"Yep. Hopefully you never need it, but I thought you might want a way to carry around that sword should you ever decide to link to it."

"What do the runes do?"

"Most of them are a Look Away charm so you can carry it around in the city without being stared at. Now, don't do that around any police or other high-ranking mages, as they'll see through the glamour, but for every-day chums, it'll work great. The other runes are to keep the blade sharp and oiled."

"Thanks, Lily. This is amazing."

"Alice helped too."

"I'll tell her next time I see her."

Lily gave a side eye to Remi before leaving the room with the door closed behind her.

Remi settled up close.

"What did you get me?"

She pulled a box from behind her back. He shook it. The box rattled with metal.

"Sounds interesting."

The interior contained a pair of padded handcuffs and a blindfold.

"For later," said Remi.

"We've got the room to ourselves," said Damon, reaching over and turning the lock.

"I have to..."

"You have to what?"

Remi grabbed a piece of cake and smashed it into his face while laughing.

He scraped it off, grabbed her around the thighs, and lifted Remi onto the bed.

"I think you have some cake on your scrubs," she said.

"I guess I'd better take them off."

He leaned down to kiss her as she cinched her legs around his waist.

FOURTEEN

The EMTs were leaning against the outside of their ambulance smoking when Remi came up to them.

"Hey."

They glanced suspiciously at her.

"Ronnie and Jess, right?"

Jess smirked.

"You're Half-Pint. I've heard a lot about you."

Remi grimaced with a smile.

"That's me."

"What do you want? Spell Jockies don't normally talk to the Ditch Doctors unless they lose a bet," said Jess.

"I didn't lose a bet. But I could use your help."

Jess raised an eyebrow at Ronnie, who lifted his shoulders ambivalently.

"No promises, Half-Pint."

"I need a ride."

"We're not a taxi," said Jess.

"I know."

"Then get one."

"You said you've heard a lot about me. You know where I was before Golden Willow?"

"Ludwig's Max Arcane Security? Didn't you, like, rob D'Agastine Industries?"

"What? No. I was underage. It was juvie in upstate New York. And it was only some petty theft."

"How long?"

"A year."

"Doesn't sound petty."

"I stole from the wrong people. But look. Some of the women from jail kinda hate me and they've been hanging out near the hospital, causing problems and looking to get back at me. I was wondering if I could ride in the back of the ambulance until you get away from the hospital and then I'll take the train to where I'm really going."

"I already said, we're not a taxi."

Remi reached into her pocket and produced four small vials of silvery liquid. She used her body to shield the items from anyone who might be looking from inside.

"What if I give you these?"

Jess stiffened and immediately glanced around.

"How'd you know?"

Remi tilted her head.

"You're not the only one who hears things."

"Fine. Get in. We've got to get rolling anyway," said Jess, flicking her cigarette into the sewer.

Remi climbed into the back. Once they were out of sight of the hospital staff, she handed over the four vials to Jess.

"It's a Jeb special, so you know, be careful."

"You don't know the half of it."

They dropped her off outside the train station. Remi checked to make sure the Scythe Sisters hadn't figured it out and then boarded the train. The trip to the Charm & Hammer passed slowly because she was constantly checking over her shoulder to make sure she wasn't being followed. After the close call when the Scythe Sisters nearly got Lily, they knew they couldn't leave the hospital without precautions.

Remi flipped the bartender off on the way to the secret passage. He shook his head and kept cleaning the counter with a rag.

When she burst through the door, she found Warnock talking to two hard-looking men that were openly displaying handguns on their hips.

Warnock shook his graying dreadlocks when he saw who it was. The two men reached for their weapons, but Warnock put a hand on their shoulders.

"Bloody hell, Remi."

"I need to talk and I don't have a lot of time."

Warnock growled under his breath.

"Gentlemen. Why don't you go up to the bar and have a drink on me. I'll try to get rid of this one right away."

After they were gone, Warnock crossed his arms. His ice-blue eyes were burning bright.

"I never should have showed you that secret passage. Barging in here without warning could get you killed."

"Those two assholes?" she asked, jutting her thumb in their direction.

"They work for a gang in the Undercity."

"Not really my expertise."

"Why are you here, Remi?"

She glanced past the owner into the secret bar. A group of businessmen in the corner spot were leaning over to snort pink powder from the table. As one of them leaned back, his body shifted in three directions at once.

"Greta and Archer are in town."

When he didn't answer right away, she scoffed.

"I know they came to see you," she said.

He sighed.

"They came to see me a few months ago, not long after they arrived."

"Why didn't you warn me?"

"I didn't know that was part of my responsibilities. Besides, I thought they'd already talked to you." He hunched his forehead. "What do they want?"

"You remember I spent a year in Utica?"

"Yeah."

"They want the pendant I stole."

"Then give it to them. Or sell it and split the profits."

Remi gritted her teeth. "They used me. I caught them turning my room looking for it."

"In your room? Wow. That's insulting."

"Tell me about it."

"Can I ask what this pendant is for?"

"It's not valuable on its own. It's a key, of sorts."

"Do you not know or don't want to tell me?"

Remi kept her lips squeezed tight. The pendant led to a mythical Horn, but not very many people knew that and the more that did would be a problem.

"Good kid."

"They told me they were working for someone else. They never told me that before. Now whoever it is, they want the pendant. You wouldn't happen to know who that is?"

"Except for their visit, I haven't seen them in years."

"Come on, Warnock. You've had to have heard something. Rumors, anything?"

He sighed.

"Back around the time you went to jail, I heard they were mixed up with some heavy hitters."

"A big gang?"

"No. The *real* heavy hitters. Legitimate corporate heads, or big-time Hall mages, something like that. Never heard any details, but they're not petty crooks."

"Hall mages?"

"Rumors, Remi. Nothing more. I wouldn't put too much stock into it."

She thought about the Horn, which she knew little about except that it was valuable. Maybe it had hidden powers that some Hall mage was looking for? Rich people liked to collect artifacts.

"Do you want some advice?" he asked.

"I can always ignore it."

Warnock chuckled.

"If there really are some big-time hitters after this pendant, you'd best get rid of it as soon as possible. You don't want to get into the crosshairs of people like that. If they have your parents spooked into turning your room, who knows what they'll do to them, or who else they'll send after it."

"I know, but—"

"But what?"

A fire burned in her belly.

"I feel used. Like I'm not even their kid." She leaned against the desk. "What was Greta like when I was little?"

"Like they always did, they disappeared for a few years, and when they returned, they had you. Greta's not very motherly. I know that much. Not everyone's born with that gift. But they did their best, as far as I can tell, having not had any kids myself."

"That you know of."

Warnock snorted with laughter.

"That I know of."

"Did they really lose a bet to give me my name?"

Warnock stared into the bar as a group of women at the bar wearing sashes were downing glowing elixirs.

"It wasn't a bet. But I don't know the real reason. That was just something they started saying when people asked."

"Do they actually know how to tell the truth?" asked Remi, shaking her head and scowling.

"It's easy to lose track of it in our line of work. You know, I'm glad you got out, Remi. Maybe this is an opportunity to get all the way out. For good. Focus on the life you're making at Golden Willow. I know your parents might not be able to express it, but I'm proud of you, and I think deep down inside, they are too."

"Lousy way to show it."

"Think about it, kid. Don't carry on their mistakes. Break the cycle. Move on with your life."

"They're not paying you to say that, are they?"

He shook his head and she believed him.

"Free of charge."

"Thanks, Uncle Warnock."

He opened his arms for a hug.

"Makes me wish I had a kid. As long as they'd be as cool as you."

"I should get back to the hospital. No rest for the wicked."

When she reached the door, she turned back.

"Please don't tell my parents I came here."

Warnock nodded towards the secret bar.

"They'd kill me if they knew you had."

Remi left the Charm & Hammer, thinking about turning over the pendant the entire ride home. Warnock was right. If she got rid of it, she could move on with her life, making a clean break from the life of crime that she'd been born into. She wasn't ready to hand it over right now, but maybe after she had a chance to talk to her friends she would. It was the best way to keep them all safe.

FIFTEEN

Only half the Spire was visible beneath the thick cloud layer that covered the city as Lily exited the train car in the third ward. A homeless man was huddled beneath a pile of blankets, muttering what sounded like an incantation.

Remi threw a few crumpled bills at the guy's feet. A dirty hand snatched them up before disappearing into the covers.

"Thanks for coming with me," said Lily.

"Safety in numbers."

Lily paused at the top of the stairs.

"Speaking of."

She stepped out of the way of the crowd and pulled a milky orb from a pocket. After a few words, the object glowed a faint pink.

"I don't think they're following us."

Remi screwed up her face.

"Does that really work?"

"Not if they're actively trying to defeat it, but if they're just on our tail, then it should work fine. You really think they're capable of higher-end magics?" asked Lily.

"I wasn't expecting Halley to come back from the dead with weird powers. Who knows what she can do?"

"Good point. We should keep our fingers to the air."

The blue line station was on the edge of the ward, which meant it was only a short three-block stroll to reach the twelfth. They crossed the ring road using a pedestrian overpass. The fencing was covered in colorful zip ties and other detritus that fluttered in the wind from the speeding cars.

"Are you sure this is the right location?" asked Remi as they crossed into the outer ward.

"Alice assured me that this was where he worked."

Remi shook her head.

"I can't imagine Dr. Broomfield doing pro bono work in a clinic."

"The hospital changes everyone. Not always for the better," said Lily.

The twelfth had once been the industrial center of the city in the previous century, but now it was a mix of empty lots covered in trash, or old factories in a state of disrepair. Gang tags were painted on the walls, some of them glowing with lingering alchemical agents.

"Neko's with you?" asked Remi as she shoved her hands deep in her pockets.

"Of course. Why?"

Remi covertly nodded towards the roof of a nearby building where two men in heavy clothing and holding automatic weapons were watching.

"Should we worry?"

"I don't think so. But eventually someone is going to check us out. Just act natural and don't make any sudden gestures."

Lily frowned.

"I'm glad you made us put those enchantments on before we left the hospital."

"They won't stop a bullet, but they'll make it easier to heal afterwards. And hey, before we get to this clinic, I want your opinion on something."

"Speak the wind."

Remi sighed heavily.

"I'm considering giving the pendant to my parents."

Lily raised an eyebrow at her friend.

"I know, I know. After everything I went through to get it."

"No, that's not it at all. That thing was nothing but bloody trouble for you. I'm surprised you kept it this long."

"That's exactly why I'm thinking about giving it up. Even if it might have changed my life."

"What is so important about it?"

Remi lowered her chin to her chest.

"I'd rather not say."

Lily could see the decision was more about her parents than the pendant. There was something dark and painful coiled in her friend's chest.

"I'll support you whatever you decide."

"Thanks."

As they rounded a corner, two men and a woman stepped out of a doorway. The men were wearing painted masks that turned their faces into fearsome beasts, while the woman had her head uncovered. She was a hob with snaggle teeth and dark ochre skin.

"You're not welcome here."

"We're healers from Golden Willow," said Lily.

"Do you not understand the meaning of not welcome here?" asked the hob woman.

Remi pulled her hands out of her pockets and after a twirl of her fingers, a folded set of bills appeared.

"We just want to see if the hospital can offer support to the local clinic."

The hob woman's gaze shifted to the money. She reached out and tried to snatch the bills, but Remi snapped her fingers and they were empty.

"I can take it from your dead body," said the woman.

"We're not here to scrap," said Remi.

The hob woman glanced between the two of them.

"I hate mages."

"Please," said Remi, holding out the money on her flat open hand.

"Fine. But if you cause any problems, you're not leaving the twelfth."

Lily followed her friend deeper into the ward.

"I'm glad I brought you."

"That wasn't as bad as it looked. They just wanted to shake us down. You have to make them feel like they earned it," said Remi.

Lily looked up to the street sign on the corner.

"The clinic should be around here."

Remi clucked her tongue and pointed towards the industrial buildings.

"In there."

"It looks like it's about to fall over."

"Smells like cooking fires."

Remi took the lead. From the street side, the buildings looked uninhabited, but as they got closer, Lily saw the way the chain link fences had been covered in tarps and other materials to hide the signs of civilization.

When they came around the corner of a graffitied outbuilding, Lily came face-to-face with an enormous woman around ten feet tall. Her hands looked like they could crush a skull easily. She had all the markings of the Fomorians.

"I smell mages," said the woman in a deep voice. "No entry."

"We're here to visit your clinic. We come from Golden Willow."

The enormous woman leaned into Lily's face and gave a deep sniff.

"You smell like a witch."

Then she turned her head slightly.

"And you smell like bones."

"Can we come in?" asked Lily.

The guard growled under her breath.

"Would you like some gum?" asked Remi. "It's from a candy shop in the third. It tastes like your favorite memories."

The enormous woman gently removed the package from Remi's hand and ushered them past.

Between the covered chain link fences and the building were dozens of makeshift buildings or tents where humans and non-humans alike were lounging around small cooking fires. Everyone was covered in a patina of dirt and had haunted, hungry gazes.

A man with tentacles for arms was playing a wooden flute near the entrance to the industrial building. He was using the suckers to hold down the fingering holes on his instrument. The song was tranquil.

"You ever been in a place like this?" asked Lily.

"This? No, but similar. They all have the same feel of quiet desperation."

Inside the factory the buildings had a more structured feel as if it were a mini-city. Lily observed a big hob getting shaved by a barber in a corner hut, while kids ran through the passages playing tag. She saw humanoids from all different realms, including a blind woman with autumn leaves swirling around her head.

Eventually they came to a building with a line of people waiting outside. A bloodcurdling scream from inside had Lily on high alert despite the lack of reaction from those waiting.

"Is this the clinic?" Remi asked.

"Get in line," said a guy with no front teeth and one eye that looked like it'd come from a cat. "Been waiting for three hours."

"We're not here to be served. We're healers," said Lily.

Remi grabbed Lily's hand.

"Come on."

There were cries and callouts as they pushed through the opening. The interior looked like a waiting room, except there was no television keeping people occupied.

A second awful scream came from deeper inside.

Lily went up to the window. A hob woman in a nurse's outfit from the previous century was sitting behind a desk, painting her fingernails a bright orange. Her makeup and outfit were meticulously crafted. She looked like she was getting ready for an old-time pinup shoot.

"May we talk to whoever is in charge of the clinic?" asked Remi.

The hob woman barely looked up from her nail painting.

"You have to wait with all the others."

"We're healers from Golden Willow. We came to offer our services," said Remi as she slid folded bills across the table.

The hob woman deftly snatched the money, which quickly disappeared inside her sleeve, then she nodded towards the doorway.

"You want Dr. Marcie."

Before they went in, another building-rattling scream sent shivers down Lily's spine.

"What in bloody hell?"

They followed the noise through a curtain to find an enormous woman like the guard at the gate lying half-naked in a kiddie's swimming pool with her legs spread. A woman with a black braid entwined with bones and other trinkets that went down to the middle of her back was bent over between the woman's legs.

Three sets of eyes drilled into them as they entered the room. Neither the patient or the doctor was looking at them, but the three women helpers who were carrying buckets of warm water to the pool gave them nasty looks.

"Augh..."

The enormous woman in the pool looked like she was in the throes of pain. Or birth. She had to weigh over five hundred pounds. Her long canines looked like they could rip through steel.

"Marcie, we have visitors," said one of the women as she dumped water into the pool.

"I think they can figure out that we're busy right now," said Dr. Marcie.

Lily stepped forward.

"We're healers from Golden Willow. We wanted to ask you questions about Dr. Broomfield."

Dr. Marcie turned her head slightly.

"We could use the extra hands. You, witch, help me with Lucy. She's crowning. Your friend can carry water."

Remi smirked as she headed towards the kitchen where multiple pots were on the stove.

Lily started to pull the bottoms of her pants up but realized the water was too deep and she'd likely have to kneel, so she waded into the warm water next to Dr. Marcie. Lily caught whiffs of brimstone within the big woman's musky scent.

"What do you need me to do?" asked Lily.

"Ever helped with a birth?"

"A few times," said Lily, though most of them were foals or other barnyard animals. She'd done a brief rotation in the maternity ward of Golden Willow, but it'd focused on the problems after birth, rather than during.

"The baby is stuck sideways. I can't get the shoulder past the pelvic bone. I need a second set of hands to help me turn the baby."

"Let me clean first."

The quick spell sanitized her hands.

"Ready."

With guidance from Dr. Marcie, Lily shoved her hands past the huge head sticking from the cervix. Nubs that would eventually turn into horns were sticking from the front of the baby's head.

"Do you feel the shoulder?"

Lily felt around the side as Remi dumped a new bucket of heated water into the pool. The baby was as big as a small child, which made it harder to reach around it. Towards the shoulder blades, her fingers ran into bony extensions.

"There's more than a shoulder here."

Dr. Marcie's head dipped.

"Fuck," she whispered under her breath.

"What's wrong?" asked the mother between deep exhales.

"Everything will be fine, Lucy. You focus on the deep space. Bring the dark sun forward."

While Dr. Marcie was talking, Lily felt around the bony structure.

"They feel like nascent wings."

"That's why she's stuck," said Dr. Marcie, shaking her head. "I don't know what to do without a real set of facilities. Do you think we can pull them past?"

"We can try."

"Let me get my hands on her neck to support the spine, then we'll pull together."

Lily didn't think it was going to work, but she was willing to try.

"One, two, pull!"

She put her back into it, trying to pull hard without causing issues for the baby, but within the first few seconds, Lily knew it wasn't going to work.

"Baby okay?" asked Lucy in a concerned, booming voice.

"Everything will be fine," said Dr. Marcie with a fake smile, but when Lucy looked away, it turned to pinched concern.

"I have one more idea and then I don't know. We'll try and spin the baby to face downward so we can fold the wings."

The two of them tried to maneuver the big baby, but between the wide shoulders and the wing bones, she wouldn't move. Dr. Marcie let her hands drop into the water with her head hanging low.

"I have an idea," said Lily.

"I'll try anything."

"Hey Remi, I need you. Can you perform the pain blocking charm? You'll need to maintain it while we try something else."

Remi furrowed her forehead.

"I'll cast it, but why maintain? Won't that just knock her out?"

"Remi..."

"Got it."

She situated herself near the mother's head. A few gestures and words later, the big Fomorian woman's eyes had rolled backwards until there was nothing but white.

"What are you going to do?" asked Dr. Marcie suspiciously.

"I'm going to break the bones in the wings so we can maneuver her past the pelvis and then we can set them when the baby is free."

"I can see why you knocked her out first. She'd kill you if she heard you say that," said Dr. Marcie.

"Let me block the baby's pain first."

Performing a pain charm on a child that was mostly in her mother's birthing canal came with challenges, but Lily managed to get it right the first time.

Then she reached around the baby until she'd found the wing bones. The infant's wings were still nascent and thin, which made them as weak as twigs. Lily snapped the supporting bones, which made her sick to her stomach.

"Okay, we can pull now."

This time, the two of them made progress on sliding the baby out. It took twisting, but within a few minutes they'd freed the child from the cervix. The baby plopped into the pool looking like a three-year-old human with limp wing structures on her back. Dr. Marcie leaned over and cleaned out her mouth to confirm that she was breathing.

Lily hadn't realized how long it'd been since she'd applied the pain blocker on the baby when it suddenly screamed. The high-pitched wail went right through Lily.

"My baby!"

The Fomorian woman sat upright despite Remi maintaining the spell.

Lily had her hands on the wing bones, preparing to reset them when the mother growled with anger.

"You hurt my baby!"

The Fomorian woman reached out to grab Lily around the neck, but she scrambled out of the pool, splashing onto the concrete. As Dr. Marcie scooped the screaming child into her lap, the mother climbed to her feet.

"I'm gonna kill you!"

"No, Lucy! She was helping you!" yelled Dr. Marcie.

The half-naked Lucy climbed out of the pool, knocking over a pot and pushing one of the other helpers out of the way as she tried to come after Lily, who was racing around the pool.

"Lucy, stop! It was the only way! The wings were stuck!"

Lily made a lunge for the exit but Lucy grabbed her around the shoulders and tossed her against the wall.

The impact knocked the wind out of Lily's chest. She slumped to the ground as the Fomorian woman reached her hand back. Lily was certain her head was about to be crushed in when Dr. Marcie stepped into the way holding the enormous baby.

"Stop! If you kill her, she can't fix the wings."

Lucy's arm halted mid-thrust.

"She hurt my baby."

"She didn't hurt your baby. She's *fixing* your baby. Lucy. I need you to get out of the way so we can mend the wing bones. Or do you want your child to be permanently malformed?"

Lucy shrank, pulling her arms to her chest.

"Fix baby. Please."

Remi ran over and helped Lily to her feet. They brought the baby to a table, laying the child on its stomach.

Repairing the wing bones didn't take long, but Lily felt the mother breathing over her shoulder the entire time.

"There," said Lily, stepping back. "The bones are fixed."

Lucy pushed them out of the way and scooped up her child, immediately pulling up her shirt to nurse the baby.

"Come on, everyone. Let's let Lucy have her moment alone," said Dr. Marcie, ushering everyone out of the room.

They entered what looked like a hall closet with a single chair and a stubby table with a few old tomes in a pile.

"Welcome to my office..."

Dr. Marcie looked exhausted, with dark rings around her eyes. She fidgeted with the bone trinkets in her braid.

"And thanks for the help. You came at a good time. If the child would have died, we probably would have had to kill Lucy."

"I thought things at Golden Willow were bad," said Remi.

Dr. Marcie furrowed her forehead.

"What *are* you doing here?"

"Did you work with Dr. Broomfield in this clinic?"

"Marcus? Yeah, but that was a long time ago, before the Event, before a lot of things."

"What was he like?"

Dr. Marcie pursed her lips.

"What's this about? It certainly doesn't look like professional curiosity."

"I don't know," said Lily. "He's our new instructor. While he's more stable than the previous guy, he's done some odd things."

"That doesn't sound like Marcus. Are you sure we're talking about the same guy?"

Lily gave a brief description that had Dr. Marcie nodding.

"That sure sounds like him, even as it doesn't. When he moonlighted at the clinic, he was the kindest, gentlest, and most patient doctor we've ever had. The fact that he knew the medical side and the Aura Healer side made him invaluable. I was really sad when he moved out of the city."

"Where did he go?"

Dr. Marcie tapped on her chin.

"After he went on a long vacation, he came back and told us he'd gotten a job with some private equity alchemical research facility. That was the last we'd heard from him. Until now."

"None of that makes a lick of sense," said Remi, grimacing. "The alchemy research does, but not your description of him. Unless he was working a con somehow."

"It doesn't sound like a con to me," said Lily. "What's there to gain at a clinic like this?"

Remi bunched up her lips.

"I have no idea, but it smells like bullshit. Were there any problems when he was here? Missing supplies or something odd?"

Dr. Marcie broke into laughter.

"Supplies? You saw our birthing room. A cheap kiddie pool and hot water. If anything, Marcus brought us supplies from Golden Willow. We really missed him after he was gone."

"Nothing weird?" asked Remi. "Missing people?"

Dr. Marcie exhaled deeply.

"I don't think you understand how on the edge we are here. While we live in a ward of the city of sorcery, we might as well live in a backwater realm. The people that live in the enclave wouldn't be accepted anywhere else."

"They can't go to Golden Willow?" asked Lily.

"The more human presenting ones can, but anyone with visible changes aren't accepted."

Lily furrowed her brow.

"That can't be true."

"Think about it," said Remi. "How many hobs or others have you seen in the hospital?"

"Morwen Clover didn't have any problem moving through the hospital," said Lily.

Remi tilted her head.

"She's a cute girl with a charming personality. And then think about Regina. Even the therianthropes can get away with looking human."

"Right," said Lily with a tightness around her chest.

She'd always thought of herself as open-minded but the last few years at Golden Willow had taught her she had many blind spots.

Dr. Marcie was staring with her hands clasped in front. Lily could feel the judgement but their host was polite enough not to say anything.

"So no missing people?" asked Lily.

"I wouldn't have the slightest idea if people were missing or just left to find other lives," said Dr. Marcie with a shrug.

"Do you happen to know what firm he went to work for?" asked Lily.

"Nope. We grieved his loss and then moved on. It's all I can do here. I'm sorry, but I really need to get back to my patients. I have a long line."

"Thank you for your time," said Lily.

"Thank you for the help with Lucy and the baby. Things would have been much worse without you."

As they headed out, Lily turned back before Dr. Marcie called the next patient.

"I'll see if we can get some supplies sent your way. I don't know how much, but you look like you could use the help."

"Anything, even a single bedpan, would be an improvement over what I'm using now. Thank you."

They worked their way out of the enclave in silence. When they reached the street, Remi glanced back, shaking her head.

"I don't get it. She made Dr. Broomfield sound like a saint. You didn't buy that, did you?"

"No. Something doesn't add up."

"We need to find out who he worked for. Private equity alchemical research sounds like a load of bull to me," said Remi.

"Me too, but I don't get the motivation. Then again, I'm a healer, not an investigator."

"Bullshit," said Remi. "Every patient is an investigation. We just need to treat this like one and find out what the root cause is and then cut it out, if necessary."

Lily chuckled under her breath.

"Never change, Remi Wilde. Never change."

SIXTEEN

The old woman was lying on the ceiling with tentacles undulating from her open mouth. The bright, sunny day outside the Hospice Ward failed to penetrate the frightening scene inside the room.

"Hand me the teacup," said Dr. Morsdux in a calm voice with his hand out.

Remi couldn't keep her eyes off the old woman, expecting a tentacle to snatch her up to be swallowed.

"The teacup?"

"Unless I'm mistaken, there's only one in the room."

"Yeah, I know, but I still don't understand."

"Remi?"

She slid over to the table, never looking down, and managed to grab the porcelain teacup on the first try.

"Thank you, Remi."

Dr. Morsdux muttered over the teacup. It was an incantation she was unfamiliar with.

"Miss Arbor. Can you hear me?"

"I'll rip your black heart out and eat it with a spoon," came a voice that wasn't the old woman's.

"I think she can," said Dr. Morsdux with the quirk of a smile at the corner of his lips.

"How can you be so calm?" asked Remi under her breath.

"Besides the risk of getting torn apart by her spectral tendrils, why there's nothing to be worried about."

Remi was regretting coming to the Hospice Ward.

"Bolster that resolve, Remi. We've a Voron to banish. Poor Miss Arbor didn't sign up to be a vessel of malice, but it's our job to save her and put things right."

"Couldn't we have just turned the entire room into an inferno? She was on her final days."

"Which made her vulnerable to the Voron. Come now, Remi. It's our job to usher them into the void peacefully."

"I know, I know."

Dr. Morsdux held the antique teacup in the air.

"Miss Arbor. Are you there? I have your favorite teacup. If you don't come out, I'm going to smash it to bits on the tile floor."

The spectral tendrils stiffened for a moment while the facial expressions turned back to that of an old woman.

"No, please!"

"That's it, Miss Arbor. Fight the Voron," said Dr. Morsdux.

Her wrinkles deepened with shadows as she cried out in a silent scream.

In sotto voce, Dr. Morsdux said, "Get the silvered salt."

Remi grabbed the bottle.

"Put some in the palm of your hand."

She did as he requested as Miss Arbor fought with the Voron.

"If you don't win this battle, I'm going to smash the cup!"

"No, please!" she cried. "It was my great-grandmother's."

Dr. Morsdux spoke under his voice.

"Get ready to throw."

Remi cocked her arm back as Dr. Morsdux set the porcelain cup on the bed and began chanting a spell that would help push the Voron back into the Veil.

As bright lights exploded from his upthrust hands, he yelled, "Throw!"

Remi launched the silvered salt onto the ceiling, which made the Voron scream. A shadowy tendril shot downward and knocked Dr. Morsdux spinning into the wall. Another nearly hit Remi, but she ducked under it and grabbed the teacup.

"Stop or I'll break it!"

The tentacles writhed with indecision. Then one shot out and tried to grab the cup, but Remi slammed it downward onto the tile in hopes of startling Miss Arbor into action.

The teacup bounced off the tile, ricocheting into the corner before bouncing around.

"Oh crap."

Dr. Morsdux was finding his feet, looking unsteady from the impact with the wall. Remi realized what the earlier spell she hadn't recognized had been. He'd protected the cup from being smashed, but now the threat had been proved false.

The Voron's tentacles were whipping outward, looking for purchase, but Remi kept ducking beneath them.

"Grab the salt!"

She made a lunge for the bottle, but a tentacle grabbed her around the midsection and yanked her into the air. She was pulled towards the open mouth which somehow seemed much larger up close.

Before she could be shoved into the Voron's mouth, Remi punched Miss Arbor in the forehead.

To her surprise, the tentacle dropped her. She half-landed on the bed, catapulting off to slam into the wall.

"Remi, with me!"

Dr. Morsdux spoke, his voice turning gravelly with power. She joined him in the incantation, the twinned words making the Voron flinch. As they kept up the banishing spell, Miss Arbor began to scream again. It was the easiest way to get rid of the Voron, but it would cause the host great pain.

"In Vecto Morbi Dalaci!"

As a bright flash of white light exploded from Miss Arbor's mouth, she fell onto the bed face-first.

"Quickly, quickly. Turn her over."

Remi helped Dr. Morsdux put Miss Arbor on her back. She was moaning and twitching, until he put a calming spell on her that gently put her to sleep.

When the patient was finally unconscious, Dr. Morsdux leaned against the bed looking older and more frail than usual.

"I used to be able to banish them in my sleep. I'm glad you were here, Remi."

She shook her head as she breathed heavily.

"I don't know how you stay so calm when they're trying to kill you. Or keep the dying woman's favorite teacup safe when smashing it might have helped her win the fight."

He put a hand on her shoulder.

"It's the last thing they'll remember, and if we do our job right then they'll make it through the Veil without getting stuck. We owe it to them."

Remi wandered to the window and pulled it open so she could enjoy some fresh, chilly air. As she leaned against the edge, thinking about how different her life was from before, she spotted a white van with a fresh decal on the side reading: Spot Cleaners.

"You've got to be kidding me..."

"Is there a problem, Miss Wilde?" asked Dr. Morsdux as he examined Miss Arbor.

"I have to check on something."

Dr. Morsdux tilted his head.

"I'll be right back," she said as she ran out of the room and pulled out her phone.

Remi first dialed Lily and then Damon, but neither of them answered. When she hit the elevators, she paused, thinking long and hard about what she wanted to do about her parents.

"Think, Remi, think."

There was a chance they could have let her see the van, knowing she'd clock the real owners and rush to the location of the pendant, thus giving it away. On the other hand, they could have found someone to divine its location using magic so they wouldn't even need her.

In the end, she decided that the chance she would see the van while working was pretty slim, so she decided it was probably the latter. Remi burst into the stairwell, running up to the roof, and headed straight for the HVAC unit where she'd hidden the pendant.

She nearly ran into Big Al wearing a white carpet cleaners jumpsuit with the Spot Cleaners logo. Remi backed up as the former Utica prisoner slowly turned.

"You were right, Miss Wilde. She came running just as you said, but I still don't know why," said Big Al.

Remi was confused, thinking that she was talking about her until Big Al stepped out of the way, revealing the other two Scythe Sisters and her parents.

"Hey, kiddo," said her father.

"What in the seven hells?" spat Remi.

Nina pulled out a blade and began to advance until her mother put a hand on Nina's shoulder.

"Remember, we said no one touches her. She is our daughter, despite what happened between you all at Utica."

Remi felt like a hole had opened up on the roof and she was falling forever. The sight of her worst enemies with her parents didn't make sense. Nothing did.

"What are you...?"

"Remi, tell Big Al why you knew we were in the hospital," said Archer as he leaned under the HVAC unit and pulled the box from its hiding location.

"Spot Cleaners. It's their favorite bad joke."

Big Al screwed up her face.

"I still don't understand."

"Spot as in mark. The person who gets conned. They're cleaning out the mark. I've always told them reusing that logo and bad pun was going to get them in trouble."

"Very clever," said Big Al.

"Not really," responded Remi. "What the fuck is going on? Why are you all working with each other? Have you been on the same side this whole time?"

"No, kiddo," said her father as he rattled the box against his ear. "But when you wouldn't reveal the location of the pendant, we knew we had to find it another way. And then we ran into these lovely young women who understand how the world works. We've partnered with them until we can complete the job."

"They tried to fucking kill me!" said Remi, extending her arms.

Greta gave her a sour look.

"Maybe you shouldn't have tried to kill Halley. She's seems like a lovely, but odd, young woman."

Remi's stomach did flips. She felt like she was having a panic attack with nothing making sense.

"Ahh...here it is," said Archer, pulling the pendant from the box. "It really doesn't look like much, does it? To think we've been after this thing for two decades."

He wrapped the chain around his palm and shoved the pendant into his pocket.

"Do I get to cut her now?" asked Nina.

"No, no," said Archer. "Remember, that's our daughter, and while she's chosen another path, we need to respect that and let her go on with her sedentary life. I can't say I understand it, but we shouldn't interfere now that we have the pendant. There are riches ahead for us."

Big Al gestured her way.

"We can't let her interfere with us leaving."

Her parents glanced between each other before Greta nodded to Halley.

"You can do your thing, but don't hurt her."

"Mother!"

"Enjoy your new life, daughter," said Greta as she strolled past.

"I—"

The words barely left Remi's mouth before Halley swirled her arm in a circle and skeletal arms broke free from the tarry roof and grabbed her ankles. Before Remi could counter their hold on her, a heavy slumber rose up from the depths and she felt herself sinking to the ground.

§

Remi woke to Lily shaking her shoulder. The rooftop was empty except for the Irish witch.

"No, no!" she said, sitting up.

"What happened? I saw your message once I was done with procedures, but it took three spells to track you down. Why were you unconscious on the roof?"

Remi gave her the blow by blow of the events.

"I'm so sorry, Remi. That's bloody awful. Your parents working with the Scythe Sisters? I can hardly believe it."

"Sadly, I can." Remi walked to the edge of the roof to witness the empty parking space where the van had been earlier. "Maybe it's for the best. That pendant has been nothing but trouble. Better to be rid of it and with it the Scythe Sisters. We can go back to leaving the hospital without precautions."

"Are you sure?" asked Lily by her side.

Remi felt the weight removed from her shoulders.

"Yeah. I mean, I think so. Good riddance, right?"

Lily grabbed her hand and leaned against her shoulder.

"Your parents are twats."

"I know. But they *are* my parents."

SEVENTEEN

"I'll take the number three, the number five, make that two number fives, and the stack of flapjacks with extra syrup and a pot of coffee," said Damon, leaning back in the seat.

The waitress stared with her jaw hanging low while his friends smirked on the opposite side of the bench.

"These aren't for them?" asked the waitress.

"All me. I'm a growing boy," he said, winking.

The waitress turned slowly and headed back to the kitchen. A short time later, he spotted the staff in back peering at him through the gap.

"I get hungry after a change," he said with a shrug.

Lily raised an eyebrow at Remi next to her.

"Have fun last night?"

Remi was staring at the opposite side of the diner while clutching her steaming coffee mug.

"Huh?"

Damon leaned back to see what she'd clocked. A faint apparition was floating through the spaces between the tables, nodding at the customers. A little boy was waving enthusiastically at the ghost.

"How is it any different from a ghost taxi? Or that band Boon raves about with the ghost drummer, the Sticky Wickets?" asked Damon.

"We have our fair share of benign ghosts, but too many require interventions. I can't imagine how insane it'd be if we hadn't fixed the hospital wards last year."

"Seen the Stranger recently?" asked Lily after sucking her chocolate milkshake through a straw.

"Not in a few weeks. The last time was when we were there at Mr. Tester's end."

"The Stranger?" asked Damon. "Should I know this?"

"It's some bloody poser she sees in the Veil sometimes," said Lily.

"I didn't think humans can live there?" he asked.

"We don't know who or what he is. That's why he's called the Stranger."

Lily's phone rattled on the table. She leaned over and cursed under her breath.

"I hate that bloody eejit. Wants me back in the ward."

"He's a menace," said Remi, shaking her head. "I swear he doesn't want you to get a moment's rest."

"He's not that bad," said Damon, receiving twin glares of annihilation from across the table.

"Bloody hell he isn't. I know you've got to suck up to him to get into the Institute, but he's trying to bury me in the bog," said Lily.

Damon lifted his shoulders.

"He can be rough, but he's got good intentions. I mean, didn't you learn as much at that clinic?"

"I don't for a second believe that bullshite that Dr. Marcie told us about him," said Lily.

She picked up her milkshake and sucked on the straw while staring out the window. Damon was about to add another good point about Dr. Broomfield when Remi shook him off.

"Any luck on the pendant?" asked Damon, hoping to change the subject.

Both of the ladies shook their head.

"It's protected for a reason," said Lily.

"We tried focusing on my parents, or the Scythe Sisters, but that didn't work. They're either warding themselves, or the pendant is doing that for them."

"So much for letting it go," said Damon.

"I'm not going after them," said Remi. "I mean, probably not. It doesn't matter. We don't know where they went or how to catch up with them. It's not like we could leave the hospital anyway."

"It's probably not that cool of an artifact that it leads to anyway. They're probably after a minor trinket that the ancients used to trick people," said Damon.

"It's a stupid Horn," said Remi, offhand.

"Horn?" asked Damon, sitting up straight. "I didn't think you knew what it led to?"

She shrugged.

"It's not a secret if you tell someone, and at the time I was going to try and find it, I thought you were a try-hard wanker," said Remi with a wry grin.

"Which Horn?" asked Lily with her head tilted.

Remi looked between them both.

"It's just a Horn and it's supposed to be worth a lot. What more is there to know? Fine, it's called the Horn of Bran Galed and it's not that cool. It'll produce any drinks you want, which is pretty lame if you ask me. Who cares about beer or soda on permanent tap?" said Remi.

Lily slapped her hand flat on the table, startling the guests a few spaces over.

"Remi..."

"What?"

Damon leaned forward and spoke under his breath.

"My father told me stories about that Horn. Don't you understand how important it is?"

"What are you two freaking out about? The Horn can produce anything you want to drink. So what? That might have been cool back in the Dark Ages, but I can go to a convenience store and pick up a thousand different flavors of Mage Blast."

The waitress appeared with a massive tray covered in plates of food. They halted their conversation while she handed them their breakfast. The entire time she was staring at Damon.

After the waitress left, Damon leaned forward. "The Horn of Bran Galed doesn't produce any liquid that exists to drink, it produces any liquid period. Even ones that don't exist yet."

The piece of bacon in Remi's hand snapped in half.

"Wait, what?"

"Branch and bough, Remi. Did you not know?" asked Lily.

Damon set his fork down. "The legends my father told me were a mix of good and evil. The Horn can produce anything, even poisons and plagues. It was sometimes called the Twilight Horn, because it was thought that if it ever got into the wrong hands, it would be the end of humanity."

Remi slapped her hand against her forehead.

"And I just let the Scythe Sisters have the pendant."

"Damon's right," said Lily gravely. "The legends about that Horn tend towards the gruesome and horrific."

"There was nothing you could have done about it," said Damon. "It was five against one."

Lily put a piece of bacon into her hair. "And let's be honest, that Horn has been lost for centuries. It's probably hidden in a place that would be impossible for them to reach, or put their lives in grave danger. Sorry, Remi."

Remi stared at her plate of eggs, bacon, and hash browns. "Any liquid? Could it fix the Summer Fae?"

Lily shifted her mouth to the side.

"Doubtful. The realm isn't a person. You can't fix it that way."

"It doesn't matter now," said Damon. "We've no way to go after the pendant. It's someone else's problem now."

"Unless the Scythe Sisters somehow end up with it," said Remi.

"The people who hired your parents would have something to say about that," said Damon.

Remi shivered. "Whoever they are..."

No one spoke for a while as they ate their breakfast. Damon wasn't as hungry as he was when he ordered. He only managed to get through two and a half plates before his stomach started aching.

"Hey, Remi," said Lily. "Did I tell you who I saw the other day? A video, not in person."

"Who?"

"Remember your NOCAT?"

Remi sat up straight.

"No way. The hag?"

"Yeah, she has a video channel called Cauldron of Secrets. She brings people on and tells them secrets about their lives that they didn't know, or gives them advice on how to use magic to enhance their life. Calls them enchanteers, or something like that. It's a bloody good time. She has real presence. You wouldn't think she was once a swamp hag," said Lily, smirking.

"She was awake the entire time, listening to what everyone was saying. I imagine she learned a lot," said Remi.

Lily's phone buzzed again.

"Bloody hell. He says if I'm not back in ten minutes, I can consider myself kicked out. As if he could do that."

"You'd better go," said Remi.

Lily stood and stretched.

"You cover my bill, wolf boy? I mean, you'll hardly notice given yours," said Lily as she collected her things and prepared to leave.

"I'm going to head out with Lily," Remi said. "I want to check on Miss Lionel before the afternoon. It's when she's most lucid."

Damon waved them off.

"Go on. I'll take care of this."

After the two women left, he leaned back and stared at the many plates of food. His stomach grumbled as he stretched, right as the waitress arrived.

"Do you want me to clean this up? Or bring you a box?"

Damon grabbed his fork with one hand and the carafe of syrup with the other.

"Just got my second wind. I should be good, but you can bring me another pot of coffee. The fresh one, not that old bitter stuff that's been sitting on the burner for the last hour."

The waitress' eyes rounded with horror.

"I'll be right back."

Damon shot her a wink and pulled Remi's half-eaten plate across the table.

EIGHTEEN

The spell bypassed the alarms on the back door of the hospital. Lily smirked at how easily she defeated the protections thanks to Remi's guidance over the years.

"Are we going to get in trouble for this?" asked Daryna for the third time.

"Probably," said Lily. "You don't have to help. I can understand the danger this puts you in for your career."

Daryna appeared pained by the decision.

"If you think it's important."

Lily smiled as she thought about her past.

"Yes, I think it is. Let's get our patients into the building before anyone sees."

She stepped outside and waved at the white panel van sitting in the front row of the nearly empty parking lot. The lamps buzzed with electricity as the door slid open, revealing a hulking man with gray skin and glowing tattoos over his face. Others much like the first quickly climbed out, including a young woman with translucent wings and eyes the size of half-dollar coins.

"Down the hallway, through the plastic sheets, and into the waiting room. There will be someone there to check you in," said Lily.

The last one out of the van was Dr. Marcie. She'd worn her white jacket and kept the bones in her braids.

"Are you sure about this, Healer Lily?" she asked as she eyed the hospital suspiciously.

"Absolutely. There's no reason we can't treat your people. You shouldn't have to be human presenting to be able to be seen in the hospital."

"I only brought fifteen, as you requested."

"Thank you. I thought we should start small."

Lily walked down the hall with Dr. Marcie, who was staring at the scaffolding and construction equipment.

"We're in the middle of a ward renovation, but one of the examination rooms is finished and not being used. We'll be working there."

"It's been a long time since I've been here," said Dr. Marcie.

"You worked in Golden Willow?" asked Lily, surprised.

"When I first came to the city. Before they found out who I really was," said Dr. Marcie, tight-lipped.

Lily had suspected that Dr. Marcie was more than she let on, but she didn't want to embarrass her with probing questions.

The waiting area was surprisingly packed as if more had somehow snuck in than were in the van. The first year was circulating through the group handing out clipboards to fill out their information.

The examination room smelled like fresh paint. Lily had stocked the shelves herself which included additional custom elixirs she thought might be useful based on the list that Dr. Marcie had sent ahead.

The first patient was the big guy with the gray skin and glowing tattoos. Lily smelled the brimstone right away, but kept her face neutral as Dr. Marcie examined his throat with a penlight.

Dr. Marcie had been apprehensive about the idea when Lily had contacted her, but she'd eventually been won over with the idea that they could help her patients on the down-low. To Lily, it'd been strange to be on that side of the argument after battling Balor the year before in the basement, but as she'd learned with the Clover sisters, or Alice's hob boyfriend, being from a particular realm didn't make someone bad, and continuing to treat them as lesser would only make them resentful and angry at society.

Everyone in the waiting room had been prediagnosed in the clinic with the information sent ahead so Lily could prepare the treatments, but Dr. Marcie wanted to do a confirmation check first. The patient had picked up a bacterial infection from working in the sewer system for the city. The affliction had magical origins, as old potions and leftover faez collected in the tunnels beneath the streets, which made it more difficult and dangerous to treat.

Lily had to cast three cleansing spells to eliminate the fungus and then they gave the patient an elixir that would help keep the growth from coming back.

The two of them with help from Daryna worked through the packed room, which Lily swore had grown in number when they stepped out after the first patient.

The next person they saw was the woman with translucent wings. Lily didn't understand why she wasn't able to use the regular hospital, as she was a cute young woman, until she smelled the odor of rotting meat. The scent was so bad it brought bile up in Lily's throat, but she forced herself not to make a face.

"You're from the Summer Fae?"

"Yes," said Irabell. "I fled last year. There's very little that isn't affected by the kalkatai. I wish I would have left before this happened."

Lily's gut contracted at the remembrance of her visit when the corruption tried to trap her. She couldn't imagine how bad it was for those that lived there.

Using a sequence of spells, Lily managed to isolate the cause of the awful smell, but without a lab analysis, they wouldn't be able to fix it.

"Will I smell this way forever?" asked Irabell. "No one will let me work for them. I couldn't even get a job in one of the skin bars."

"We'll figure it out," said Lily. "I'll get your sample processed during the day and see if we can find a solution. Once I do, I can have it sent over to the clinic."

Most of the stories were like the first two. Either they had a job in the city doing work that no one else wanted to do, or weren't able to get a job because of who they were. Lily had thought the city more accepting, but she couldn't ignore the reality that these patients were faced with on a daily basis.

They worked through the night and managed to meet with every patient, and even if they weren't able to fix their ailments, they made a plan for next time.

When the waiting room was finally empty, Lily sent Daryna to bed since she had a shift in a few hours.

"Thank you again for your help," said Dr. Marcie as she stretched her neck and massaged her jaw. "We got more done tonight than I normally do in a month."

Lily peered at the list of patients, which was four times longer than originally agreed upon.

"You're not mad, are you?" asked Dr. Marcie when she saw what Lily was looking at.

"I'd do the same if I were in your shoes."

"Speaking of, when can we do this again?" asked Dr. Marcie.

"I'll have to check the construction schedule and when I'm free again. Might be a few weeks."

"We really could use it sooner. I brought the easiest cases tonight. There's a bunch that need more serious treatment sooner rather than later."

"That will make it harder to treat them. We can't get caught."

"I know, Healer Lily, but you came to me with this idea. And if you want to treat them, we need to treat all of them, not just the easy ones. I know you're resourceful. I sense that about you."

Lily stretched her back by pushing with both hands until her spine shifted with a satisfying pop.

"I'll see what I can do to move that up."

"Thank you."

Before Lily realized it, Dr. Marcie hugged her tight. As they embraced, Lily felt like she was holding onto a body full of bees as the clinic doctor's body vibrated. Dr. Marcie pulled away sheepishly, looking embarrassed about something. She left without saying anything further.

Lily was about to head to bed when she remembered that she had to clean up. If the construction crews found any leftover materials, they'd report it and then she wouldn't be able to use the facilities. She checked the time to see she had two hours before rounds with Dr. Broomfield. Time enough to get things cleaned up and swing by Jeb's for a double shot of his best energy elixir.

"Remember, Lily," she told herself as she grabbed a cart and started collecting the empty potion bottles, "you were the one that contacted Dr. Marcie."

NINETEEN

The train ride to the seventh ward was short, but it gave Remi enough time to watch a few of Ruby Thistleheart's web shows. Remi found it hard to imagine that the gorgeous, raven-haired woman with a fanciful streak of white was the same wrinkled old NOCAT that had been bedridden for over a century. She looked even younger than when they'd first released her from her curse-induced slumber and sounded as if she'd been playing the arcana influencers' game for decades.

Ruby's stream involved her answering questions about how to get revenge on cheating exes, or improve one's sex life using simple spells and potions. The last one had gotten pretty graphic, which had forced Remi to put her earbuds in when a mother with her young son shot her a nasty look.

Her apartment was near the Canal District, which was where the college-aged students hung out at night. It made sense Ruby would pick that area as a place to live since that was the majority of her online clientele.

When Remi lifted her fist to knock, an illusionary image of Ruby's head floated before the door.

"Welcome, Remi Wilde. I was expecting you. Come in and make yourself at home."

The announcement startled Remi, and at first she wondered if Ruby had been scrying her, or was prophetic, but then she remembered the scams they ran when she was younger. People couldn't help but believe in supernatural predictions. It was easy to make them think they were about to come into a large amount of money, which would make them reckless when it came to trusting people.

The apartment walls were painted crimson and covered in hit movie posters from the last few years like *Men with Wands*, *The Last Stand of Raggedy Vance*, and *Enter the Mage Tower.* As she looked closer, she saw they were all personally signed by the cast to Ruby.

A tabby cat was lying on a tan chaise lounge with its three tails hanging over the edge lazily undulating. Remi heard muffled conversation through a black door. She hesitated, wondering if she would be interrupting a stream, when the cat spoke in a cockney accent.

"She's waitin' for ya, luv. Don't be a stranger."

Remi opened the door a crack and saw there was an entire sound booth on the opposite side. Remi found a seat on the couch next to a black-and-white photo of Pythia Silverthorne during the infernal invasion, facing down a demonic giant. But Remi didn't have time to study the picture because she was drawn to what was happening beyond the glass.

Ruby Thistleheart was seated on a black stool in front of three cameras and a laptop. She was wearing a slinky black dress that accentuated her cleavage. Her lips were so thick and crimson, they looked cushiony enough to melt in.

"—and remember, my little enchanteers, you don't want to get all hexed up about a simple mistake. You are as golden as faez, so don't even let that wannabe-other make you all sparklebrained. You deserve better." Ruby winked at the camera and stuck her tongue out to the side. "That's it for today's stream. Tonight, we'll talk about how to be the charmcaster you want to be. I have an amazing spell to teach you called Glowflux. It's going to be so fade. Be good, enchanteers, and don't forget to put a spell on those follow and like buttons."

Ruby made quick finger motions and the lights on the cameras all went out at once. Then she snapped her fingers and the laptop in front of her shut.

When she stalked out of the sound booth, Remi found her heart jumping around in her chest. She'd never been attracted to women, but Ruby's presence made her question her sexuality.

"Oh, sorry," said Ruby, reaching underneath her hair and removing a platinum necklace from around her neck. "It helps with the conversions to paid subscribers."

As soon as the chain was unlinked from Ruby's neck, Remi found she could think again.

"It's way worse in person. Don't worry. I can't scramble their brains *that* easily."

"You seem to be doing quite well for yourself."

"Thanks to you," said Ruby. "Please, this room is so impersonal. Let's gab on the balcony."

Her host swung by the kitchen and grabbed a tray with a teapot and two cups. The balcony had a view of the Canal District, which since it was daytime wasn't packed with drunken college students.

When Ruby poured two cups of tea, the liquid came out steaming.

"Black tea with a touch of honey, just like you like it," said Ruby when Remi opened her mouth to ask.

"Thank you," said Remi, impressed despite knowing how easy it was to trick people. "I still find it hard to believe you're the same woman as the one in our hospital beds."

Ruby arched an exquisite eyebrow.

"I'm sorry to hear about Dr. Decker. He was quite the kisser."

"You know about him leaving?"

"I like to keep up on my knight in shining armor. Too bad his heart was already taken, or I would have tried to steal it."

Remi took a sip of the tea. It was, as advertised, exactly how she liked it.

"Do you know why I'm here?"

Ruby crossed one leg over the other as she stared across the city. The Spire reflected the thin clouds stretched over the buildings.

"Not the exact reason, but I can see your life is a tangled mess of influences. Some are more recent, but they're all quite powerful."

Remi cradled the warm cup in her hands.

"This isn't influencer bullshit, is it? I don't know how you knew I was coming, but I know how to make a scam look legit."

The smirk was like a dagger to her heart. Remi hated that she didn't know how the trick was done.

"It's not a trick. Not like that anyway. I take my business seriously. It's almost hard to remember those early days, the ones that got me stuck in a bed for over a century, but I know they were full of fear and loneliness."

She lifted her cup towards the people wandering the canal and sighed heavily.

"This is all so wonderful. I don't have to be afraid of frightened villagers with pitchforks, or of quick-fingered rivals. I can have it all in the palm of my hand without breaking a single law. Man or otherwise."

Ruby set the cup down and stared intently at Remi. Eventually she realized that meant she was expected to speak.

"Before I came to Aura Healers, I was a thief. I stole a pendant from some very dangerous people and got sent to jail for a year. I managed to hide the pendant, because it leads to a powerful artifact, but then a few weeks ago, the pendant was stolen from me. I want to know where it is, and how to get it back."

Ruby contemplated the explanation while her leg bounced.

"You clearly had it for a long time. Why do you care now?"

"Because I spent a year in jail for it."

"Sunk costs. I know you're too smart for that. What's the real reason?"

"My parents stole it from me."

Ruby exclaimed as she leaned back in her chair, clearly surprised. She let her tongue rest on her bottom teeth.

"That's a revelation."

"Tell me about it."

Ruby tapped a fingernail on the porcelain cup.

"If I were my old self, I'd use this against you. Twist it in your gut until you did whatever I wanted."

"Who's to say you're not going to do that now?"

"Please, Remi, let's be friends."

The offer made Remi's gut tighten with suspicion. The more someone talked about their honesty, the less inclined she was to trust them.

"Then tell me how to find the pendant."

Ruby set the teacup on the table.

"Are you sure? No guarantees I can help, but if you want, I will give it my best effort. But I can see that road leads to dark roads."

"Is that prophecy?"

"There's no such thing as true prophecy, but sometimes it's easy to see where a person's path leads," said Ruby.

"I want your help."

Ruby stood and strode to the door.

"Come. Let's not make a spectacle of ourselves."

Remi thought that was rich, coming from an online influencer, but she followed the gorgeous woman into the apartment. Ruby took a seat on the chaise lounge and patted the spot next to her. As Remi sat next to the ancient woman, the hairs on her arms rose in anticipation.

When Ruby held out her hand, palm up and flat, Remi was confused.

"I want you to lick it. Don't be shy. From palm to tip. Give it a little faez too."

Remi leaned over and extended her tongue, flattening it against the palm and licking upward until she'd covered the entire open hand. When she pulled back, she saw Ruby give a shiver.

"What…?"

The old witch held out a hand, silencing Remi. Ruby had her eyes closed and rocked in place trance-like. The smoothness of her skin wrinkled as she went through minor convulsions, lips mouthing unsaid words until eventually her eyes popped open, revealing what Remi could only interpret as pity.

"I'm sorry, Remi Wilde."

"Why?" she asked aggressively.

Remi was certain it was a con, but there was something real and visceral that made her believe regardless, too.

"Your past, your present, your future. They're all tangled."

"I thought you said prophecy is bullshit."

"It is. I'm reading your aura. There are so many demands on your being. This is unexpectedly complicated. There are links to the Fae on you—"

"The pendant."

"Maybe," said Ruby with lips pursed. "And the Veil. I caught a glimpse of a dark, brooding figure."

"The Stranger," said Remi, truly surprised. There was no simple way for her to know about the person she'd been seeing in her dreams and her rituals.

"What's in your past that connects you to the Veil? It's very unusual for someone to have that connection because nothing can live there. It's not a realm like any other."

"I wish I knew."

"It's why you work in the Hospice Ward."

"How does this help me find the pendant?"

The corners of the hag's eyes creased.

"Because if you decide to go after it, your world will never be the same," said Ruby.

"Just tell me where it's at."

Ruby closed her eyes.

"There's a hint of Fae trailing from you."

"You already said that."

"Not from you, but from when the pendant was in your possession. It's from the Summer Fae, but there's a glamour from the Autumn on it."

"Autumn?"

"The glamour is old, so it was probably breaking down. It left some residue on you. If you want answers, you'll likely find them there."

Remi's stomach tightened. The Fae realm was a dangerous place, especially for a human. While she knew her parents had ventured there decades ago, it was lucky they'd made it out alive and without getting trapped.

"What are you doing to do?" asked Ruby.

Remi wondered if Ruby knew that the pendant led to the Horn of Bran Galed. She'd given no indication, but since she could sense things others couldn't, Remi wouldn't be surprised. If it were just about what her parents had done to her, Remi thought she might be able to give it up, but after hearing about what the Horn was capable of, including the destruction of the entire human race, she feared that leaving it up to her parents was a mistake.

"I'm not done looking for answers."

"But do you know the right questions?"

"Is there anything else you can tell me?" asked Remi.

"I wish there was more, but that's all I can do."

Remi didn't think that was true.

"Thank you for your help," said Remi, standing and shifting towards the door while Ruby watched with half-lidded eyes.

As her hand touched the handle, Ruby said, "Do you want to know how I did it?"

"You shouldn't give up your best tricks."

Ruby arched an eyebrow. "As if *that's* my best trick. I knew you were coming because you were watching my stream. I saw your name pop into the channel. After that it was a simple spell I learned from a kind Cyber-magics neighbor that let me know you were on your way here."

Remi shook her head as she thought how easily Ruby had fooled her.

"Good luck with your enchanteers."

"Luck's got nothing to do with it."

Remi shut the door behind her and exhaled deeply. She'd gotten the answers she wanted, but somehow felt unresolved. After her parents stole the pendant, she'd felt untethered as if the parts of her life that she thought she'd understood had been scrambled into a new and confusing order.

Ruby had been right. She didn't know the right questions to ask, but was certain that the only way to learn them was to go after the pendant—and the Horn.

TWENTY

Lily watched Damon fidget with the straps of his pack as the train rumbled around the track. It looked over a hundred pounds, but he seemed to be carrying it easily.

"It's not too much, is it? We have to bring all our food and drink with us, but we can drop some if you want. You look worried."

Damon scoffed.

"I'm not worried about the weight. Are you sure we're not going to be gone long?"

Remi glanced up from reading her phone on the seat with her pack between her legs. The train was rather empty due to the snowstorm blanketing the city.

"If you don't want to go..."

"I'm going, I just want to, you know, know that I'm not going to come back with my career in shambles. I feel like I'm close to finding a solution for Marcus' challenge, and the twins have events coming up in a few days."

"Time can be wonky in the Fae," said Lily.

"Damon, seriously," said Remi. "If you don't want to come, I understand."

"You know how important that Horn is. And there's no way I could let you go without me. If something happened, I'd hate myself forever."

"What did you tell Dr. Lara?" asked Remi.

Damon grimaced.

"I messaged her this morning that I was sick with the elixir flu. I hate lying to her."

"Well, if there's one thing that should be believable, it's that you've taken too many elixirs and need a few days to clean it out. Speaking of…" said Remi.

Lily tapped on her pack.

"I mixed them myself."

"What about you two?"

"Dr. Broomfield prefers not to interact with me directly," said Lily. "I think he would have kicked me out months ago, but Dr. Fairlight knows about what happened last year, so his requests have gone nowhere. As long as I don't give him a real reason, I think I'm safe. Boon and Sasha are going to cover my extra shifts so nothing happens with my patients."

Remi shoved the phone in her pocket and stood to join them. She slipped into her pack and grimaced from the weight.

"I told Dr. Morsdux where we were going. He was cool with it."

"What? You told him?" asked Damon.

"No specifics, but I wouldn't put it past the old man to know the truth."

Lily had only interacted with the head of the Hospice Ward a few times, but he had what her mother would have called the Old Magics.

The train reached their station. Lily reapplied her weather enchantment before heading into the storm. The snow battered her face, but it felt pleasant after a rough week in the hospital. She led the way through the streets, and without the use of the iron armbands. Since she'd been visiting Alice regularly, she'd learned how to navigate Lady Nimueh's glamours.

"Oh, the snow's letting up," said Remi, craning her neck.

"Not really," said Lily as the mists rose from the streets.

After a few turns, the hazy eyes of the Mists' gas lamps greeted them.

Alice was standing outside in black leather pants and a cream top that exposed the ring in her belly button. When Lily gave her a hug, she could smell faint rot beneath the scent of perfume.

"You look like you've lived in the city forever," said Lily.

Alice curtseyed.

"And you look like you're headed back home."

Lily tugged on her loose forest green skirt.

"It feels more comfortable to travel to the Fae like this." She glanced to the red door. "Is the Lady still going to help us?"

"I think so, but you're not going through there," said Alice. "Come with me."

The youngest de Meath led them through a wrought iron gate along the side of the Mists. The alleyway seemed to go on for much longer than the size of the house would suggest. After a minute's walk, they broke into a manicured garden with high hedges and silent statues.

The stern figure of Lady Nimueh appeared out of the mists. She approached the group, staring directly at Lily.

"Greetings, Lady," said Lily, inclining her head. "Thank you for agreeing to help us."

"I've done nothing of the sort."

Lily stiffened, but she kept her head lowered.

"I agreed to meet and hear your request personally."

Lily glanced to her sister, but Alice had her eyes lowered and was standing with her hands behind her back.

"We wish passage to the Fae."

Lady Nimueh raised an eyebrow.

"These days the traffic is going only one way."

"Not to the Summer. We wish to enter the Autumn Fae."

"An unusual request. Queen Kiutian does not entertain visitors. She'd be more likely to turn you into one of her projects than allow you to see her."

"Still, our task requires it."

"And what is this task?" asked the Lady with chin held high.

"To retrieve an item of great importance."

Lady Nimueh glanced to Remi, suggesting she knew the real reason.

"Some people stole a pendant from me that leads to a great artifact. They're working for someone, and I fear if they can find the item, there will be many problems," said Remi.

Lady Nimueh slid closer to Remi and held a clawed hand against her neck. Fingernails as long as knives rested against the flesh.

"This is the danger I saw in you when you first darkened my door. I should have ended you then. Tell me why I shouldn't do it now."

Damon growled and extended his claws.

"If you even touch her—"

"Lady Nimueh, please," said Lily, trying to calm the situation by waving Damon back. "She means no harm."

"Then why did she lie to me?"

Remi's eyes shifted nervously as she remained still.

"She didn't lie."

"By omission she did. Who stole this pendant?"

"My parents," said Remi.

"Another lie," said Lady Nimueh.

She raised her arm back, readying to strike. Lily saw there was nothing she could do to stop her. Even Damon was transfixed by the sudden shift.

"Lady!" said Alice, stepping forward and receiving a glaring rebuke from her mistress. "I do not think she believes it to be a lie. Give her the Kiss of Truth."

"Alice..."

Her sister shook her off. Lily didn't agree, but her sister knew the Lady better, so she kept her lips squeezed tight despite the danger.

"Would you consent, trickster?"

Remi gave the Lady side eye.

"It's not like I have a choice."

"I'll take that as a yes," said the Lady as she released her hand from Remi's neck. The blade-like fingernails disappeared.

"What do I do?" asked Remi.

Lady Nimueh leaned over the short woman.

"Do not resist."

When she pressed her lips against Remi's it wasn't like two years before when she'd kissed Damon. The Maid of the Mist gave a chaste kiss, more pressure than exploration, but the pain it was causing Remi was clear. Her friend whimpered the longer the Lady's lips were pressed against hers. When the Lady finally pulled away, the two of them appeared greatly relieved.

Remi wiped her mouth with the back of her hand, glancing angrily at the Lady, who looked like she'd eaten a bad piece of fruit.

"Lady?" asked Alice when the silence had gone on for a while.

"To my surprise, you are right, she does not lie, but that doesn't mean I shouldn't kill her. Right here and right now, and save the world the trouble she presents."

"What danger?" asked Lily.

"She's not the friend you think she is," said the Lady.

When Lily glanced to Remi, she was as confused as ever, and for a brief moment, Lily questioned her friend's intentions. It was only an instant, but she wondered if this was an elaborate scam. Faith in her friend returned right away, but she felt terrible for even having that moment of doubt.

"No," said Lily defiantly. "She's better than that. Despite all her cocked upbringing, she's been a right, good friend. The best of friends. She's put herself in danger to save others. I couldn't ask for a better companion on this journey."

Lady Nimueh straightened her shoulders.

"I did not say that she wasn't a friend to you, girl. Maybe I should let you go. It's doubtful that you'd return from such a trip, wet behind the ears pups that you are."

The derision and anger from the Lady confused Lily. There must be something else going on that she couldn't see.

"My sister and her friends have good intentions," said Alice.

"And we all know how much good intentions are worth." Lady Nimueh spun on her heel to face Alice. "But I will allow them passage. Only because you have served me well."

"Thank you, Lady."

"Before I send you on your way, know that I cannot send you directly. You'll have to go through Summer to reach Autumn. Not far, but the dangers remain. Do you still want to go?" asked the Lady with eyebrow raised.

Lily shot Remi a glance. She nodded profusely.

"We do."

The Lady lifted her arms and the mist rushed in, swirling around them. Lily reached for Remi, but she was fading to whiteness. A moment of vertigo brought Lily to her knees, despite her experience with realm travel.

When the mists finally faded, Lily found herself surrounded by twisted vines, choking trees with trunks bent with scoliosis. The air held the rich scent of rotting.

She climbed to her feet and spun around, finding she was the only one in sight.

“Hello?” Lily called, hating the way the foliage swallowed her voice.

No answer returned.

TWENTY-ONE

Damon fell over a decomposing log. His knee crushed the soft wood, which exploded into mush and released a host of winged creatures. The flash of a malformed tiny humanoid passed his eyes, trailed by black dust falling from its wings.

"Blood and bone."

He grabbed a vine and yanked it down, exposing a hole through the thick foliage. Every step had been a battle. They'd been within a dozen feet of each other in the Lady's garden, but now he had no idea how close they were to each other.

"Hello? Lily? Remi?"

Each time he yelled, he felt the hair on the back of his neck bristle with warning. His friends had yet to hear him, but other beings of the Fae had.

Damon fought through a thorny patch, coming away with bloody, scratched arms as thick rivulets of sweat poured down his cheeks. The weight of his pack wasn't bothering him, but the oppressive humidity was.

A mad giggle had him spinning in place. He saw nothing but intertwined branches and leaves covered in spots and brown scales.

"Who's there?"

He felt foolish for even asking. Whatever beings were left in the Fae, they'd been twisted by the kalkatai.

Damon let his claws grow.

The last words of Lady Nimueh rattled around his brain. What had she meant when she was talking about Remi? She had a complicated life before she'd come to the Halls, but he'd never thought she was lying to him. Not since the early months when they were at odds with each other.

He stepped through a gap to find a trail cutting through the overgrown forest. Multiple split hoofprints in the soft soil suggested that it was frequently used. He was considering the safety of traveling it when he heard crashing ahead.

Damon prepared to blast whatever it was with a force bolt when a shape exploded through the space between two narrow trunks and fell onto the ground.

"Merlin's tits, Remi, you scared the life out of me."

She looked up from her knees, dark hair plastered to her forehead, then checked behind her.

"Do you hear anything? Something was chasing me."

"No," he said, helping her up.

Remi threw her arms around his chest the moment she was standing.

"I thought I was alone here," she said eventually.

"The Maid of the Mist has it out for you. Do you know why?"

Remi pulled away and crossed her arms.

"You think I do? I swear she's gone mad. Maybe the corruption got her too."

"Have you seen Lily?"

"No, and I hate to say it, but we'd better find her fast, or we're screwed. You and I know jack shit about traveling in the Fae."

Damon knew something was wrong when Remi froze. She was staring past him to the path.

He turned to find a four-legged creature with tendrils undulating from its haunches.

"Neko?" he asked.

The creature nodded, which brought a sense of relief. Neko headed the other way, looking back to make sure they were following. A few minutes later, they stumbled into a tight clearing where Lily was cleaning her boots of mud. Half her lower body was covered in rich soil.

"What happened to you?" asked Damon.

"Bloody quicksand. Only thing that saved me was all the stupid vines that make walking anywhere a nightmare," said Lily.

"Where are we?" asked Remi.

Lily shook her head.

"I'd like to put my boot up Lady Nimueh's arse the next time I see her. She's trying to get us killed."

"Should we be concerned about that?" asked Damon.

Remi punched him in the arm.

"I'm not a danger."

"I didn't say that, but she was acting pretty weird."

"I think it's the corruption," said Lily as she finished cleaning off her boots and slipped them back on. "I hope, anyway. Come on, we need to get moving. I don't like the feel of this place, and unless she was lying, passage to Autumn shouldn't be far from here."

"I should have brought a machete," said Damon.

Lily spoke to Neko in a low voice. Her companion put his nose to the ground and led them to a new path that Damon hadn't seen before.

"No, you shouldn't have. They don't like iron, and especially not sharpened iron here." Lily reached down and scooped a hunk of mud from her hip. "And don't eat or drink anything. Only what we brought."

"What about me?" asked Damon. "Since I'm King Nuada's blood."

"Not unless you've been cleared by the Oak Father. I might be able to get away with some small things, but I'd prefer not to test it," said Lily.

Neko led them for a half hour. No one spoke, but the trees seemed to be listening to their every breath.

When they passed through narrow gaps between the trunks, Damon swore the branches were reaching out to touch him. His pack was covered in green smears by the time they stopped for a break, which was near a little waterfall that fell into a crystal-clear pond.

"I really want to take a swim in that," said Remi as she sipped from her water bottle. "I feel like I'm basting in my own sweat. Is it always this hot here?"

"No," said Lily. "It was always pleasant like a cool summer evening when everything is just perfect."

"My parents talked about waterfalls like this when they came here. Even with the overgrowth, it's still breathtaking."

"I still can't believe your parents visited the Fae," said Damon, shaking his head.

"They can be brilliant about some things and idiots about others. They had help coming here. Or they would have never been able to manage it on their own."

"What were they after?" asked Damon.

"A shortcut to a better life," said Remi, frowning. "There was always another job, another scam, another bullshit con that would only leave us with just enough money to make it to the next city. There was a time I thought the Fae heist never happened, but they had too many specific details about it, and some secret language between them whenever they'd talk about it."

"They never said what it was?"

"Only that what they took was important and that it was the key to their better life. A few times I overheard them talking about the woman they stole it from. She'd gotten stuck in the Fae. A thief just like them."

Damon froze when he heard crashing coming from the path leading to the waterfall. Neko made a squeaking noise and darted into a gap between the vines.

"Hurry, go," said Lily as she made two brief arcane gestures. A silvery sigil released from her fingertips and faded into the grass.

The four of them ran over the narrow path, the sounds of the pursuers always right behind. It felt like they were just out of sight.

When the trail split, Lily led them through a gap in the vines to a little space that barely fit the four of them. She cast a spell that obscured the space around them as if it were their own private bubble.

Damon positioned himself near the front in case they were discovered.

The crash of footsteps came more slowly and deliberately, suggesting they were searching rather than blindly following the path.

Damon leaned against the rough bark as an insect landed on his cheek and stuck to the sweat on his skin. He heard tiny screams from the creature, but ignored it, fearing discovery from their pursuers.

When the first one came around the corner, he had the impression of a pair of horns sticking from a tangled knot of hair that had been pulled out of a vacuum bag. Then he saw the backwards-facing knees, the split hooves, the extended groin area, and finally, the clawed hands still bloody with the viscera of fallen foes.

The hairy horned figures stalked to their position, sniffing the air and probing the gaps in the trees. There were two of them. Taller than a basketball center and twice his weight. Damon doubted he could take even one of them.

The bigger one stood outside their hiding place, peering between the leaves.

Damon held himself perfectly still. He could hear it breathing through its nostrils.

A hand touching his shoulder nearly made him jump. It was Lily, moving closer in preparation for a fight.

The horned figure reached out to touch the vines covering their hiding spot. It wrapped its long, clawed fingers around the foliage. Damon could hear the strength in its fist when it squeezed and the vine cracked and splintered into dust.

The beating of Damon's heart confused him when he heard the distant thrumming.

The creature heard it too, turning its neck to peer further down the trail. It grunted like a silverback gorilla, which was answered by the second creature that was sniffing further up the trail.

In the span of an eyeblink, the creatures were gone, galloping down the path and disappearing into the overgrown forest.

"What the hell were those?" asked Remi.

"They are, were, satyrs," said Lily with clear disgust. "I don't know what they are now, but bloody frightening."

"I heard drums. Who drew them away?" asked Damon.

"I don't know. Could be a friend or foe, but let's get moving before the satyrs come back," said Lily.

They made it a short distance before Damon sensed another presence in the trees. He didn't see her at first, but his therianthropic senses picked up her scent, and then he found her crouched on a branch twenty feet above their position.

She was covered in thick clothing and wearing goggles, but tufts of blonde hair stuck from beneath her hood. Their watcher leapt from the branch, plummeting to the ground quickly, but grabbed a vine at the last second to halt her fall.

"Follow me before they come back."

TWENTY-TWO

The path the stranger took through the overgrown Fae forest wasn't immediately visible to the eye, but Remi was barely paying attention to their surroundings. She wanted to know who was helping them and why.

Not that she was concerned about the motivation of their savior. For once, Remi found herself trusting someone she just met. Maybe it was the close call with the satyrs, and the understanding that this stranger had been the one to save them. It wasn't like the Fae was a place that could easily be manipulated for a con.

The path went up rather than across the forest. Fallen trunks had been hauled into the mid-level branches, providing easier passage over the tangled foliage. Their guide brought them over waterfalls and meandering brooks choked with leaves until she stopped at a gap through the vines. The woven creepers looked like the web of a trapdoor spider. The woman made brief sigils in the air that floated with golden faez before disappearing.

"Step through. Be quick."

The three of them climbed through the opening between the vines. The woman came through last then made another sigil and the opening grew hazy with obscuration magic.

"Where are—" asked Damon, but the woman used her hand to slice through the air.

She led them down a spiraling path until they reached a clearing by a waterfall-fed pond choked with lily pads. The crash of water sent a soothing mist into the air. Their savior led them to a stone path that went behind the falling water. A door built into the stone opened to her touch. Remi was certain there was a secret to opening it, but she didn't see exactly how the woman had performed it.

The inside of the cave home felt homey and comforting. A banked fire in back radiated soothing warmth into the cool space, the smoke going up a hole in the back of the cave. The walls were covered in faded tapestries of Fae lords and ladies dancing in the Summer Court. Other trinkets and shiny objects littered the shelves and flat spaces, but Remi only had eyes for their mysterious benefactor.

The woman pulled off her goggles and hooked her fingers around the front of her hood, drawing it back until she was revealed. She had a hawk-like face with spikey blonde hair and an intensity to her gaze that made Remi feel like all her secrets were being exposed.

"Did you come through a shimmer?" asked the woman.

Remi looked to Lily at the same time as Damon.

"No," said Lily.

The woman's lips wrinkled with disgust.

"You came here on purpose? Are you mad?"

Remi detected a New York accent worn away by time. She looked to be in her early thirties, but something about the eyes suggested she might actually be older.

"We're trying to get somewhere else," said Remi.

The woman narrowed her gaze suspiciously at the obvious obfuscation.

Damon stepped around her.

"Thank you so much for saving us. I assume that was you who drew them away with those drums. I'm—"

At the moment he was going to say his name, Remi gave him a tight shake of the head. She wasn't sure why, other than an abundance of caution in a dangerous realm.

He hesitated, so she leapt into the gap.

"He's Darion, I'm Regina, and this is Bridget. We're Aura Healers from the Hundred Halls."

"Aura Healers?" she scoffed. "Not Explorers, or Animalians, or anyone else, really?"

"Might we have your name?" asked Damon.

She hesitated.

"Coraline."

Remi stilled her face from reacting. There was unlikely to be another Coraline in the Summer Fae, which meant this was the woman that her parents stole from. The one they'd met two decades ago.

"Do I know you?" asked Coraline, directing her question to Remi.

"Doubtful."

"You're clearly from our realm," said Lily. "How did you get here?"

Coraline stared at them before letting out a heavy sigh as she started pulling off her thick gloves.

"Let me get out of these clothes and make some tea, then we can talk about how stupid the three of you are to come here."

Remi tried to hide her grin, but it was hard because she found herself immediately liking the woman. Coraline gestured at a small table in the corner.

After stripping off heavy layers of clothes until she was only in a simple green cotton shirt and embroidered tan pants, Coraline moved around her cave home with grace and intention, boiling a pot of water.

When she started pulling out extra cups, Lily said, "We can't drink that."

Coraline hung her head. "Shit. You'd think I'd remember something like that given that's how I ended up stuck here. Did you bring water? I can boil that. The tea is from home. Before the corruption made travel impossible, I traded with some folk passing through."

She threw out the boiling water and started anew.

"Where were you from?" asked Remi.

"New York. I was on a hike with a boyfriend at the time upstate and got lost and mistakenly walked through a shimmer. Been here ever since."

"How long?" asked Damon.

"I don't really know, but it's been long enough to see the corruption take over this realm."

Lily surged forward.

"You watched the corruption take over? Do you know how or why it started?"

Coraline glanced up, then a second time when she noticed the intensity on Lily's face.

"You seem to have more than a passing interest."

"I… it's important to my family to understand how it happened."

Coraline chewed on her lower lip as she poked the fire from a crouched position.

"It happened far from here. I heard about it long before I saw the signs and then it was too late. Those that could leave, did, and those that stayed too long were transformed by it."

"But not you," said Lily.

"I'm not from here."

"What's with all the gear?" asked Remi, receiving a flat look from Lily, who was still interrogating their host.

Coraline's eyes shot towards the heavy clothing she'd worn outside the cave home.

"There are vines covered in a sap that will drive you mad for a time. I mistakenly got some on my arm when the corruption first reached this area. I spent a few days hiding in here thinking the air itself was out to get me. There are other contagions that are much worse. I watched a pixie friend that I used to trade with get dissolved by a puddle she thought was water."

"Blood and bone," exclaimed Damon.

Coraline's face was pinched with sadness.

"When I first got stuck here, I thought I was cursed, then over time I grew to love it. It's a place like no other. I made enough friends to make the Fae feel like home, but then this happened. It breaks my heart."

"Would you go back if you could?" asked Remi.

The wistful smile on their host's lips spoke of heartbreak and loss that had only become bearable over time. After a pause, Coraline stared back at Remi with the intensity of a supernova.

"There's someone I love back in your world."

Remi felt a tightness in her throat.

"I'm sorry."

"It's okay," said Coraline, looking away. "I've made peace with my luck."

The kettle whistled, prompting their host to begin tea making again.

While she waited, Remi investigated the room with her eyes. It wasn't much. A space for a bed, a small kitchen area including the fireplace, and the table, which had four chairs. She spied a colorful box shoved under the bed with tiny handprints on either side of the lock.

Remi's observations were interrupted when Coraline poured the tea.

"I've told you my simple story. Would you indulge me with your own tale? Is this about your family?" asked Coraline, nodding towards Lily.

"Yes and no," said Lily, cagily.

"We're after some people that stole something important from me," said Remi, receiving a pinched face from Lily.

Coraline was about to take a sip but let the cup drift away from her lips.

"Must be important to risk your lives coming here. But I fear you've made a mistake. You can't move far in the Summer Fae anymore. The roving packs of wild satyrs and other dangers make it treacherous. It's more likely they're dead."

"They're not in summer. We need to get to Autumn."

Coraline shook her head.

"A different kind of trouble. While Autumn isn't affected by the corruption, you'd put yourself to the whims of Queen Kiutian. Few except the heralds of the Courts dare enter her realm, and even then, they sometimes come away changed. She is as capricious as she is formidable. I'm sorry, you're fools or worse if you go there."

"It's something we have to do. Can you show us where to go over?" asked Lily.

Coraline appeared saddened by the request. "What I should do is refuse you this information and bring you to the shimmer so you can return to your world alive and well. But you seem like the kind of folk that aren't dissuaded by simple warnings. So show? No. But I can give you directions. I'll not risk myself for your foolish quest, no matter how important you think it is. I speak from experience in that it's better to let whatever happened fade into memory than let it destroy your life."

The anger bubbling beneath the surface of their host's expression was like lava beneath the crust in an active volcano. It'd neither faded nor been forgotten, but Remi didn't think their host realized that.

"Please," said Damon. "It's that important. What the Wildes stole could—"

Coraline nearly dropped her teacup in surprise.

"Who?"

Damon checked back to Remi for reassurance, but he'd already said it, so she shrugged to let him know he might as well continue.

"The Wildes."

Damon's arm raised, headed in Remi's direction. "Yeah, that's—"

"Greta and Archer," said Remi, interrupting Damon before he said too much. "They stole something valuable from me. It had a glamour from the Autumn Queen protecting it. We thought she might be able to tell us where it is."

Coraline slumped into the chair, the teacup slipping out of her fingers and spilling tea onto the table. She made no move to clean it up as she stared into the distance.

"I never thought I'd hear those names again."

"You know them?" asked Damon incredulously, leaning forward and then glancing back at Remi.

She made a face at him, hoping he understood not to reveal any more.

"They stole something from me many years ago. More valuable than gold. It was a priceless gift."

"Then you understand our need."

Coraline sat with her eyes closed for a moment. It lasted long enough the three of them glanced between themselves to check if they should interrupt, or just leave.

"I'm sorry," she said. "I wasn't expecting to have to relive those memories. What did they steal from you?"

"A key that leads to a powerful artifact. They're working for someone else and we fear what will happen if that artifact gets into those hands."

Coraline's forehead wrinkled with thought. Remi suspected a memory from before had surfaced.

"Who are they working for?"

"I wish we knew."

Coraline scoffed quietly.

"I wonder if it's the same people they were working for when I met them so long ago."

"Do you know who they are?" asked Remi.

"No," said Coraline as she smoothed her hand across the table. "They never said. But it was easy to guess that they were powerful folk. Someone equivalent to a Hall patron, or the head of a realm, or one of the other powerful beings that have been around for centuries."

"It seems more than coincidence that we should meet," said Lily, cradling her cup between two hands.

"I refuse to believe there's such a thing as fate," said Coraline. "But I do believe in choices. I have made mine. I will take you to the crossover for Autumn."

"Great," said Lily, starting to stand.

"I can't take you now," said Coraline. "I risked much to save you from the satyrs. They'll still be in the area and it's almost night. We need to wait until morning. They're rarely active after an evening of sex and revelry."

"Are you sure?" asked Damon. "We can't be gone from the hospital for that long."

"Would you rather be late or dead?" asked Coraline.

"We should wait," said Remi. "I trust her to keep us safe."

Coraline's eyes creased at the corners.

"Thank you. There's room enough on the floor for sleeping. You'll have to eat your own food, of course, but at least you can rest safely. I'll take you to the crossover at first light."

The idea that they would have to stay the night settled on them. Remi reached into her pack to grab a bite to eat as her stomach had started to rumble. While she was digging, Lily asked Coraline questions about the corruption. The two conversed on the topic for a while. Remi found a spot by the fire and Damon joined her.

"I hate sitting here," said Damon as he shifted in his spot.

Remi held her hands out by the fire. She wasn't cold, but the heat was comforting.

"I don't know. This is kind of nice. I haven't had a chance to sit around and do nothing in forever. I don't even have my phone to distract me."

Damon leaned over.

"Do you trust her?" he whispered.

Remi checked back to their host, deep in conversation with Lily.

"Yeah. I think I do."

"What gives? You don't trust anyone."

"I trust you and Lily. I think that makes me a good judge of people," said Remi.

Damon stared into the fire.

"But we just met her."

Remi lifted both shoulders.

They sat by the fire in silence until Damon was snoring softly on his side, and the conversation at the table ended. Lily sat in the corner by herself, clearly upset that Coraline had nothing new for her about the corruption.

Sensing Coraline wanted company at the table, and to sate her own curiosity, Remi joined her.

"Thank you again for your hospitality."

"No, thank you for adding a bit of spice to my relatively boring life. Since the corruption overtook everything, I have to stay in my cave except when I'm foraging. Would you like to play a game?"

"Sure."

From a high shelf, Coraline pulled a board covered in pieces that looked similar to chess, except there were four sides and colors rather than two.

"It's called the Game of Courts. Supposedly, the kings and queens of the four courts play it to resolve minor issues rather than war like the olden days. It's thought that chess was derived from it."

"Sounds interesting."

"I had it made for... It doesn't matter now."

After Coraline explained the rules, they each picked two sides and started playing. Remi lost the first game rather quickly, but the second one, she found the gameplay less confusing. By the third, they had a long back-and-forth battle that ended with Coraline winning. Barely.

"You're quite adept at Courts. I felt like I was playing myself."

"I rather enjoyed it. Shall we play a fourth?"

Coraline checked back to the fire which was only embers.

"We should probably sleep. We need to be out the door at first light."

Remi didn't know why but she didn't want to go to bed. The time with Coraline quietly playing Courts had been some of the most pleasant hours she'd spent in years. It made her feel like she was leading a completely different life than the crazy one that she'd found herself in.

"What were you like before here?"

Coraline had started cleaning up the board, but paused mid-thought. She blinked as she looked away.

"It's hard to remember details since it was so long ago, but mostly what I remember is that I was in a punk band in the city, hanging with my friends and trying to figure out what I wanted to do with my life besides always getting in trouble. I wanted to join the Halls, but didn't have the money for the Trials. Thankfully, living in the Fae has given me some measure of protection from faez madness. Does that answer your question?"

Remi wanted to say no, but she sensed her host was wanting to get to bed.

"Yes, thank you for indulging me."

Remi found her spot next to Damon near the fire. Lily was on her side facing the other way, status of slumber unknown.

"Good night, Coraline," said Remi.

Coraline was sitting on the edge of her cot, pulling a necklace from over her head and hanging it on a hook.

"Good night, Regina."

Remi thought it would take a while to fall asleep given their location and the strangeness of the day, but slumber claimed her quickly as she felt warm and safe as if she were lying in her own bed.

TWENTY-THREE

Damon thought he'd be first to awaken, but he found Coraline making tea by the fire while Lily was at the table with a white rat in her lap. He didn't remember her introducing Neko to their host, but the woman didn't seem to be worried.

"Good morning. First light hasn't touched the horizon yet, but it's soon," said Coraline as she poured from her kettle into four cups.

Damon rubbed his eyes with the meat of his palms.

"I haven't slept that good in years."

"Is it busy at the hospital?" asked Coraline.

"Busy doesn't even begin to describe it. Even if we had twice the staff, I still wouldn't get a chance to rest. But the good thing is we're learning faster than we would otherwise," he said.

"Do I smell breakfast?" asked Remi, rising from her slumber with her messy black hair sticking in all directions.

"I have tea. But I'm sorry, you'll have to eat from your own stores."

A wistful smile drifted across Remi's lips.

"That's okay. It's kinda nice to wake up somewhere other than my dorm room."

"Or in someone else's," quipped Lily.

The brief morning period was spent mostly with Lily asking Coraline more questions about the corruption while Remi sat quietly nearby staring at their host.

When it came time to leave, Coraline donned her heavy clothing and handed them strips of cloth to wrap around their hands. She led them out of the cave home and they climbed back up to the platform that traveled above the forest floor.

The passage to Autumn was a few hours of travel, and most of it on the ground where they'd be exposed to danger. Coraline told them once they hit the forest floor that they'd need to stay silent and move quickly.

The first light of morning peeked through the gaps in the trees, sending dappled light upon them. For a few minutes, Damon could get a sense of the beauty of the old Summer Fae, the one untouched by the kalkatai, but then almost as soon as the soft light faded, a weird howl wavered through the trees followed by a half dozen similar voices.

The pace picked up. Damon thought they might be followed but saw no signs. At times they had to fight through the vines, and other times, Coraline detoured them off the path when she sensed something ahead. Damon mostly saw the surroundings through his nose, which was constantly assaulted with alternating smells of deep rot and floral intensity.

Coraline stopped when they reached a grove of towering trunks that seemed untouched by the corruption. The undergrowth was made up of saplings and old leaves that crunched underfoot. A strange light drifted through the trunks like glowing mist.

"This is the passage to Autumn," said Coraline, pulling up her goggles and exposing her face. "I would ask you not to go, but I see you're not easily dissuaded. So instead, I'll wish you good luck."

They traded a round of hugs.

"Will you be safe getting back?" asked Remi.

"I have many tricks to keep them off my tail."

As if responding to her taunt, a gargling howl echoed through the trees.

"I should go."

Remi turned her head towards the noise.

"We'll stay a moment and draw them here to give you time to get away."

Coraline hugged Remi again, holding her tight.

"Thank you. And please stop by if you ever come through Summer again. I'd like another game of Courts."

"Me too."

Coraline donned her goggles, and as a new round of howls started up, she sped back the way they'd come.

"You want to do the honors?" asked Remi.

Damon tilted his head. "What?"

"Answer their howls."

He leaned his head back and let a mournful tune echo from his chest. Damon rarely had the chance to howl, so he found great joy in its practice.

Even the responses, strange as they were, felt pleasing, and he wondered what it'd be like to hunt in a pack.

"Neko says we should go," said Lily after a minute.

Remi held out a hand. "Not yet. We need to give her as much time as possible."

"Remi..."

"I know, Damon. I know. Another minute. They're not here yet."

"While we're waiting," said Lily, "did anyone else see what was on the end of her necklace? I was first up this morning and saw it before she put it on."

They both shook their heads.

"A mortanis hound talon. A small one, but I don't doubt what I saw."

"That's strange. What connection would she have to the Veil?" asked Damon.

A low growl from Neko had them turning towards the forest. Damon sniffed the air, smelling warm odorous flesh.

"Run!"

He pushed Remi towards the gaps in the trees. The four of them sprinted towards the strange light.

Behind them a pack of wild satyrs burst into the clearing, bounding effortlessly on their split hooves. They were catching up quickly. Damon worried that they'd delayed too long and the satyrs would catch them.

He checked over his shoulder to see a big satyr a few strides behind. Damon thought about turning to fight to give the others a chance to make it through the passage, when he felt a quiver of vertigo.

When he turned his head, he no longer saw the satyr and the trees had changed noticeably. Rather than the dark green foliage tinged with brown rot, the canopy was a burst of bright yellows, reds, and oranges.

"Whoa. It's like the trees are on fire," breathed Remi.

The terror of escape was quickly replaced with wonder. They meandered through the grove with their heads tilted, gawking at the sights above them.

They exited the grove, reaching a cliff edge that overlooked rolling hills cloaked in the colors of Autumn. Damon choked up from the beauty. It was like nothing he'd ever seen before. He worried that he'd gone mad from the sight when he started laughing, especially when Remi joined him.

"If I die today, I don't know if I'll feel sad, knowing I saw this," said Remi.

Lily was subdued as she viewed the vista with lingering sadness.

"What's wrong?"

"Summer used to be like this in its own way. So much has been lost by the corruption."

"Where do we go?" asked Damon.

Lily extended her arm towards a distant hill. An enormous pagoda stuck above the colorful trees.

"We can try there first."

A well-trampled path led them down from the cliff. The trail meandered into the valley, taking them past sights that seemed to increase in wonder. A cloud of insects that looked like living fire danced around the base of a waterfall, turning the rising mist into a furnace of gold and orange. Past a rope bridge over a deep chasm, a group of slender humanoids no taller than their knees dove into turquoise waters, then burst from the surface with shiny, angled rocks in their fists.

When they reached the valley floor, Damon's hackles rose in anticipation of hidden dangers. His friends were equally spooked by the thick mist that made it difficult to scout ahead.

"Are we being followed?" asked Remi.

"Neko says yes."

"By what?"

Lily shrugged.

Damon checked over his shoulder as they moved through the mist. He never saw what was following, but he smelled the creatures surrounding them.

"Hurry. Don't run, but hurry."

The pace picked up. As the mist started to fade, he felt the creatures growing impatient.

Damon turned around and held out his claws with a throaty roar. He didn't see anything move, but he felt them shift away. After a few seconds, he caught up to his friends. A few minutes later they exited the mist.

"What was that?" asked Remi.

Damon shrugged.

"I don't know."

Crossing the valley floor took a few hours. Damon felt like they were being watched the entire time even though he never saw anything. Neko reported the same thing to Lily, so they never let their guard down.

When they happened upon a strange statue in the middle of the forest, they stopped for a break. The statue was of a humanoid figure in mid-song with his arms outstretched. The material of the creation was not stone or concrete, but thousands of tiny small rocks that glimmered in the sunlight.

"Any ideas what's watching us?" asked Remi as she chewed on a rod of spiced jerky.

"I heard laughter earlier," said Damon.

Lily said nothing, but Neko was pacing near the statue and staring into the colorful trees.

"I have a feeling we'll find out soon enough," said Damon.

After eating, they traveled through a narrow canyon covered in moss and little waterfalls that connected at the center to form a meandering stream. Little rocks were occasionally knocked off the edge, which alerted them that their observers were still with them.

When they crested the hill, they saw they had another valley to cross before reaching the pagoda. Beyond it, a range of angled mountains reached towards the cerulean sky. They decided if they hurried they could reach it before the end of the day.

On the next valley floor, their journey was stymied by a colorful swamp covered in bright flowers that floated on the surface of the water. A few tentative attempts to wade through were quickly ended when they realized the mud was trying to suck them downward.

"I guess we'll go around."

At times, bits of mist covered the water, and small glowing creatures flitted through the trees. The entire experience was enchanting, and Damon had to remind himself not to get lulled into a false sense of security and keep his senses on high alert.

An hour after they reached the swamp, they came to a sturdy, but narrow one-person bridge that provided a path across the water, leapfrogging the small islands to reach the opposite side.

"Do we dare?" asked Damon.

"This swamp feels like it goes on forever. I say we take it. Looks solid enough for me," said Remi, bouncing her foot on the first planks.

Neko sniffed the anchors and put a tentative paw on the first wooden board before looking back to them and giving a small whine. The sides were made from woven rope.

"I don't think Neko likes it," said Damon. "I don't think I like it either."

"I'd rather risk it and make it to the pagoda before night falls. We don't know what kind of creatures live in Autumn," said Remi.

Lily frowned.

"I tend to agree with Remi. The Fae is not the kind of danger that we're used to, but it's more dangerous than an Irishman with a grudge."

"Fine. Let Neko take the lead and I'll bring up the rear," he said.

While Damon felt uneasy about crossing the rope bridge at first, his unease quickly dissipated as he marveled at the sights further into the swamp. Slender rainbow-scaled fish zipped right below the surface, while birds that looked almost like folded paper flitted amongst the canopies.

He didn't realize anything had changed until he nearly ran into Lily. The other three had halted on a small island before a long stretch across deeper waters. Damon wasn't sure what the problem was until he spotted the figure on a nearby island.

Damon thought the figure was unusually constructed with too-long arms and short stubby legs stuffed into bright, checkerboard clothing until he realized that they were standing on their head and juggling fruit while taking bites at random moments.

"...and time is rhymed but never the prime is sublime as they climb towards crime—"

The figure made a fearful squeak at realizing they were being observed, then flipped onto their feet, never missing a catch of the six spinning fruits. But as soon as they were upright, the objects disappeared.

"Why do you think?" asked the figure in a light, playful voice.

The words traveled across the water. Damon shared glances with his companions at the odd question.

When he looked back, he realized the figure was wearing a mask of leaves and displayed a frightening expression of a wide mouth filled with fangs. The colors of the mask were white, black, and an earthy crimson.

"Who are you?" asked Lily.

"Kabo."

He bowed deeply.

"And who are you?"

"Travelers to see the queen."

Kabo leaned his head back and laughed hysterically. The response seemed to break the figure as he danced around his island, stomping his feet, until at last he turned back towards them.

"A fine time to seek the queen's line, oh so divine, you mine to find if she can design your decline or the perhaps benign, but never the shrine, but beware the sign."

Remi turned her head away from Kabo and spoke under her breath.

"Is he an idiot or playing with us?"

"I heard that, Remington Wilde."

Remi stiffened as she slowly turned her head back.

"How do you know my name?"

"The queen does not tolerate visitors without knowing their identity."

"She knows we're coming?"

"Of course not. She's busy doing queen things. There's no time to worry about the whims of mortals. I mean, she has time. All the time in the universe, but it's precious, precious, precious. You can't just fit *everything* into your schedule. But she's going to try. That's why she has us. We deal with the pesky problems that beset her kingdom."

"Would you take us to her? It's important," said Remi, leaning against the rope side of the bridge.

"Everything's important. Nothing's important," said Kabo, throwing up his arms with faux exasperation. "Work, work, work. Play, play, play. Die, die, die. It never ends, does it?"

"Please," said Damon. "There's much at stake."

Kabo snapped his hand together like a mouth closing.

"Hush. I'm talking to the trickster. Yes, I know what lurks inside your heart, Remington."

"I don't like this," said Damon under his breath.

Lily turned her head slightly, concern baked into her expression.

"I think we're going to have to trust Remi to get us through this one."

TWENTY-FOUR

Remi leaned against the rope as she stared at Kabo on his island. She hated that people called her a trickster without her knowing why.

"Have you been following us?" she asked.

"Why would I do that? I have a busy schedule myself. I had to put on a beetle play. It was quite the production, except for sewing all those little costumes. You can't imagine how many pixies I had to murder to get them done in time."

Remi didn't know how much Kabo was being truthful. Part of his little speech felt like the edgy crap that young boys on the internet liked to post, but she also sensed a darkness in the strange Fae.

"You've been waiting for us," she said.

"That's as plain as the drain on an unlevel train."

Remi checked the sky.

"We don't have time for this."

She headed across the section of bridge. The longer span was less stable and it started to rock around the quarter mark. Remi checked behind to see her friends were watching cautiously rather than following, a choice she didn't understand until she turned back to see Kabo on the island ahead of her, sitting astride the two ropes like a ballet dancer stretching.

"You don't scare me," she said as she continued forward.

"I should. You know they call me Kabo of the Lovely Terrors. Or the Prince of Terrors for short."

"I know a con man when I see one."

"And I know a twit when I see one," said Kabo, turning up his chin.

"Take off your mask, or are you afraid to show your face?"

Kabo did a backflip off the ropes and landed on his feet with his arms wide in a pose that suggested he was waiting for applause.

"Who says this isn't my face?"

At the halfway point between the islands, the bridge began to sway. Remi shifted with the movement, but it was making it hard to cross. She clamped onto the sides.

"Stop messing with the bridge."

Kabo crossed his arms.

"You insulted me."

"You're not a con man?"

His head snapped back towards her.

"Con man? No, that you said I was waiting for you." He shivered. "What kind of being would that make me that I, a prince of the realm, would reduce myself to being a handmaid to mere mortals?"

"Are you really a prince?" she asked.

"Are you really a twit?"

Remi opened her mouth for a retort when the sides of the rope bridge collapsed, leaving only a flat, unstable platform that was swaying precipitously.

"Hey!"

The words barely left her lips when she tipped over the edge, plunging beneath the surface of the water. The heavy pack on her shoulders dragged her deeper as she struggled to swim back to the surface. Remi fought with the straps to free herself as the air in her lungs screamed to get out.

When at last she was no longer sinking, Remi kicked upwards. She was almost at the surface when she saw a trio of rainbow fish darting towards her belly.

Three narrow fish heads slammed into her gut, forcing her mouth open in surprise. A lungful of water rushed in, right as she broke the surface, coughing and sputtering.

With eyes burning from the achy chest, Remi ungracefully paddled to the island wishing she'd had a normal childhood. She crawled onto land dripping wet and coughing uncontrollably, only to look up into the shocked faces of her friends.

"How did you get over here?"

Lily and Damon glanced between themselves.

"Why did you dive in?"

"Dive in? That bastard Kabo knocked me in."

"That's not what it looked like," said Lily. "You leapt over the rope edge."

"I'm okay now," she said, pounding on her chest to free up the water that had gotten lodged there. "Minus the loss of my pack."

The looks her friends were giving suggested otherwise.

"What? Do I have a leech on my face or something worse?"

"Remi," said Damon, stone-faced. "You drank the water."

The realization settled on her bones.

"Oh. Maybe it wasn't enough, to you know..."

She knew the answer even if she didn't want to admit it to herself.

Damon helped her to her feet. She looked around for Kabo, but he was nowhere to be found.

"Where's the twit?"

Lily frowned.

"He disappeared off the island when you started walking across. Then you were shouting at no one in particular and then you dove in. We were right behind you, but it didn't matter."

"Would it help to explain that's not how I experienced it?"

Lily batted a glowing insect away from her hair.

"I suppose that's possible. But it still doesn't change the fact that you drank the water, Remi. You can't leave. This was a one-way trip."

"Then I guess we'd better make sure it was worth it," said Remi, trying not to think about it. There would be time enough for regrets later.

A half hour later, they were off the bridge. Kabo was sitting on a rock eating a bright purple fruit. As soon as Remi neared, he leapt off, startling her to bring her hands up defensively, but he bowed deeply and with a twirling arm-flourish.

"Welcome to the other side of the swamp. You look damp, Remington Wilde. Did you encounter some difficulties on your journey?"

Remi crossed her arms as a hundred different quips appeared on her tongue but kept her lips clamped until the urge to say them passed.

"My apologies for my earlier comments. It's been a long day and I was rude."

She sensed amusement under the mask.

"Apology accepted. Let us put aside our petty squabbles. Allow me to lead you to my queen. It's only fair, and frankly, you'll want to get there as soon as possible, for night is when the Yosati come out, and you don't want to meet them. It's only a short walk from here. All uphill, of course, but you look like sturdy...what are you again?"

Before Remi could respond, Damon stepped forward.

"That would be lovely, thank you."

She glared at him.

"I was going to be nice."

"One can never know."

Kabo did a backflip off the rock he was sitting on and then trotted up the path, beckoning them onward. Remi found it hard to believe he was a prince of the realm. He seemed more like a jester, but she decided there was no point in antagonizing him further. He'd proved his point when he'd knocked her off the bridge—a problem she decided was better to think about at a much, much later date.

The trail brought them through a wide forest covered in mist, much like the one they'd passed earlier. Remi sensed the mist-creatures, but like before, never saw one.

"What are the creatures that lurk here?"

Kabo halted and turned his head.

"Best not to speak of them. Or think of them really. It only encourages them."

After that, Remi found it hard *not* to think about them. She felt the mist swirling tighter around them, occasionally receiving exasperated looks from Kabo. She wasn't paying attention when she felt a cold, moist touch along her wrist.

"Hey!"

The mist retreated, laughing in bright tones, until the trunks were visible at a distance.

Remi stared at her flesh where the mist-creature had touched her. Her friends had similar confused expressions.

"What did they do?"

Kabo tilted his head.

"They're thieves is what they are."

Remi patted her pockets.

"I don't have anything left, what could they have stolen?"

"Same," said Damon. "Nothing's missing, that I know of."

Kabo cupped his ear.

"They steal more precious things than possessions. I can hear them tittering about it. It seems one of you lost what it's like to taste cinnamon, while another can never see the color of aquarai in the realm of Senasalia. It's a real shame. I would give my fourth eye for a chance to see aquarai again. It's breathtaking."

"How can they steal something none of us have experienced?" asked Remi.

"There you go again with your strange, easily disproved lies," said Kabo.

Remi decided that silence was better as she contemplated whether or not she could remember what it was like to taste cinnamon. She couldn't quite decide if there was a hole in her memories, or the long trying day made it hard to conceive.

The path that Kabo led them on wound up the hillside. The trees and surroundings were still breathtaking, but Remi's legs were tired. She'd not walked this far, maybe ever, and the lingering worry about drinking the water earlier was weighing her down. Which she found quite contradictory, since she'd shed her pack in the swamp.

As shadows lengthened, Remi felt like they were no closer to the top. She focused her attention on the shifting of the light for a time until she was certain that Kabo was misleading them.

"Stop."

Her friends halted, but Kabo kept moving, checking behind and making motions to catch up.

"Hurry, hurry! We want to reach the top before night. While I'm in no danger from the Yosati, I cannot say the same for you."

Remi's foot shifted forward unconsciously, but as soon as she sensed it, she growled under her breath.

"No. We're not moving. You're leading us in circles and not up the hill. If you're not going to lead us correctly, we'll find our own way up."

Kabo's shoulders slumped.

"You're no fun, Remington Wilde. Come, let us take the real path."

Within a few steps of following, Remi was certain that it was still a false one.

"Come on," she said to her friends and cut uphill, right through the undergrowth.

Kabo stood to the side silently.

"That's not the way. You're going to get lost and eaten by the Yosati," he said in a singsong voice.

Remi ignored him and led them directly upward. There was no path, but it wasn't like the Summer Fae. The saplings and other undergrowth were easy to avoid.

About halfway up, the sun set behind the hill and strange lights appeared in the distance. Kabo was still following, but he had his head down and made noises under his breath like a petulant teenager.

"Are you sure about this?" asked Damon when they had to bring out mage lights to see the way forward.

"I only need to look at Kabo to know we're going the right way."

But the truth was that she was worried that Kabo had baited her into this decision as she sensed tiny smirks behind the mask. This lasted until she saw the warm glow of faerie fire through the trees and she spied a towering pagoda rising above the valley.

Remi turned to say something to Kabo, but he was gone. She thought she heard laughing but the others were too entranced by the sight of their destination.

"Come on," said Damon, marching forward. "Let's get this over with."

TWENTY-FIVE

A cool wind whipped across the hilltop, bringing a slight chill. Damon shivered as they ascended the final stretch towards the base of the pagoda, which rose at least a hundred feet above their heads.

The bottom of the structure was open, with archways on either side. The glowing embers of a firepit reflected off the walls, pushing out a radiating warmth that countered the brief cold. A woman with black hair, wearing a bright red cloak, stood near the spent fire, gesturing over the red-orange coals.

The Fae woman clearly sensed them, but made no motion to acknowledge as she was focused on a task that involved the crackling embers. When Damon reached the pit's edge, he saw not a lump of old wood burnt down to char, but the outlines of a carnival, including a merry-go-round and a team of horses pulling a carriage. The mix of coal-black and bright oranges and red provided the colors of the ember-painting which made his heart soar in appreciation, though he didn't understand the meaning of the crumpled light green silk shirt near the fire bowl.

Damon shifted his attention to the Fae woman as she conducted changes to the embers as if she were pulling invisible threads. The presence of fire was unusual in a Fae realm, but he knew the others were not like the summer realm.

"Is it customary for your kind to sneak upon royalty with no regard for their station?"

Damon quickly bowed, pressing his hands against his thighs, noting that his friends were doing the same.

"I'm sorry. We were led here by Kabo. He disappeared right before we reached the pagoda."

The Fae woman faced them, which made his heart skip. She was beautiful, alien, and fell. Her painted eyes, with extended corners, made her almost cat-like, while the long face and high cheekbones gave her the look of a runway model.

"I am Lily de Meath, and these are my friends Remi Wilde and Damon Wolfhard. Our deepest apologies for sneaking up on you. We've had a long day since leaving Summer, and were only joyful at finding a place to rest."

"Yes," said Damon, bowing again. "We're pleased we can finally meet you, Queen Kiutian."

The sharp laugh that exited the woman's lips felt like knives against Damon's flesh. He knew his error immediately, doubly so when Lily frowned in his direction.

"I'll do you the favor of never speaking of that mistake, or you'll find yourself a permanent fixture of our capricious realm. I am Lady Aki, sometimes known as the Lady of Embers, or That Bitch Who Likes Fire."

A soft snort slipped from Remi's lips.

"Was there something funny?" asked Lady Aki.

Remi shook her head.

"Not at all. I like that last name."

Lady Aki made a noise in the back of her throat. She peered into the darkness.

"Where is that wearisome Kabo?"

"He disappeared the moment we reached the pagoda." Damon gestured towards the embers. "I enjoyed the pictures in the coals."

Lady Aki sighed.

"Unlike our queen, I prefer my art to be ephemeral. The murmurings of thornwings, the patterned death of a mammoth tree, or the embers of a volunteer dryad." The corners of her eyes creased as if she realized who she was speaking to. "What did Kabo promise you?"

"He said he would lead us to the queen," said Damon.

"And what would you ask of the soul of Autumn?"

Before Damon could speak, Lily stepped forward.

"A question only for her ears."

"I am a Lady of her Court. You would dare to keep this knowledge from me?" asked Lady Aki with her chin raised.

"I mean no disrespect—"

"Yet your lips give it."

Lady Aki towered over Lily, who had her head inclined. Damon sensed the ancient Fae gathering power.

"It has to do with the kalkatai," he said.

The Fae woman's head snapped around.

"What do *you* know of the kalkatai?"

"It has reached the city of sorcery where we come from. We're healers at Golden Willow. A corrupted Green Man came to our city and attempted to spread its corruption."

Lady Aki turned away, her cloak flowing around her like flame.

"The kalkatai is a problem for Summer...and your realm it seems. It is not our problem that the Oak Father could not protect his realm."

"But who knows if once it's finished that it won't spread to the other Fae realms. Please, let us speak to the Autumn Queen, and then we'll be on our way," said Damon.

"The queen is not here. This is but a way station. A place of rest and contemplation."

"May we learn her location so we can go to her? Is she at the Autumn Palace?" asked Lily.

"She's not been there for centuries. Our queen has little interest in the machinations of her Court. Her projects are more important." Lady Aki turned back swiftly. "But no more questions. Your presence tires me. You may spend the night and in the morning I will decide if you are worthy enough to pass or if I will feed you to the flames."

Lady Aki strode from the base of the pagoda, disappearing into the gloom as the embers of the fire winked out as if they'd been turned off with a switch, leaving them in near darkness except for the faint floating mage lights.

Damon turned to address his friends only to find the strange mask of Kabo staring at him from two feet away.

"Is she gone?" he asked in a whisper.

Damon startled and nearly fell over stepping backwards.

"Have you been here this whole time?"

Kabo tilted his head.

"Lady Aki is cross with me."

"I can't imagine why," said Remi.

"Where can we rest?" asked Lily, craning her neck at the tower.

"Oh, not there," said Kabo. "It's best if you stay in the grass, but the nearness of the tower will keep you safe from the denizens of the night."

They set up camp near the outer wall. Remi had lost her gear, so Damon loaned her the thin blanket he'd brought as a cover. The tower blocked the wind so the air was warm enough to be comfortable.

Kabo watched them while they worked as he sat in the grass and picked at his fingernails.

Shortly after they'd settled, Kabo popped to his feet, looking out over the valley. Damon followed his gaze to see a bloodred moon climbing from the trees. They watched in silence as it rose above the valley until the deepest crimson washed away and there was only an orange patina.

With the excitement over, Damon settled down to sleep, but found it hard with Kabo sitting on a round rock watching them.

"Are you going to sit there all night?"

"Close your eyes, little human. Don't worry. I'll keep watch."

Damon didn't trust him, but there was no choice if they wanted to get some sleep. He set his head on the rolled-up shirt that acted as a pillow and promptly, and unexpectedly, found slumber.

§

He woke to laughter.

There was no sun, but the daylight was warm and shining in his eyes. Damon sat up, finding Remi and Kabo sitting in the grass on the far edge of the slope, laughing and slapping their knees like old friends.

Damon was suspicious about the change, wondering if it was like Remi's admission that she hadn't dived into the water, but in this case, he was unsure what Kabo's game was. They'd already been in the Fae much longer than they'd originally planned. He felt like they were constantly pulled just a little bit further. And then again. And again.

"Good daylight, Damon Wolfhard," said Kabo. "Is that the correct greeting?"

"Almost," said Remi, laughing. "Good morning is more correct, but I rather like good daylight."

Lily was also awake. Eating something from her pack and sitting away from the others. Damon reached into his for pack only to find it missing.

He surged to his feet, towering over Kabo.

"What did you do with my pack? It's got all my food and water. I can't stay here without it."

Kabo held a hand to his chest.

"Why would you accuse me?"

"Because you're the only one besides us that was awake, and none of them would have stolen it."

Remi looked up with a pained expression. He saw the fear in her eyes about being trapped permanently in the Fae.

"It couldn't be Kabo. We've been talking all night. I couldn't sleep and so we started chatting. But it's okay. I feel rather refreshed. A good part of being stuck in the Fae, right? I won't need sleep. Or very little of it."

"Then who took it?" asked Damon, fists at his side.

"There are more thieves in the Fae than stars in the sky," said Kabo.

"Damon," said Lily, holding out a package of jerky.

He took the offering and found a spot near the wall to eat, glancing suspiciously at Kabo as he worked on his food. He wasn't given long to enjoy himself before the Lady of Embers came sweeping down stairs that he hadn't seen before.

When she appeared, a feverous rustling from the nearby forest had him checking to see nothing but the trees. He thought he heard a whimper, but his eyes detected nothing.

"I will take what I wish," said Lady Aki.

Damon thought she was speaking to him, until he realized her head was turned towards the forest.

"Good morning, Lady Aki," said Lily, approaching with a bow. "Have you decided on our request to see the queen?"

The Fae woman was even stranger in the light. Pale and thin like a reed. She had an almost parchment quality.

"I have."

She seemed distracted by whatever was going on in the trees. Whenever Damon looked away, he sensed movement at the corner of his vision, but could never spot it directly.

"Let us speak above, away from these distractions."

Lady Aki swept towards the tower.

Damon quickly grabbed his gear, fearing to leave it to the quick hands of the forest. As he fell in behind the Fae Lady, he noticed that Kabo was no longer around. He'd disappeared again, and Damon wondered if that was the most prudent action around the Lady.

Each level of the towering pagoda was an open area containing new and strange sculptures. They passed quickly, so it was hard to study, but he saw what was once a thick trunk burned down to the shape of a woman that suspiciously looked like their host. Another floor held a trio of dancing flames that moved around each other like moons in an unstable orbit.

They stopped on the top floor, which had no walls and a grand view of the surrounding autumnal forests. Damon's breath caught in his throat at the mists collecting in the valleys, shifting and moving like a living thing against the bright oranges, reds, and yellows of the leaves.

"It's so beautiful," said Remi near the edge, thumbing away a tear.

Lady Aki blinked and checked back to where Remi was looking with a faint expression of sadness.

"Oh, to look upon these hills with fresh eyes again."

While both he and Remi were distracted by the view, Lily was facing their host with her hands behind her back like an obedient servant. Damon followed her example and joined her, while Remi continued to gawk at their surroundings.

"Last night, I couldn't decide between feeding you to the flames or sending you back to Summer, but then I realized I'd been given a gift that I shouldn't waste."

The mention of a gift had Damon nervous. He wanted Remi to come away from the edge and join them in respectful audience, but she seemed enraptured and Lady Aki seemed not to care.

"I offer you this proposition. Answer my question successfully and I will help you get the truths you need from my queen. Give the wrong answer, or fail to give one by the time the blood moon rises again, and I will let the flames reveal your true form beneath that wretched skin."

"What kind of question?" asked Lily.

"An honest question."

"Will we know the answer? You could ask anything, even something mundane and trivial, but so intensely personal that we could never stumble upon the answer in a thousand lifetimes."

Lady Aki smirked.

"You are well versed in the ways of the Fae. But I am not like Kabo, or the other tricksters of the realm. The only truths that matter are the ones that flame can reveal. Do you accept my proposition?"

"Remi?" asked Damon.

When she turned, Damon saw both radiance and sorrow. He realized what she'd been looking at, and talking about with Kabo. Now that she knew she was stuck in the Fae, she was coming to terms with her fate.

"I accept under the condition that it is only me that will pay the price if we fail, and that you'll send the others back without further harm. It was my responsibility and my quest. I should be the one to bear the load."

Lily took a half-step forward.

"Are you sure?"

"I'm already a prisoner. Let me make the most of my sentence."

Lady Aki smirked, which felt unusual to Damon, but he hadn't quite figured out their host so he kept quiet. Besides, his heart was aching at the idea that no matter what happened, they wouldn't be taking Remi back to Golden Willow.

"Wait," said Damon, catching the error of his thoughts. "It doesn't matter. You can't leave Autumn. I don't know if just the two of us can find the Horn."

"You have to try. Please. Let me make something of this sacrifice."

A second soft snort from Lady Aki brought heat to his cheeks.

Before he could stop her, Remi marched in front of Lady Aki and said, "I accept your challenge."

Lady Aki lifted her chin as she regarded Remi with half-lidded eyes.

"What leads the spectral arrow on its eternal chase, bound by fruitful misfortune and the drumbeat of the night's calendar?"

The question lay heavy upon them. Damon looked to his friends with equal confusion.

They gathered away from the heavy gaze of Lady Aki, who was pleased by the effect the riddle had on them.

"Ideas?" asked Damon. "Riddles aren't my thing."

"I'm decent at them. Nyx never met a riddle she couldn't solve. It would be better if she were here," said Lily.

Remi put a hand on her shoulder.

"I wouldn't choose anyone else in the world to help me with this."

"You realize what you've signed up for? The Lady's paintbrush is not kind," said Lily.

"I have faith in my friends."

"I wish I had faith," said Damon quietly.

"Focus on the riddle, not what might happen if we get it wrong," said Remi.

He wanted to pull her into his arms and spend their potentially last day in blissful embrace, but knew that wouldn't help them solve the riddle. For the next few minutes, they threw out a few bad ideas, but quickly fell into silence.

"Let's each think separately and come back together in a short while," said Remi.

Damon sat on the edge, looking out upon the fiery leaves of the rolling valleys. His thoughts trended towards the artworks on the lower floors, the promise of fate for Remi if they should get the answer wrong.

"Damon—"

He hadn't realized how long he'd been sitting and staring at the mist collecting in the valley until Lily got his attention. When he checked back to the sky, he saw that it was taking on darker tones.

"How long have we been apart?" he asked.

"Time passes strangely in the Fae," said Lily.

Remi turned on Lady Aki, who had been watching them silently.

"No cheating."

"I haven't cheated. The three of you have been staring into the valley for many hours. It's not my fault your minds are too weak to resist the fell beauty of the autumnal forest."

Damon marched over to the Lady, anger rising in his chest.

"You steal what you cannot earn."

She laughed in his face.

"Children, all of you. You know nothing of this realm and throw your accusations around like sparks in a dry forest. Do you want to wake the flame?"

A soft hand pulled him away. Remi set her hand against his cheek.

"Don't. It's not worth it. Focus on the riddle. Please. We've not much time."

They gathered with Lily, who was pacing near the edge. Faint stars were starting to appear, announcing the advent of night.

"What leads the spectral arrow on its eternal chase, bound by fruitful misfortune and the drumbeat of the night's calendar," said Damon.

"It sounds like nonsense to me," said Remi.

"What is the spectral arrow? A ghost that goes places? And why is it always chasing?" asked Lily.

"I don't know," said Damon. "But that's not the part I've been focused on and I think I have an idea about it. What is the drumbeat of the night's calendar? Is that not the moon? Calendars mark when it moves through its phases."

"But that's a human thing. Why would the Fae mention a calendar?" asked Remi.

"Good point, but I still think it holds true," said Damon. "I think it has to do with the changing of the moon. Is there something in Autumn that matters? A ritual or other event?"

Lily shook her head.

"I don't know."

"Then it can't be that. It has to be something we have knowledge of," said Remi.

Their ideas went round and round as Damon felt the ticking of the clock in the back of his head. He peered at the sky, watching in slow horror as the stars twinkled into existence, one by one, announcing the shortness of their time like the ticking of seconds.

Lady Aki stayed silent at the center, quietly amused by their flailing around the riddle. Sometimes Damon checked back to see if a topic was resonating with her, but she had a skilled poker face.

"What about the fruitful misfortune? A curse, but not a curse? What is that?" asked Remi.

Lily's expression was wracked with concern as she stared out over the valley.

"Remi..."

All eyes turned towards the horizon where a reddish glow was spreading like spilled blood.

"We've not long. Focus. What is a beneficial curse?" asked Remi.

Damon snapped his fingers.

"Wait, why didn't I see it before? I don't normally associate my therianthropy with the moon, but that's a thing that people believe. It's a beneficial curse that I'm a werewolf."

"Yes, yes," said Remi. "But what about—"

"That's time," said Lady Aki, gesturing towards the horizon where a sliver of the red moon was peeking over like a shy child.

A hole opened in Damon's heart at the thought that they'd lost. Remi had lost. He immediately put himself in front of her, which prompted Lady Aki to lean back her head and laugh.

"The rage of mortals, how precious."

"It's not over," said Remi. "You said, by the time the blood moon rises. It's not finished. It has to be over the horizon."

Lady Aki clasped her hands in front like a priestess getting ready to perform a sacrifice.

"The girl is correct. But you'd better hurry."

Damon found it hard not to stare at the rising moon. It was already a quarter over the horizon. The images of what would happen to Remi were already creeping in.

"Spectral arrow. Eternal chase. Full moon. Werewolves."

Damon repeated the phrase again. And again, as he watched the bloodred moon ascend.

"Spectral arrows. No arrow. A single object. What does a werewolf have to do with a spectral arrow? What. What." He turned to Lady Aki. "Is it a what or a who?"

Her gaze shifted to the horizon. The final quarter was draining away in reverse. He could only think of Remi on a pyre being reduced to ash, but his fears were not helping him with the task at hand. Damon closed his eyes and focused on the riddle. Spectral arrow. The full moon. Werewolves.

"It has to be something we know. That I know."

He opened his eyes to see the final piece of the moon still connected to the horizon like a tether.

"Shit. Could that be it?" Realizing they had no more time, he blurted out his answer. "A human in wolf form, leading the Wild Hunt, and not just any werewolf, but the original, King Nuada."

His words and the moon timed their exits simultaneously. He stared at Lady Aki, waiting for the acknowledgement of the riddle.

She turned and strolled to the edge of the platform. Damon joined her.

The four of them stood in a line, toes kissing the edge, overlooking a forest covered in the reflections of the blood moon.

"Tomorrow morning we shall travel to the queen, but before we can ask her this boon, I must understand the nature of your problem. Tonight we palaver."

TWENTY-SIX

The flame at the center of the platform was neither warm nor bright. Remi found she could sit with her knees almost touching the blaze as she stared into the shifting purplish flames, watching what could only be described as a fire show.

The four of them sat on opposite sides like the points of a compass. Since Damon had successfully answered the riddle, Lady Aki acted subdued, yet amused. Remi couldn't understand these emotions, except that the being across from them had lived for many times longer than the three of them combined.

"Tell me of your burden. No more obfuscations. No more lies. I am bound by the terms of the riddle. I will do my best to aid you on your quest."

Sensing that the earlier confrontations were over, Remi reached for the porcelain cup containing the fire water Lady Aki had poured for them.

While her friends would not partake, there was no reason for her reluctance, so she downed the liquid, feeling it burn on its way down to her belly. A small boon for the curse of being trapped in the Fae.

"A number of years ago, I stole a pendant from an ancient and powerful human family. This pendant is a key that leads to the Horn of Bran Galed. I did not wish to go after the Horn, but some others stole the pendant on behalf of some powerful people, and we want to get it back. We know the pendant was glamoured by your queen, so we thought she might be able to tell us where the Horn is hidden."

"Give me your hand," said Lady Aki, holding out hers in the middle of the flames.

Remi did as she asked. The flames did not burn, but the elder Fae's touch felt hot like the handle of a pot that had been on the stove. It took all of Remi's self-control not to yank her hand away.

Lady Aki pried Remi's fist open and stared at her palm. She scratched her fingernails across the flesh, revealing faint eldritch lines.

"There it is. The imprint of your pendant. I see it now. A key made in Summer, but glamoured in Autumn. A strange combination. I know this pendant, and the Horn, though I have not thought about them in a very long time.

"The Horn is a terrible thing. Capable of great acts, but ultimately it always ends up being used for tragedy. After an ancient trickster stole the Horn and wreaked havoc upon your world in the form of plagues and viruses, the Keeper of the Veil, having seen too many souls pass through her realm, decided to take matters into her hands. Together with her assistant, she found the Horn and brought it here, knowing that despite its dangers, it might be necessary in the future, and asked Summer and Autumn to help her disguise the trail."

It was too much. Remi tried to yank her hand away, overwhelmed by the news, but Lady Aki held fast.

"The assistant. Is that a brooding young man that lurks in the Veil? Some call him the Stranger."

"It is. He was human once, but long ago found himself a creature of the Veil."

"That shouldn't be possible," said Remi.

"Yet it is."

She peered at him in her mind's eye. The dark-haired stranger lurking in the Veil, watching from a distance.

"Maybe that's why he's been spying on me. Because I held the key to the Horn."

"Have you seen him since it was stolen?" asked Lily.

"No."

"Remington Wilde. Yours is a twisted past. Bound with invisible threads. If you choose to follow the path of the Horn, I see a great tragedy unfolding."

"Is this prophecy?"

Lady Aki shook her head.

"There's no such thing. But sometimes it's easy to see where a life is headed. It's like seeing a fire in the forest and knowing which way it will burn by the dead trees, the old leaves, and the swirling winds."

"Will you take us to your queen?"

"In the morning we'll leave for the Kiutian Peaks. It's not far, but we should be on foot at first light if we want to reach the queen by evening."

"Why does it matter if we see her by evening?" asked Remi.

Lady Aki inclined her head as she swept away, disappearing down the ramp as the purple flame disappeared.

In a quieter voice, Remi asked again, "Why does it matter if we see her by evening?"

Lily followed the Lady of Embers down the ramp.

"One can never know with the Fae. We should rest."

"Come on, Remi," said Damon. "All this tension has exhausted me."

Remi didn't head down right away. She watched the blood moon climb into the sky, slowly losing its color until it was a pale orange.

"This is my home now."

A part of her thought that returning to Summer and living with Coraline would be the best course of action. It might be more dangerous in Summer due to the kalkatai, but at least she'd have someone normal to spend the time with. Remi couldn't imagine spending the rest of her days with the likes of Kabo and Lady Aki without going stark raving mad.

In the morning, Lady Aki was waiting for them when they awoke.

"Come, children. We must hurry."

They packed in a hurry and joined their guide as she strode down the hillside in the opposite direction of the moonrise. She moved like a flame through dry tinder, forcing them to make haste. Even the spells they knew that bolstered their endurance weren't enough to keep them from panting every time they were given a brief stop for rest.

Lady Aki admonished them frequently for lagging behind. Remi almost had the impression she was enjoying the journey, like a parent taking a group of kids on a field trip.

Kabo was with them as well, but he stayed out of sight. Remi caught glimpses of him lurking in the trees, sticking his tongue out of the mouth hole of his mask of leaves, or making rude gestures with his hands. She couldn't help but laugh, which brought strange looks from her friends because she was the only one seeing him.

"What's with you?" asked Damon.

"Nothing."

Unlike the previous day, time passed more slowly as they hurried up and down the hills towards the peaks where the queen was supposed to be.

The pace quickened as night drew near. Remi's legs burned from the constant climbing and descending. Her thighs were tight enough to bounce a quarter off. Lily was similarly spent, with only Damon with his werewolf blood making the travel look easy.

When Remi didn't think she could push herself any more, Lady Aki halted them on a clifftop that had a good view of the mountains. They were stark, blasted sections of rock that rose to jagged peaks. There was something strange about them that Remi couldn't quite figure out. They looked unnatural, but not in an obvious way.

"What is wrong with those mountains?" she asked.

Lady Aki stood with her hands behind her, wrapped up in her crimson cloak, a benign smile resting on her lips.

"We've arrived just in time."

"In time for what?"

"Quiet, child, and watch."

The appearance of the red moon gave Remi a brief thrill in memory of the previous day, but that wasn't the direction that Lady Aki was pointed. She was watching the strange mountains in breathless anticipation.

Remi watched back and forth, first the moon, then the mountains, until she started to see what the Lady of Embers was looking at.

As the bloodred light fell upon the mountains, the rocks sparkled in response. Slowly, and gradually, a pattern formed on the mountainside as if it were a giant movie screen. The image that formed in the sparkling rocks was of a woman, Remi could only guess that it was the queen, slender and fierce, wielding a blade and rushing towards a horde of unspecified creatures. As the moon rose, the pattern shifted, displaying new scenes of the queen, first in triumph, then in sorrow cradling another figure in death, then finally seated on a throne of leaves, heavy with burden.

When the moon started losing its thick, bloodred color, the mountains faded to stone.

Remi spotted Lady Aki thumbing a rolling tear of flame from her cheek.

"What was that?" asked Damon.

"Noyamatu. Mountain art."

"That shouldn't be possible."

"You know nothing of what's possible, child. Come. We'll finish the journey at a less hurried pace."

The previous anticipation in the Lady's stride was no longer present. She seemed burdened by their presence, carping at them when they failed to keep up with her less frenzied pace. Eventually, she grew so frustrated that she spelled them in a way that gave them a burst of energy.

They reached the mountains by morning, sustained by Lady Aki's fire magic. Remi was expecting a building or place of rest nearby, but there was only stark white stone that seemed glossy and odd.

"This is where my obligation to you ends. The queen will return here soon. Be careful. She is a capricious soul. Anger her and you might find yourself a part of one of her projects."

"You're leaving? You said you'd help us with the queen," said Remi.

"And I have. You would have never found her otherwise. She does not tolerate visitors. This is the best I can do."

"You're afraid of her, aren't you?" asked Remi.

The Lady of Embers looked away as she gathered her crimson cloak around her person. She made it a few strides away, before she turned back.

"It is unlikely that she will help you, but on the slim chance that she does, good luck with the Horn. May the flames of fate burn a path to its door."

And then she was gone.

The three of them stood on the plain stone, staring at each other, wondering what was next.

Remi ran a hand through her messy black hair.

"Well, fuck."

TWENTY-SEVEN

A meeting with any Fae was fraught with danger. Long lived, almost immortal, their interests had grown so queer that it was hard to fathom with a mortal mind.

Lily knew this from her interactions with Medb, who was far, far younger and less strange than most Fae she'd had the opportunity to meet. Medb at her core was a simple warrior who had chosen a life outside the Fae to protect the witches that had come to rely on her.

But now, not only were they meeting a long-lived Fae, but a queen, no less, and one who clearly was avoiding the company of others.

"What do you want, Kabo?" asked Remi.

Lily turned to see the leaf-masked trickster approaching in a low crouch as if that would help keep him from being spotted.

"You must flee. The Lady of Embers has led you into a trap. Queen Kiutian barely tolerates other Fae, and despises humans especially. Your quest will end here."

"Why didn't you tell us this before?" asked Lily.

"Nobody asked."

"Bullshit, Kabo," said Remi, crossing her arms.

Kabo tittered with laughter. He looked ready to speak again when he squeaked instead and scurried away like a tumbleweed in a brisk wind.

Lily didn't know what to expect of Queen Kiutian. The leader of the Autumn Court was the least known to her, and for reasons that were more clear upon coming to the realm. Lily worried that she'd be more strange than Kabo, more erratic than the Lady of Embers.

What she saw when the figure appeared from around the ridge was neither.

"Is that her?" asked Damon.

"Your vision is better than mine," said Remi, squinting.

The Fae woman that came down the rocky slope was built like a blacksmith, with broad shoulders, hands covered in chalky white dust, and an auburn braid that hung over her shoulder. She wore what could only be described as strapless overalls the color of cut stone.

She also might have been the most beautiful woman that Lily had ever seen.

Except for the eyes.

As the queen drew closer, Lily couldn't help but recoil from the maelstrom in her immortal gaze. It was like looking into a supernova mid-burst.

"You are trespassing."

The queen's final approach had barely been witnessed. Her aura left Lily swimming in her own thoughts.

"Lady Aki brought us," said Lily with the deepest bow she could muster.

"I thought I smelt the odor of burnt wood. I smell another," said Queen Kiutian, head roving in search of Kabo. "It's unusual for your kind to be traveling with a single Fae, let alone two."

"We apologize for interrupting your work, but circumstances require it. We have a grave and important task."

The queen approached, looking them over individually. She wasn't as tall as Lily had expected upon first seeing her, but she had the weight of the mountains she was working on her shoulders.

"What do others call you? Or are introductions a thing of the past?" asked the queen, nostrils flaring.

"I am Lilith de Meath, formerly of Medb, and current student at Aura Healers of the Hundred Halls. This is—"

"I want to hear it from their lips, witch." The queen stepped close. "Medb is of Oberon, is she not?"

"She is."

"And why have you forsaken her? Is your oath that meaningless?"

"I left her service with her permission to find a cure for the kalkatai in the Halls."

"Ha! The arrogance of you humans. Mere fireflies in the eternal forest, yet you think you can remake it in your own image. If Oberon hadn't lost himself to this corruption, I would recommend he punish you for your insolence."

Queen Kiutian approached Damon, who had his head down.

"I smell an old mutt of Oberon's."

Damon cleared his throat.

"I am Damon Wolfhard, Zev Clan, and descendent of King Nuada."

"His kin has fallen far, begging for scraps in another realm. Why should it be my responsibility to help another who turned his eye when I needed him? This tragedy is of Oberon's making. A just response for his past arrogances."

"There is more at stake than just the Summer Fae. The Horn—"

"Silence. I did not ask for your opinion."

Queen Kiutian stepped to Remi, who hadn't bothered to avert her eyes or incline her head.

"A curious addition. Do you know who your friend is, or has she failed to tell you?"

Remi's forehead furrowed as she met Lily's gaze and shrugged her shoulders.

"I'm not hiding anything."

The queen leaned into Remi's face, studying her like a bug crawling across a dinner plate.

"You stink of the Summer *and* the Veil."

"Of Summer? Not Autumn?"

"Why would a whelp like you smell like *my* realm?"

Remi swallowed.

"I fell in a pond, drank your water, and have since consumed your food and drink. By Fae law, I am bound here."

The queen put a dusty finger under Remi's chin and lifted it up until they were eye to eye.

"You really don't know," smirked the queen. She marched away, laughing quietly to herself. "I'd forgotten how amusing you children were, playing games on a stage that doesn't involve you."

With Remi deep in contemplation about the queen's words, Lily dared a question.

"We're on the trail of the Horn of Galed Bran to keep it from unsavory hands. Our path has led to you with the understanding that you once glamoured its key."

The queen rubbed her palm in an almost human-like gesture. The ache of working with her hands. Or maybe it was the memory of an old wound.

"The Horn. Yes. That would explain much." She glanced to Remi. "Yes, I helped hide the Horn from unworthy hands. But it is no longer my responsibility. I was only doing a favor for one that it was owed."

"If the Horn gets into the wrong hands, it could cause havoc across the realms. With so many portals and other means of transport, it's not like the days of old when others' problems could be ignored. The Horn is powerful enough to affect any realm. Imagine a poison designed perfectly for the Fae of Autumn."

"I might deliver it to the Court myself and put an end to their eternal scheming." She raised an eyebrow. "But that would require stepping foot in the Court of Leaves. I much prefer it here where the stones give honest counsel."

"Please—"

The queen's sharp gaze felt like a thousand swords against her throat.

"Do not dare interrupt my thoughts, child of Medb. You might be a strong witch, one capable of traveling across the Fae, but you are not strong enough to demand my attention when it desires to be elsewhere."

Lily squeezed her lips closed and bowed deeply.

"No. I do not care. Not for your Horn, not for your realm, not even for Oberon's now-twisted home."

"Queen Kiutian," said Remi, stepping forward. "It is but a small boon that we ask. To give us some hint to the Horn's final resting place and then we'll be gone, or at least they will, and you won't have to see us again."

"I am not like Lady Aki, child, that I find amusement in torturing your kind with pointless riddles. Or that annoying Kabo who peddles falsehoods as easily as breathing. No, I am Autumn incarnate! This is my realm to do as I please."

A great, fell power filled the queen and the mountains shook. A few times in Medb's presence, Lily had felt the extent of her strength, and had rightly been cowed by its intensity. This was to that experience like a mountain was to a boulder.

Lily found herself on her knees, clutching the earth as if she were going to be thrown off as small rocks bounced past.

She managed a glance up, regretting it instantly, as she was faced with the queen's true visage, not the humble stoneworker that she'd first presented, or even a powerful Fae Queen. Lily saw Kiutian as she was: the avatar of the harvest and renewal and most importantly, death.

TWENTY-EIGHT

When Remi dared to look up, the queen was gone. Her friends were still prostrate against the ground. Remi wasn't sure it was safe until she heard the tittering of Kabo, who had taken position on a boulder that had rolled near.

"And to think I was bored before you arrived. What a thrill. You should be quite pleased that you witnessed the true queen and came away unscathed."

"But we're no closer to the Horn," said Remi, who had shifted to a cross-legged sitting position.

Damon climbed to his feet unsteadily, checking himself as if he wasn't sure he was alive, or whole.

"I've never been so frightened in my life. I felt like I was trapped in a burning building with no way out."

"She's like that, our queen. Once, long ago, she could be quite fun, but that pyre long ago burnt to ashes," said Kabo.

"What do we do now?" asked Remi. "We've no idea where the Horn is, and I'm stuck in the Fae for all time. This trip has been worse than a disaster."

"I'm sorry, Remi," said Damon. "It was the right thing to do, but we've come to a dead end."

Remi rubbed her palm with a thumb, feeling the ache of past magics. She was in quiet contemplation when she looked up to see Lily staring at her.

"Let me see your palm."

"Why?" asked Remi. "Of course you can."

Lily held her hand and studied her palm.

"This is where Ruby tested you, and Lady Aki scratched away until she could see the glamour. And the queen, well...maybe we can follow the path ourselves."

"I don't know any magics that could do that. Do you?"

"Not to the potency of these Fae royalty, but perhaps they've scratched at this old wound long enough that it might be visible to a less skilled hand."

"I don't know what you're talking about, Lily. You're the most powerful mage I know."

A wistful thought passed across her friend's face.

"I like to think that myself, but I was witness to true power a little while ago. I know how insignificant we are."

Lily fussed with her hand, drawing a rune on the palm using a light blue paint marker from her pack. The tip felt cold against her flesh until the magic was wakened with Lily's arcane touch.

"Ahh—"

"What?" asked Remi, trying to understand what her friend was seeing.

Lily turned her head with her eyes closed as if she were experiencing pain.

"That's enough."

She pulled away, releasing Remi's hand.

"Did you learn anything?"

Lily swallowed and rubbed her temples.

"It was like touching a live wire. I don't know if their prodding caused it, or it was imprinted from when you owned the pendant, but I could see where the path led."

"And?"

Lily grimaced.

"The Veil."

Kabo tittered from his rock, so Remi flipped him off, which only made him laugh harder.

"From bad to worse. We can't go there," said Remi.

"I thought you were learning ways to enter the Veil from Dr. Morsdux?" asked Damon.

"I was, but I'm not very good at it. Nor can I even take you, since I'm stuck here."

Kabo broke into belly laughs, slapping his leg and eventually rolling off the boulder to lie on the ground heaving. The display broke loose anger that was building up. Remi marched over to the trickster, nudging him with her boot.

"Why are you laughing? You're the cause of this. Your stupid trick on the bridge. If it weren't for it, I could at least try to go to the Veil."

This only made his laughter worse until he was rolling around, rubbing under his leafy mask to wipe away tears. Remi reared her boot back to kick him when she had a revelation. His behavior and the constant reminders from others that she had trickster blood put an idea into her head.

"I'm not stuck here, am I?"

The laughter subsided until it was only a shaking of Kabo's belly.

"No."

Remi looked to her friends, who were equally confused.

"Why?"

"I cannot tell you that, even if I knew the truth."

"There's only one reason that could be true," said Lily. "You'd have to have been born in the Fae. Nothing short of that would matter. Not even Damon or I with our familial links qualify."

"Shit," said Remi. "I should have seen it before. They came to the Fae around the time I was born. I could have been conceived or born here, right before they came back. It still doesn't tell me why the Veil is involved too, but at least it makes sense."

"Why wouldn't they tell you that?" asked Damon.

"I wish I knew, but maybe now we can ask them. I assume they've gone to the Veil too."

"Are you sure? The Veil is not a place for living souls. Can you keep us safe?" asked Damon.

"I can try, but we have to find a safe way over."

"I thought that was one of the things you learned in your ward," Damon said.

"I could take myself, but not the two of you. I'm not that good yet. We either need to find a portal, or a place that is thin enough, but I can't imagine there are any nekyia trees in Autumn."

Lily marched over to Kabo, who was sitting cross-legged on the ground, listening to their conversation.

"Where do we need to go?"

"Why would I know that?" asked Kabo, trying to make himself small.

"Because this is Autumn, and death is not far away. I saw it when your queen revealed herself to us. Which means the Veil is probably not far away from this realm. I would guess you even know something about it."

Kabo lowered his head.

"Please, Kabo. We've played your games and entertained you during our visit. Show us where to go. You clearly know something," said Remi.

"You won't like it," he said.

"We're going to the Veil. Nothing about that trip will be enjoyable. Not like this one in its own weird way," said Remi.

"The other option is we can take out our frustrations on you," said Lily with her hands on her hips. "Tricking Remi to fall into the water, stealing Damon's pack, trying to lead us astray on the way to see Lady Aki. You haven't exactly been helpful."

Kabo made a show of standing up and dusting off his dark green pants.

"You see—"

A burst of colorful leaves exploded into existence, forcing Remi to stumble backwards. She looked to the spot he'd been standing, but it was empty.

"That little bastard."

"Remi."

She turned to find Kabo dangling from Damon's grip away from the group. His feet were still moving as if he still hadn't come to terms with the fact that he'd been caught.

"How did you catch me? I tricked your vision."

Damon touched his nose.

"You can't fool this."

Remi got into Kabo's face.

"You can take us to this Veil-thin place, or we can feed you to the werewolf."

"I'm rather hungry since you stole my pack."

"You won't be able to leave then."

"A small price to pay for a just revenge," said Damon, revealing long canines.

"Fine. Let me down and I'll lead you to the place."

"We're not doing that again," said Damon.

Lily unshouldered her pack.

"I have a solution."

The Irish witch pulled out a nylon rope and after a few minutes of quiet spellcasting over it, she handed it to Remi.

"You do the honors. You're the best with ropes and knots."

Kabo flinched when Remi put the rope around his wrists.

"It hurts!"

"Quit being a baby. Besides, this is your own fault. We have no way to trust you otherwise."

Before long, Remi had Kabo tied up in a makeshift harness that went around his neck and hands. Damon held the other end of the nylon rope while Remi and Lily took up the rear.

"Lead on."

"You humans are so mean."

Damon gave Kabo a swift kick in the rear.

"We haven't shown you mean yet."

The leaf-masked trickster capitulated and led them into the valley. He kept his head down and mumbled in a language none of them understood.

"Can we really trust him?" asked Lily, when they hung back to talk quietly.

Remi frowned as she thought about their captured Fae.

"No. I half think he let himself get caught on purpose. He might be leading us into a trap, or he's just having fun. It's hard to tell. His tricks so far have been harmless on the whole, but that might only mean he hasn't had the opportunity to do otherwise."

"I won't let my guard down."

Twice during their descent, the earth shook, but except for the falling of leaves, there was no obvious danger.

They traveled for the entire day, heading away from both the queen's mountain and Lady Aki's pagoda. If Remi hadn't been worried about their destination, she might have enjoyed the journey more. She'd seen pictures of the northeast during fall colors season, and this was so much more, the bright leaves imprinting themselves in her mind. At times she had to shake off the spectacle to remind herself that they had a task to complete. At other moments, she found her thoughts returning to the news that she'd been born in the Summer Fae. The reason she'd been called a trickster or Fae-touched in the past became clear. But the reason that her parents kept that knowledge from her was still a mystery. Maybe they were waiting for the right moment, or feared that knowledge would reveal who they were working for. It was all speculation until she could talk to them again. If she ever got to talk to them again.

"We're getting near," said Kabo when they'd reached the valley floor.

The air was thick with mist and the trees felt less festive and drearier than seeing discarded Halloween decorations in the trash. Remi shivered with cold, even though the air was pleasant.

"Stop."

Damon had Kabo by the back of his neck, like a disobedient pet.

"What's wrong?" asked Remi.

"He seems too happy. Like we're headed somewhere bad. I can smell it on him."

Kabo giggled under his mask.

"I'm happy because I'm soon to be rid of you."

"Maybe we'll take you to the Veil," said Remi.

Kabo's shoulders shrank inward.

"Please, no," he whined.

Remi crossed her arms.

"You protest too much. What's ahead, Kabo? What trap are you leading us into?"

"It's not a trap. But these lands are a thinning. Not quite Autumn, not quite the Veil."

"You've been here before," said Remi.

"A curious Kabo seeks out new experiences. So yes, I've been here. It's dangerous, but only for the unwary. You've survived the Lady of Embers and our frightful queen. What could a few creatures in the mist do to endanger you now?"

"If you lead us into a trap, we'll drag you to the Veil and leave you there without a way back," said Remi.

She wasn't sure how she could do such a thing, but the threat seemed real enough to Kabo. She guessed enough people had mentioned her connection to the Veil, a link she still didn't understand, that the threat held weight.

"Come on. Let's get moving," said Remi. "The sooner we can be rid of him, the better."

She didn't like the smirk she sensed under the mask.

The mist grew thicker as they pressed further into the damp forest. It was unlike the mist they'd encountered a few days prior when she'd supposedly lost her taste for cinnamon. The air seemed to wrap its cold fist around them. They huddled closer for fear of losing each other.

The swamp held fewer colors than the forest, both due to the fog and because the lands seemed to be dying. The only bright spot of color was a crimson bloom they occasionally saw at the base of the trees. Damon took a sample and shoved it in his pocket, calling them floremus or death blooms.

"How much further?" asked Damon, shaking the trickster.

He tittered beneath the mask.

"Not much further."

"Keep your spells at the ready," said Lily.

Remi noted that Damon had extended his claws. She liked when he did that, but vowed not to get distracted by his increased virility.

The crack of a snapping limb had them turning to see Lily staring at the soggy soil.

"Sorry. This bloody ground is hard to see with all this mist."

"Lily..."

"What?"

Remi gestured towards her boot.

"That's not a stick."

The gray bone was broken in half. One end stuck up past her boot while the other was trapped beneath.

"There are bones everywhere," said Damon.

Now that she knew to look beneath the mist, Remi saw them littered across the ground. They looked like fallen sticks after a storm, but that wasn't why they were there.

"We must be bloody close," said Lily.

Remi sniffed the air.

"We are."

A few minutes later, Lily yelled for help. She was sinking into soft mud. Already up to her thighs, Remi tried to grab her friend's outstretched hand but the wet soil tried to drag her in too when she stepped close.

"Let me help," said Damon, but Remi waved him back.

"Keep watch on Kabo."

Remi searched for a limb or something to reach Lily, who was already up to her waist and sinking fast.

"Remi..."

"I know, I'm looking."

"Behind you."

Remi didn't see what Lily had indicated, so her friend cast an elemental spell that blew the mist away in a stiff breeze, revealing an ancient woman that looked like she'd crawled out of a grave recently. Her hair was stringy and falling out. Teeth were yellowed and uneven. And power crackled from her fingertips.

The blast came so quick, Remi barely had time to dive out of the way. Jagged bolts of electricity reached out and slammed into the spot where Remi had just been, leaving a bright image in her vision.

She rolled out of the way of a second blast, aware that Lily was almost to her chest in the mud pit.

A roar was followed by Damon rushing through the trees after the hag. He reached her before she could summon her magic. Damon swiped his claws at her head, but she backhanded him across the swamp to land against a small tree which snapped in half.

Remi was aware that Kabo was no longer visible, but that wasn't their biggest concern. She scrambled after the upper half of the trunk that Damon had broken and swung it around towards Lily.

"Watch out!"

A blast hit the ground right next to Remi, and the impact threw her spinning into the air. She landed, out of breath and dizzy. When she looked back to the pit, she saw the branches leaning over the mud, but no sign of Lily.

With spots in her vision, Remi crawled to the edge, then across the fanned branches until she could reach into the mud where a depression had formed. She grabbed what she first thought was a root, and then realized was one of Neko's tendrils. With Remi's help, the changeling climbed out of the pit with Lily holding onto his back.

Once Lily could take a breath, Remi told Neko to help Damon, who was battling the hag somewhere out of sight in the mist. Then she started pulling Lily further out, which took all her strength because the mud kept trying to pull her back down and her friend was barely conscious.

When half her body was out, Remi turned to take a quick breather when she spotted a figure darting towards her. She brought her foot around, right into Kabo's stomach. He clawed her leg and landed on top of her, hands wrapped around her neck.

"You think you can bind me!"

As the life was choked from her, Remi jammed a hand underneath Kabo's grip and tried to knee him in the groin, but he giggled madly in response. The leafy mask shifted slightly, giving her a view of his face, which looked like it'd been sliced with a thousand knives and left to heal without medication.

She wasn't able to free herself, so she moved her free hand to his crotch, finding neither male nor female genitalia. Then she triggered the deliberator spell, which sent a heart-starting amount of electricity into his groin.

Kabo exploded off her, scrambled to his feet, and went screaming away with smoke trailing behind him.

Remi finished pulling Lily out of the mud pit as Damon and Neko came sprinting back to them.

"We have to go. Now."

"What?"

The horror in Damon's gaze shook Remi into action. They grabbed Lily, who was having trouble standing.

"Which way to the Veil?"

Remi oriented herself to an internal compass.

"This way."

They ran as fast as they could with a semiconscious Lily, dodging around old logs, buried bones, and more boot-sucking mud. Behind them, a terrible screeching arose, sending shivers down Remi's spine. It was more than one voice. At least two, maybe three.

The voices grew louder, and nearer, for a short time, and then they faded quickly as if they were headed a different direction.

They stuttered to a stop the moment the mist swirled away, revealing a bleak, endless landscape covered in greenish clouds. The air was neither warm nor cold, but it made Remi shiver regardless.

"This is the Veil. We're in the Veil."

TWENTY-NINE

The fight with the hag had left Damon drained, but his friends were worse, so he tried to appear unhurt for their sake. After Remi announced they were in the Veil, they attended to Lily, who was having trouble keeping her eyes open.

"What's wrong with her?" asked Remi.

Damon checked her eyes and cast two aura spells.

"I don't know. Maybe she ingested some mud and it's affected her. I hate to say this, but the bigger question is are we safe?"

"No."

The matter-of-fact pronouncement wasn't a surprise, but it confirmed his feeling of doom.

"What do we need to do?"

The mud covering Remi had already started to crack away in the dry Veil air. Damon was thirsty, but they'd lost all their gear in the scramble to escape Autumn.

"I don't know if I can do this, I've only had a few months with Dr. Morsdux," said Remi, kneading her hands. "We should go back. We'll stand a better chance against the hag."

"There's more than one. That's why we had to run."

A fit of coughing alerted them to Lily's condition. She hacked out a bit of dark matter that splattered onto the ground.

"I feel like I drank the arse end of a bachelor party."

"You look like it too," said Remi.

Lily reached into her hair, which was plastered to her head, covered in dried mud.

"Maintenance is going to hate me when I leave this mess in the showers."

"Yeah, maintenance," said Remi quietly.

Damon grabbed her shoulders.

"Remi, I know this is a lot, but neither Lily or I know a damn thing about the Veil. You're going to have to get us through this."

She nodded faintly.

"Not good enough, Remi."

Remi offered a thin smile and nodded harder.

"That's better. Now what do we need to do, or worry about in the Veil?"

"The first thing is that we need to control our emotions. Nothing about the Veil is well understood since people can't come here for long, but the beings that exist are drawn to strong feelings."

"That means no diddling for the two of you," said Lily as she picked mud off her neck.

The quip made Damon smile because it meant she was feeling better.

"But controlling them will only delay the inevitable. After that, I don't know. I only know a few spells for dealing with them and I'm afraid that it won't be enough. Not only that, but we've no food or water, and no way to find the Horn."

"Look at your hand," said Lily.

Remi held up her palm, which was crusted with mud, but faint glowing lines were shining through.

"Maybe we can do this after all."

As soon as the words left her lips, a bone-chilling howl rose in the dreary air.

"Merlin's tits, they've found us already."

"Who?" asked Damon.

"Her hounds. Let me put this spell on you. Hopefully it'll help keep them from finding us right away."

The spell felt like having little needles poked into his forehead. When Remi was finished, she climbed up the short ridge and beckoned them to follow.

"If we encounter anything, even the hounds, don't fight, but run. We can't kill anything here because they can't die."

"What about us?" asked Damon.

"It'll be a short trip if we do."

Remi led them across the blasted plain, using the eldritch runes on her palm to guide them. The landscape reminded him of a wasteland centuries after a nuclear blast, with nothing alive and old bits of stuff buried in the hard soil.

"Don't bother," said Remi when Damon leaned down to pry a rusted machete from the ground. "It doesn't really exist. They're called memontuorums. Memories of the dead. The people, or imprints of those that end up here, cause them to appear for short periods of time."

He grabbed the handle, but it faded to mist in his hand.

As they traveled, they saw things moving in the distance. He saw the shapes of people and other beings that made no visual sense.

"Don't think about them or you'll draw them near," Remi warned him.

"Sorry."

A second howl a short time later had him producing his claws. Remi shook her head.

"Emotions, especially fighting, will only bring them faster."

She extended her arm towards a knot of figures meandering in their direction. Damon cleared his mind of anger and the figures eventually stopped and then dissipated like fog in the wind.

"Maybe this isn't so bad," said Damon.

Remi frowned.

"Something's not right. We should have been attacked by now. I know I have a knack for the Veil and Dr. Morsdux is a good teacher, but I'm not that good."

A short time later, Remi froze, forcing them to stop. Neither he nor Lily understood the reason for her immobility until they saw the figure ahead.

Dark, brooding, and very substantial, unlike the other figures they'd seen.

"I really didn't think he was real," said Remi.

"Him?"

She nodded.

"The Stranger."

He was directly in their path and waited for them to approach. Damon didn't know what to think since the Stranger's face was hidden with shadow, but he sensed a terrible power contained within. To Damon's surprise, Neko merely sat on his haunches and tilted his head at the newcomer.

"Greetings, Remi. It is strange to see living souls in the Veil, let alone two separate groups."

"My parents and the Scythe Sisters."

The Stranger nodded.

"The youngest has the touch."

"Where are they?"

"You know where they are."

"I know what they're after, but not where."

The Stranger gestured towards Remi's hand.

"You'll find it soon enough."

Damon studied the Stranger, but he was hard to fathom. The only thing he could glean was the way Remi was reacting to him. She seemed both pained and relieved by his appearance.

"Why are you here?"

A third howl had the Stranger glancing over his shoulder.

"Don't worry, I'm keeping them away. For now. I wanted to talk to you, to know why you're here."

"To keep them from getting the Horn."

"You're not here to take it for yourselves?" asked the Stranger. "You *were* the keeper of the pendant."

"I'm only here to stop my parents from stealing the Horn for whoever they're working for. And why can't you stop them?"

"I'm forbidden to directly interfere."

"Why?"

He frowned beneath the shadows.

"My Mistress did not clarify the reason before she left."

"She left?" blurted Damon, receiving glares from both Remi and the Stranger.

"Not permanently. She'll be back. Eventually. I'm sorry, if she were here, this wouldn't be an issue, but I can do little to stop them and I've already stretched the rules to keep the hounds from visiting you."

"Thank you," said Remi.

"I need no thanks, I only need you to stop them from taking the Horn. Its history is littered with tragedy. I helped my Mistress hide it away last time. I fear with the interconnected realms, the results this time would be much, much worse if the protections were bypassed and the Horn stolen away."

Damon sensed a personal connection in the way that he talked about the history of the Horn.

"It's what we came here to do."

The Stranger stepped closer. His hand twitched as if he wanted to reach out. Damon prepared to intervene, if things turned deadly, but he didn't think they would. The emotions lurking beneath the surface suggested the Stranger had more to say to Remi than what he had already.

"Then you'll leave the Horn when you're finished."

"I...I can't promise that."

"You understand it's too dangerous to return to the living world?"

"What's to stop the people that want it from sending others? And couldn't the Horn fix Medb? Lily's family is relying on her to find a cure."

"It's not clear if the Horn could do such a thing."

Lily stepped forward.

"But you're not saying that it couldn't. Because you don't know," she said.

The Stranger flinched.

"It's hard to say, but in this case, the risk does not equal the reward. Better your family passes into history than unleash the power of the Horn."

"That's easy for you to say as an immortal being," said Remi angrily.

The backlash seemed to affect the brooding Stranger. He took a half-step backwards and inclined his head for a brief introspection.

"I'm sorry. It was an awful thing to suggest. I spend my time with the lost souls of the dead. I've forgotten what it was like to be human."

This news sent a shock through them. Remi tilted her head.

"You were human once?"

"I'm sorry. I've said too much. I should go. But my warning remains. Do *not* take the Horn. It will not end well. For everyone."

"Wait!" said Remi, surging forward, but the Stranger turned and after two steps, disappeared. "I wasn't done..."

Twin howls, followed by a third coming from a different direction, spurred them into action.

"I think he stopped protecting us," said Lily.

"Yeah, I think you're right."

They picked up the pace, hurrying across the blasted plain, each step sending up little plumes of dust in their wake or occasionally crushing a bone beneath their heels. As they drew closer to their destination, the howls grew nearer. Remi kept grimacing and holding her palm.

"How much further? They sound so near," said Lily.

Damon checked the horizon to see a four-legged shape the size of an elephant only a few hundred meters away. The shadows kept the details from his vision, but he knew when he was outmatched.

"I see it!"

Remi extended her arm to a small hill not far from their location.

"Hurry, run."

They broke into a sprint as the hounds followed, the howls making Damon feel like they were right behind. Damon wasn't sure they were going to make it. The hounds were half the distance closer than they were to their destination.

He turned, intending to fight the hounds and give the other two a chance to make it, when he saw translucent figures rising up from the earth. The beings put themselves in the way of the massive hounds, forcing them to slow down and giving them a chance to reach their destination.

"What are you doing? Hurry!" prodded Remi as she ran.

Damon couldn't help but watch, wondering why the spectral beings were interfering with the hounds. He eventually turned to run, but with uncomfortable thoughts on the meaning.

They reached the small hill, which had a dark passage leading into the depths. He and Lily were both panting from extreme effort, but Remi seemed revitalized by their journey, almost glowing with excitement.

"Quickly, inside," said Remi, ushering them onward.

The hound fell from view as they descended into the darkness, until Lily summoned mage lights to float above their heads. At the end of the short tunnel, a huge round stone covered in runes blocked their passage.

THIRTY

Lily breathed faez onto the round stone, waking the runes to glow with eldritch light. She inhaled sharply.

"They're Celtic runes. I know them like I know my own heart. What in the bloody hell are they doing in the Veil?"

"Maybe that's where our dark friend came from," said Damon.

"It would make sense," said Lily. "These are of an older style I haven't seen in quite some time. At least five hundred years or so. But I know them well. Mother made us learn all the forms."

Remi held her hand towards the stone for a few seconds before turning away.

"I hoped the imprint on my hand would open it."

"It's a good thing it's closed," said Lily. "It means your parents haven't found it."

Damon was down on one knee near the stone.

"They've been here. I think they're already through. I can smell Greta's perfume and I can see sneaker tracks."

"Can you get us through the stone?" asked Remi.

Lily studied the runes for a few seconds before she determined the counter.

"Stand back."

It wasn't so much a spell, but an answer to the question posed by the runes. Lily triggered them in the correct order and stood back.

The ground shook before the stone rolled to the side, revealing a tunnel that led into the darkness. Once they hurried through the gap, the stone returned to its original position.

"Sealed in the tomb," said Remi.

"Be careful," said Damon. "The Stranger mentioned protections. I assume there are traps and guardians."

The comment proved prescient shortly after when they came around the corner into a large chamber containing what first looked like a giant pile of bones, but eventually they realized was the promised guardian already felled by their rivals.

"This looks bigger than one of the hounds," said Damon, running his hand along a smooth white bone.

"If they were able to take this down, I'm worried about our chances," said Remi with a pained expression.

"It's only the Scythe Sisters we have to worry about. It's not like your parents are going to hurt you," said Lily.

Remi nodded, but the inward curl of her shoulders suggested she had doubts. The closer they were getting to confronting Remi's parents, the more her friend looked ready to implode.

"We're going to fix this," said Lily.

Remi squeezed her lips tight.

"We'll get the Horn and save your family too."

"Aye, that's the plan."

Damon was examining the ground after the enormous bone guardian with Neko at his side. Her changeling was sniffing the stone.

"Let's not get ahead of ourselves, ladies. I think Neko found a problem. They might have killed the guardian for us, but they managed to reactivate the traps after they passed."

"That would be my parents," grumbled Remi.

"They couldn't have known you were following them," said Damon.

Lily put a hand to her chin. "They must have known somehow, or why bloody bother to reactivate them?"

No one spoke for a short time as they contemplated the insinuation that someone had notified them that they were on their trail.

Lily approached Neko, whose sensing tendrils undulated in an unseen breeze. He stood at the beginning of a flat section of manufactured stone that led further down the ramp.

"What do you see?"

Neko scraped at the rock as if he were pressing a button, then he nosed forward without putting his snout against the stone.

"Trapped?"

Neko nodded.

"Pressure plates?"

Another nod.

"Can you lead us through?"

Her companion nodded for the third time and took two careful steps to the right.

"Get in a line, not too close in case someone accidentally triggers one, but not so far you can't see the path."

Neko led them down the ramp cautiously, spending long periods sniffing at the various blocks before deciding on a course of action. They were almost near the end when the ground rumbled slightly. Not a lot, but the reverberation through their feet was clear.

"Explosion?"

"Or something falling," said Damon. "They might not be all the way through the traps. We have time to catch them, and if we're lucky, there'll be less of them."

A worrying knit formed on Remi's brow. Those were her parents below. Lily hoped that familial tie wouldn't be a distraction when things came to a head.

They passed two more sections of traps with Neko's help. The changeling was able to follow the path that their rivals had taken, or smell the arcane traps with his nose. But eventually, they came to a section Neko couldn't help them with.

A delicate archway provided the path forward. The only problem was it lay beneath an unstable structure that was covered in overlapping enchantments.

"How did they get through this?" asked Damon, pacing with his hands on his head. "You'd have an easier time trying to slip through a funnel spider's web."

Lily was on a knee, examining the arcane barrier. At intervals, she breathed faez to wake the lines that blocked the path through the archway.

"Most of it's old, but there are a few parts that were added recently. If we needed an indication that they knew we were coming, this is it."

"We can't know that for sure," said Remi, standing behind Lily with her arms crossed.

Lily extended her finger towards a hair-trigger enchantment.

"This one in particular is a problem. They linked it to the others and I ain't never seen something this devious before."

"Can we get past it?" asked Damon.

"I don't know. There's a way to bend these. It's a technique from the Curse Ward—when someone's been hit with overlapping curses, you need to tease them apart to unravel them one at a time."

"No way we're unraveling that," said Damon.

"I didn't say unravel. I said bend."

"Can you?" asked Remi.

"I think so. Give me some time to work through the order, but I bet I could pull them back far enough to create a gap for you to slip through. Then once everyone else has passed, I'll show you how to hold it open for me."

The others stood back while she worked on the order. It would be five times more complex than anything she'd done in Golden Willow, but she was confident that she could pull it off. Except for that one thread. There was something about it that bothered Lily, but she hadn't figured out what it was, or if it was anything at all.

Working through a layered enchantment field was like trying to unravel a knot that would blow up in your face if you got it wrong. But her time in Golden Willow had given her the tools and confidence. Lily tugged them away one at a time, then bound them in place with an enchantment of her own. Not all could be held with anchors, some would have to be bent by hand and held there until the others passed, but that would be the final step. Slowly, the gap started to form, growing from barely being wide enough to put a head through to possibly being able to squeeze by sideways. But she needed it wide enough to fit Damon, who was the largest of the group.

"I'm done," she said, collapsing on the stone with sweat dripping from her forehead.

"We can go through?"

"I'll have to bend the final piece by hand, but yes, once I get a chance to rest, we can go through."

Remi put a hand on her arm.

"You're the best, Lily."

"Tell me that after you get through safely."

The effort had worked up a sweat, which made the thirst worse. She smacked her lips and hoped, one way or another, they'd get through this soon and return to Golden Willow so they could eat and drink again.

"Remi, you go first. You're the smallest, so it should be the easiest and then you can help me hold it open for Damon."

The final golden thread of the enchantment thrummed with energy when she plucked it away from its resting position. It was like pulling a bowstring taut.

"Make yourself as small as a brownie and scoot through."

Remi crouched down and duck-walked forward. As her friend grew near the enchantments, the thread quivered. Lily held it tight.

"I feel a tingle all over like I'm charged up with static electricity," said Remi with her head nearing the gap.

"Aye, keep going."

The further Remi shifted forward, the more the vibration forced Lily to bear down. As the tension grew, she worried she'd missed something. She'd expected pressure, but not this much. As it pulled harder, Lily started to worry that she wouldn't be able to hold the enchantment back.

"Hurry," she said through gritted teeth.

A pinpoint migraine formed at the center of Lily's forehead making her eyes water and her eyes feel like they were being pushed into her skull.

In a fit of desperation, she tried to reach out to Medb, forgetting she was no longer connected to the ancient Fae. A pained groan escaped from her lips, and when she opened her eyes, she saw the problem. The last thread had been tampered with. A section about the length of her finger was glowing crimson like a hot spot on a crucible. Lily could see right away that it was a recent addition, left as a trap for her friend as it'd only woken upon her passage.

"Remi—"

The name barely escaped her lips before the entire interlocking weave of wards exploded.

THIRTY-ONE

Everything hurt.

Teeth, hair, the back of her eyes, even the toenails on Remi's feet, which were strangely in open air rather than her boots.

Remi tried to open her eyes, but a bout of vertigo had her turning her head and vomiting what little she had in her stomach onto the stone.

The last thing she remembered was trying to get through the wards and then nothing. Which meant it'd exploded.

"Is that greasy little bitch awake?"

The sound of Nina's voice had Remi's eyes shooting open despite the nausea it triggered.

Remi tried to sit up but her wrists and ankles were bound by ropes that sizzled with enchantment, so she had to crane her neck in the direction of the voice. Nina was sitting on a rocky ledge peeling an apple with a knife that could have doubled as a machete.

"Hello, Princess."

"You—"

She had to bite back the rest as bile threatened to come up again.

Nina came over with the knife while eating a slice of apple. She crouched by Remi, placing the flat of the blade against her cheek. Remi was painfully aware of how close the tip was to her eye, but she refused to flinch away and give Nina the satisfaction.

"What was that again?"

Remi grimaced.

"It's nice to see you again, Nina. Shame the hounds didn't get you."

"I could say the same for you. I thought Halley was the only one able to get through the Veil, or did you bluff your way like you always do?"

"Nina," said Archer from the opposite side of the cavern. "We agreed that no one would hurt Remi. She's our daughter, remember?"

Nina grumbled under her breath, pressing the blade harder, until she pulled it away and blew a kiss. Her father appeared in her vision a moment later.

"Hey, kiddo."

"Untie me."

He grimaced.

"I'm sorry. We agreed that you're too dangerous to be let loose. I know this seems terrible, but once we've gotten the Horn, we'll take you back home and you can be free. Until then, no one will hurt you."

"What about my friends?"

He sucked air through his teeth.

"I'm afraid they're fair game. That is, if they survived the collapse."

Her heart leapt.

"Collapse?"

"When you triggered the trap that Halley laid, the entire archway fell in. Somehow you got thrown free, though you did sustain some injuries.

We couldn't hear anyone after it fell in. I'm sorry, Remi. It's highly likely that your friends died."

The world narrowed to a focus. Remi felt like she was being squeezed into a small space and she couldn't breathe.

"Cut me out."

"I can't—"

"Cut me out! Now! At least my wrists, please. Now."

Her father pulled a switchblade from a back pocket and popped the ropes around her wrists.

Remi sat up, holding her stomach, then the rest of its contents came flooding out past her feet. When it was over, she felt less pressure, but no relief. She knew she should be crying, but knowing that the Scythe Sisters were watching was holding them back.

"How could you do that? How could you murder my friends?"

Archer took the spot on the ledge where Nina had been sitting when she woke up. His expression was painfully familiar, the one he wore before he told her the hard truths about the world. Ones that she'd believed when she was growing up, but after four years in Golden Willow, she knew what real hardship was.

"Spare me the bullshit parable."

"Kiddo, that's no way to talk to your father."

"You just killed my friends!"

"We don't know for certain. And we didn't kill them. You could have turned around and gone home."

Remi spat on the ground.

"You *tried* to kill them at the very least. And at the worst, you did, or were an accomplice. And I thought when you didn't pick me up from Utica, that was the worst thing you'd ever done to me."

"This isn't easy for us either. If we didn't go after the Horn, some very bad people would have visited you. This was the only way."

"Bullshit."

"Remi, look over there."

She'd barely had time to orient herself due to her anger and sorrow. She looked where he was pointing his chin. The cavern was larger than expected, with a small, clear pond near the wall, a tunnel that went deeper, and a larger flat space where the Scythe Sisters clustered together. Remi thought her father was pointing at a pile of sleeping bags beside them, then saw bandages. It was Greta.

"Your mother is very hurt. She barely survived one of the traps from earlier. She's conscious right now, but she needs attention. Can you do that? As a healer and more importantly, her daughter?"

Inside her head, she screamed, *How can I heal her when my friends might be dead?*

"Untie my feet."

Archer stared at her and then grabbed a new section of rope, which he used to make a pair of loose manacles that would keep her from running—not that she had anywhere to go—and then he sliced through the ropes holding her to the stone.

As Remi hobbled over to her mother, the Scythe Sisters watched like vultures waiting for a sick calf to die. Halley in particular gave Remi the shivers as she stared without a trace of emotion as if she were as dead as the beings inside the Veil.

Greta was lying on her side when she arrived. The smell of rot was unmistakable, almost like gangrene.

"Mom?" asked Remi, her voice cracking.

Greta stiffly rotated with little groans escaping. The movement exposed gaps in the bandages where her entire side had been—seared wasn't the right word—but something like it had melted the skin.

"Hey," said Greta weakly with bloodshot eyes.

"What happened?"

"Thought I'd figured out the pattern, but I was wrong. Some spectral explosion got me. It was like being melted down by a ghost."

Remi knelt on the hard stone, peeking past the bandages.

"Is it bad?" asked her mother.

"The sour smell isn't a good sign, but thankfully I'm here. Let me figure out what's going on. Some of it might tingle, or even hurt, but it's necessary."

After removing the bandages and exposing the melted skin, Remi made arcane gestures over the injured areas. Occasionally, she made eye contact with her mother, which only made the surrealness of the day worse.

"What's the prognosis, Doctor?" asked Greta.

"I'm not a doctor. But I think you'll be fine. Thankfully, this looks worse than it actually is. You've been infected with a semi-benign geist. I can get rid of the invader and then apply some antiseptic spells. You'll still need to visit a hospital and get real treatment, but this should stabilize you until you can return."

For the next twenty minutes, she worked on her mother. When she was finished, Greta was able to sit up.

"Am I always going to look like a melted candle?"

"Most of that isn't real. The geist imprinted the details of its death on you. Probably burned in a fire, or something equally horrible. But had it stayed too long, the flesh would have believed it real and you'd eventually succumb to the same painful death that it had experienced."

Greta hung her head, damp blonde hair falling into her face.

"Thank you, Remi. I know the last few years we haven't been good parents. I feel bad for everything that's happened, but we're just trying to get out of a bad situation. I swear when it's over, everything can go back to normal."

Remi didn't have the heart to tell her mother that there had never been a normal.

"Is this water okay?"

"It is. We tested it. Think it came from a trap in another area that we bypassed."

"You'll want to wash off the dead skin. It'll help you heal faster."

Greta stripped down to her underclothes and slipped into the water to scrub away the dead skin on her side. Remi watched to make sure that there weren't any spots that she'd missed.

"Mom?"

"Yeah, honey," said Greta, looking up from washing her midsection.

"Where's your C-section scar?"

Greta froze mid-clean for a second before a broad smile spread across her lips.

"There are elixirs and spells for that sort of thing. You should know that."

The urge to confront her mother about the C-section lie was strong, but it would only expose that she knew she'd really been born in the Fae. Remi wanted to know why she'd been lied to all these years about it, but decided that she didn't want to air their past in front of the Scythe Sisters. That would come later if they managed to escape the Veil.

"Who are the people you're getting the Horn for?"

Greta climbed out of the water and grabbed an old shirt to dry off, leaning her head over as she scrubbed. As her hair dripped onto the stone, she frowned in Remi's direction.

"You know I can't tell you that. And you don't want to know. It's the only thing keeping you safe."

Remi knew it was bullshit, but she was too tired to call her mother out.

While she was waiting for her mother to get dressed, she stared into the shadows in the back of the cave, only to see a familiar shape. She sat up and leaned closer, but the figure was gone. Remi was sure that she'd seen the Stranger, but he was no longer there. What was he doing?

"What's wrong, Remi?"

"Thought I saw something. The Veil plays tricks on the mind."

Greta nodded.

"I can't wait to be back home. This has been a trying adventure. I'm sure you're ready too."

Remi gritted her teeth because she knew where this line of discussion was headed.

"Yeah..."

"You know, we could use your help getting past the final barrier. Halley is quite powerful. She's been able to brute force us past some terrible things, but this last thing has stymied her. We need your Aura Healers finesse and knowledge."

"What if I don't want to help?"

Greta stilled, which was usually a sign of her internal anger.

"We're doing our best to make sure that the Scythe Sisters don't hurt you. If you don't help, then I'm not sure we can stop them. It's not like we have any real magic."

The lie was skillfully told. But it was also blatantly obvious. It was the kind of lie she'd swallowed dozens of times in her young life, because it was easier and simpler to think of it as dealing with the hard truths of reality, rather than that her parents were manipulating her.

Remi checked back to the Sisters. Nina would fillet her like a fish if given the opportunity, while Big Al was staring with cold calculation, which was worse than the naked threat her sister implied. Finally, Halley was on their right, staring into the distance with the emotional range of plaster, but Remi knew how powerful the youngest Scythe sister was and that if push came to shove, she'd be the biggest threat.

"Yeah. I can help. I'm done with this place. I shouldn't have come in the first place."

"That's great," said Greta.

Remi hobbled after her mother towards a dark passage at the bottom of the cave. The others followed at a distance, but they seemed reticent to interfere while it appeared there would be cooperation.

If Remi was certain her friends had died, she might have pursued a nihilistic end to the Veil visit, but while there was a chance they were alive, she needed to delay in case they could reach her.

The lower chamber was much different than the rough cave they'd been camping in. It looked more like a temple than a tomb. Hewn stone, carefully fit together, formed the floor leading up to a symbol-filled wall. Blocks had been spray-painted with an "X" showing which places weren't safe for stepping, but a path led up to a wall that was illuminated by mini camping lamps.

At the beginning of the path, Remi conjured three mage lights into existence and sent them high into the air so she could examine the barrier.

To the left and right, ancient symbols had been carved into the stone. Remi knew the language from her studies with Dr. Morsdux, though she was hardly an expert. But that wasn't the part that most interested her.

At the center of the wall, right above a section that looked like a door, was an enormous carving of a skeletal dragon. Except that's not what it was. While the shape was of a dragon, it'd been made from the bones of hundreds of smaller creatures, cobbled together to create the larger threat. She'd seen a few sketches in the books that Dr. Morsdux gave her, the ones that had attempted to create a catalog of the Veil's denizens, which her mentor had explained was a fruitless task as it was a realm of constant change.

"What is it?"

"The Dragmha."

"It looks scary."

Remi half-turned towards her mother, who had crept up close. There was real fear in her mother's eyes, which was a rare window into her mood.

"The Dragmha is legend from centuries ago when a mad wizard tried to make his own dragon out of the bones from a charnel house. Unfortunately for him, he was successful and his creation quickly turned on him, but before he died and with the help of his apprentice, they managed to send the Dragmha into the Veil, where it supposedly exists today."

"How could you even know this?"

Remi scratched the back of her head.

"The observers of the Veil have seen it a time or two over the centuries, but not recently."

She approached the wall so she could read the written text. Every fifth word was unfamiliar, but she managed to decipher the general intention which was both warning and riddle.

"You can read that, sweetie?" asked her mother.

"Not all of it."

"That's impressive. You've been learning a lot at Golden Willow, haven't you?"

Remi kept her face neutral despite knowing that her mother was trying to butter her up. When she turned to answer, she saw the Scythe Sisters in the back of the room with her father. The way Big Al was staring at her was warning enough of what would happen if she couldn't get them past the final barrier.

"What does it say?"

"The part on the left talks about the Dragmha and how dangerous and powerful it is. At least that's what I'm getting from the partial text. I don't know this language very well."

"Why would they bother doing that?"

"In case the picture wasn't enough."

"Does that mean the Dragmha is on the other side?"

"Possibly. Though it could be a bluff."

"What about the other text?"

Remi hesitated, which she knew was a terrible giveaway, but she hadn't quite formulated how to finesse this part.

"I'm unsure. There are some words that I don't quite understand from this other part. It's a riddle. Probably the way you have to get past the barrier and into the final chamber where the Horn is kept."

"What's the riddle?"

The scuff of footsteps announced that the others had come up the path to listen to what she had to say.

"Tell us the riddle, Remington," said Big Al with her arms crossed.

"I haven't worked it all out yet, but it's something about the dead and their far vision. I'll need more time. I'm new to the Death Ward. I haven't finished my studies on this dead language."

Big Al leaned forward while Nina picked her fingernails with her blade.

"You'd better hurry. Nina's not a patient woman and neither am I."

"It's got my full attention."

"Good. You keep working. We'll stay back and make sure you don't screw anything up."

Her mother, to her credit, gave a very believable "I'm a fellow hostage" stare, but Remi knew that wasn't how the power dynamic worked. Archer and Greta would never give the Scythe Sisters all the information necessary to complete the Horn transaction, as they wouldn't want to risk making themselves irrelevant.

"If you could, Mom. I need to focus on this."

Greta offered an apologetic smile and moved back with the others.

Remi shifted to one knee as she feigned reading the carved text. The truth was she'd already deciphered the riddle, and while it was familiar, she didn't yet know how to pass it.

Under her breath, she muttered to herself, "The dead see more clearly than the living."

THIRTY-TWO

Damon woke to whining.

White dust covered everything, including a lump with a suspiciously large clump of hair at the top where Neko was crouched. Damon staggered to his knees, crawling to Lily, who was coughing from her back.

"Are you okay?"

Lily struggled to a sitting position and reached out to Neko, who pressed his hairless head into her chest.

"Everything hurts," she said after a round of deep coughs.

The dust in his eyes burned but that wasn't his major concern.

"Where's Remi?"

Lily gave him a flat stare and shook her head.

"The last thing I remember is the explosion and then everything falling. When you yanked me backwards, I didn't see Remi anymore."

"I pulled you out before the archway fell, but I couldn't see her either."

The entire cavern was blocked by fallen stone. The trap that the Sisters had laid had destroyed the path further into the tomb.

"We have to believe she's alive," said Lily.

"I'm not giving up."

Lily wiped the dust from her eyes. The hard stare was answer enough.

"And if she is dead, well, then the Sisters are going to have to pay the price."

Lily nodded.

"It's what she would have wanted."

Damon wasn't entirely sure that was true, but he was angry enough not to care. They would have time for soul searching later.

The next few minutes they took stock of the situation. Neither was hurt other than minor cuts and bruises, but the passage was blocked.

"Wish I was a Stone Singer," said Lily with her arms crossed.

A short bark had them crossing the cavern to where Neko was crouched, nose pointed into a small hole at the base of a crack in the wall. It appeared freshly opened.

"Looks like a potential path opened up."

Damon crouched and put his hands into the hole.

"My shoulders are too wide to fit. You can make it, but I can't follow and this stone is too thick to move."

"Aye, that's true, but I have an idea. It'll bloody hurt, but it'll get you past the hole."

"Do you know how to do it?"

Lily's lips were squeezed white as she nodded.

"Do it."

He sat cross-legged with his hands resting on his knees. Lily applied pain blockers that would dull the impact, but without elixirs wouldn't keep the worst of the pain away.

She knelt behind him with her hands right behind his shoulder.

"You might want to look away. And breathe deep."

Damon slowed his breath, inhaling at an eight count through his nose. At the moment he was about to transition to exhaling, he sensed the sharp tint of faez right as she blasted his shoulder with a force bolt. The pain was immediate as his arm dropped against his side.

"Keep your breathing, you gobshite, I've got one more shoulder to dislocate."

Damon grimaced and tried to focus on his breathing, but everything hurt.

The second blast hurt even worse than the first because it jarred his already injured shoulder.

Lily leaned into his vision.

"You look like someone broke their doll before putting it away."

"Blood and bone, how am I going to pull myself through that?"

"You're not going to like the answer."

Lily shimmed through and then motioned for him to follow. He placed his head into the gap and she grabbed his shirt and yanked him through while Neko pushed on his rear.

There was a point that he almost blacked out, but then he found himself on the other side, lying on the rough stone, covered in sweat and looking up at Lily.

Putting his shoulders back into place hurt just as much, but at least there was relief on the other side.

"This better go somewhere. I don't think I could do that again."

The collapse of the archway had cracked stone, forming deep fissures that they were able to slide down. They came to a stone wall with an old door covered in an ancient language.

"Any ideas?"

Lily grimaced as she pointed to a section above the door.

"Only that, because I've seen it before. It says: the Halls of the Dead."

"I'm getting the feeling that this tomb had a different purpose before they hid the Horn."

"Aye. You're not wrong."

He tapped on the door.

"I kinda wish I was."

The door opened easily, which was a warning in itself. The space beyond was larger than he expected, with stone pillars heading into the darkness.

They each summoned mage lights which floated near their heads. Neko took point, sniffing the dusty stone while his tendrils undulated behind him.

The emptiness was paradoxically claustrophobic, because it felt like something was lurking just beyond his vision. His nose detected only the dust and ancient bones, though he saw none.

"Did you see that?" asked Lily suddenly, peering ahead.

"No."

She furrowed her brow and gestured toward.

"How could you not? It was on the other side of that second pillar."

"What was it?"

"I...I'd rather not say..."

The shifting of her gaze worried him, but then again, this was the Veil, the land between the living and the dead. Seeing things should be expected.

"I have a feeling things might get a little weird. Hopefully it's not dangerous."

"How can we tell?"

His gut tightened.

"Good point."

Damon wasn't sure when or how they got separated, but one moment he was walking beside Lily with Neko ahead, and the next, he found himself alone staring into the darkness.

"Hello? Lily?"

He repeated the words three times, getting louder each one, until he heard a faint reply. She was far, far away. He moved towards her, yelling, but her answers came from different directions each time.

When he saw a shape ahead, he ran forward, only to skid to a stop when he realized they were much larger than Lily. The figure was taller and had broad shoulders. The musk of a werewolf was present beneath the dust.

"You shouldn't be here."

The voice was familiar.

"Connor?"

He stepped into the light. His uncle, Connor Black, looked no worse than when he'd seen him last.

"This isn't a place for you."

"I know, but I have to find my friends."

"Turn back. Leave the tomb and the Veil. There's nothing but heartbreak."

"Is that why you're here?"

Connor loomed forward.

"You should have at least brought the sword."

"I don't know what to do with it. I'm a healer, not a warrior."

"Then find a teacher."

"You would have been a good one."

"The sword is the key to your problems, if you just learn how to use it."

"I'm not a warrior."

"Hear my words, the sword is the key."

Damon tried to step around him but Connor held a fist before him.

"This path. The Horn. Everything. It's a trap. You're going to bring chaos and destruction to the world. Turn back before it's too late."

Damon marched past his uncle. The apparition swiped through his arm, revealing the illusion.

"I have to find my friends."

A few pillars down, he checked back to see Connor Black gone.

"Blood and bone, how do I get out of here?"

He continued in the direction he suspected was the exit for no reason other than it smelled the cleanest.

A group of figures blocked his way after a few minutes. When he grew near, he realized it was his clan, the ones slaughtered by the deathless assassin.

"Don't go! Turn back!"

They were covered in blood as they reached out to him, pleading with their hands and voices. It took all his self-control not to break into a run as he avoided their touches and continued further into the Hall of the Dead.

Then the pillars faded away, and he found himself on the streets of the City of Sorcery. He didn't quite know what was wrong until he saw the bodies on the sidewalk.

Tourists in Hundred Halls hoodies were spread out, arms and legs akimbo, their eyes sunken beneath gray skin. He knew immediately that they'd died from disease. The further he walked, the more bodies he saw.

"There's no such thing as prophecy," he told himself over and over, but it was hard not to feel the impact of his visions.

He blinked and the vision faded, revealing the outline of a doorway in the distance. Damon hurried forward until he realized there were two figures standing to either side of the exit.

There was no mistaking their forms.

Lily stood to the left while Remi was on the right. She held the Horn in her hands.

As he approached, he smelled rot.

They looked like they were either a few days after death, or so sick with disease that it had sucked the vibrancy from their skin. Bruises and crimson blooms covered their flesh.

"It was a mistake, Damon. We never should have come here. The Horn isn't safe. It will always be used for awful things."

Lily reached up to her bountiful red hair and when her hand came down, clumps of hair came away. The skeleton of a four-legged creature lay at her feet.

"I killed them all. The cure was worse than the disease. We shouldn't have come here. Go back, Damon, before it's too late!"

"Damon—"

When he looked at Remi, her eyes fell upon themselves, and grubs spilled out as her flesh turned gray and then black and started falling away.

He ran from the horror, right through the exit, immediately stumbling to his knees. It took him a few moments to realize someone was sitting nearby.

"Lily?"

She nodded grimly.

"Are you well?"

"I'm not hurt. Not in that way."

"Did you…?"

"Aye, the visions. They were not kind. Not at all."

"Are we through the Hall?"

"Aye."

He exhaled.

"That's good."

"Not really. I've been here for a while waiting for you. I sent Neko searching for an exit, but the only thing he found was a passage that leads back to the entrance."

Damon leaned his head back with his eyes closed.

"So we went through that for nothing. The shoulders, the visions, everything?"

"If it weren't for bad luck..."

Damon snorted softly.

"Then we wouldn't have any at all."

THIRTY-THREE

The stone was hard on her rear as she sat before the runed barrier with her hands resting on her knees. Remi knew she couldn't delay much longer as the Scythe Sisters were getting restless in the back of the cavern.

The heavy steps of Big Al brought tension. She leaned into Remi's ear and spoke in a rough whisper.

"If you don't get us past the barrier soon, I'm going to let Nina start cutting bits from you, or maybe your parents. We don't need both of them and we don't need them in one piece. I know you figured something out a long time ago and you're trying to figure out a way to turn this back on us, but it's not going to work."

Remi climbed to her feet. Her parents were on the other side of the cavern, talking quietly.

"Which one will it be? Your mother or your father? My guess is you'd rather see us cut on her. Something about Greta screams manipulating bitch," whispered Big Al.

Remi glared at her captor, but it only made the big woman grin.

"That's what I thought." She turned away. "Nina—"

"Stop," said Remi, putting a hand on Big Al's arm.

She might have her differences, but they were her parents. That meant something in this screwed-up world.

"I think I know how to find the way through, but I don't like the solution."

Big Al furrowed her forehead.

"I have to die."

"That makes no sense."

"It makes every bit of sense, given where we're at. But I don't want to make it permanent. Can Halley bring me back when I do it?"

"I don't know if she has that kind of power."

"She does, even if she might not know it. I'm not dying all the way, just right to the edge and then I need to be brought back."

"I'll talk to her."

Remi grabbed her arm before she could head back.

"Don't tell them," she said, nodding towards her parents.

After a brief huddle of the Sisters, Halley came over with that same dead look in her eyes.

"I can do it if you want."

Remi knew the youngest Scythe was not offering to die, but to kill her.

"I can do it. It's something I read about in my studies, but I need someone to bring me back."

After a moment of quiet staring, Remi gave an explanation, but it was hard to tell if Halley was understanding since she made no motion to acknowledge.

"Can you do it?"

Halley offered an odd grin.

"Remember what I said, don't pull me out too quickly. I don't want to have to do it again. But not too late either."

Halley didn't respond, so Remi returned to her cross-legged position before the wall. She hoped that when she fell, she could position herself correctly. It would be a shame to successfully pull off her near-death experience, but not be facing the right way and miss the solution on how to get past the wall.

"I need a knife. Don't worry, I'll give it back."

Nina brought over a blade.

The tip dug into Remi's palm, bringing a gasp. Once the blood was trickling from the wound, she handed it back.

She wasn't going to bleed to death, but the cut would make it easier to hear her heartbeat before death.

At first, she closed her eyes, but she didn't want to miss out on anything, so she opened them back up. The words of the ritual came easy to her lips as they were a variation on another one she'd learned.

The droning chant kept time with the beating of her heart which slowed as she calmed.

Drumbeats in the dark. That's how she imagined her heart. It would guide her to the edge of life.

As her consciousness dimmed, she slurred the words of the ritual, but it didn't matter anymore. The magic had taken hold deep inside her. She could feel her heart continuing to slow. The beat was already once every five seconds and getting slower.

The world had a strange, distant quality as if she were watching through a pinhole.

This is it. This is where I die.

As she descended into the tomb of her own making, she saw faint shapes moving at the edge of her vision. Souls too far gone to be visible to the naked eye, but now she could see them. A one-armed woman leaned over to inspect.

Remi wasn't sure when her vision had shifted, but she could see the entire cavern, including herself. The body—her body, she reminded herself—was lying on its side, eyes focused on the wall and a small puddle of blood around her knees.

Halley stood over the body like a deathless sentinel while the two other Scythe Sisters stood back a dozen feet, quietly chatting.

Her parents had stopped their discussion and were staring intently.

It was like Remi was seeing them for the first time.

Greta, the tall pale blonde Norwegian with ice-blue eyes, arms crossed and an almost regal curl to her judging lips. She was everything Remi wasn't.

Then her father.

Handsome like an old '60s movie star, Archer always looked like he should be holding a cigarette with smoke curling up from the tip.

How she'd come from them was a mystery to her.

Boom.

Remi thought there'd been an explosion, but realized it was a single beat of her heart. She couldn't recall the last time she'd heard one.

Time was down to the quick.

The vision rushed to the wall, which was hazy and shimmering, like an illusion before the reveal.

Boom.

Would Halley be able to pull her out? Remi wanted to shake the motionless Scythe Sister, but she had to focus on the wall.

As the runes shook and shifted, other lines revealed themselves. At first, the words were incomprehensible and she feared they were in a language she'd never learned and her sacrifice would be for nothing, but then the lines merged and she could understand completely.

I know the way through. I even know what waits for us on the other side.

Her excitement was quenched with the realization that Halley wasn't moving. She was waiting too long. Remi screamed at her to begin the return, but no voice uttered from her lips. She was a ghost trapped inside her own head.

Boom.

The beat was faint. As if the drums had moved into the distance.

Boom...

Remi didn't remember waking up.

She lay on her side, hand throbbing. She raised it into her sight to see it was wrapped with bandages.

In a panic, she tried to remember what she'd seen in the vision, but she couldn't reach it. Like trying to remember the details of a dream after waking up.

"Do you have the answer?"

Remi climbed to her knees, feeling groggy and a little sick. Big Al was leaning into her vision.

"Thank you, Halley."

The youngest Scythe made no indication she'd heard.

"What were you doing?" asked her mother, who had approached while she was unconscious.

"Finding the answer."

"So you have it?"

Remi closed her eyes and willed the memories to return. When she opened them, she could see the places she needed to touch.

"Move away, I don't know what this is going to do."

Remi touched five separate runes, each one representing an individual element.

As soon as her fingertips came away from the stone, a rumbling started deep within the ground. She worried that she'd set off a trap until a spot right ahead shifted into the stone, creating an opening to the other side.

When Nina surged forward, Remi thought the blade was going into her heart, but she helped her to her feet.

"You look like shit."

Remi swallowed her response, thankful for the unexpected kindness, especially because she knew their trials weren't over.

The next room was a cathedral to the dead.

The high ceiling arched into the shadows, past the flickering ghost lights along the walls. Four massive chains descended until they reached the massive stone disc that took up the center of the room. It was at least a hundred feet across, with a pile of bones in the center. Around the outside of the disc was a Stygian darkness that seemed to go on forever.

On the opposite side of the room was a wide alcove. Sitting on an altar was a black drinking horn that looked big enough for a giant. The tooth-shaped artifact had streaks of white and gold inlays too fine to see in detail at a distance.

"It doesn't look like much," said Nina, grinning.

"That's the Horn of Bran Galed. What we came to find," said Greta, breathlessly.

Big Al was about to leap from the ledge onto the stone disc when Archer held her back.

"What are those?" he asked, gesturing towards the tunnels along the walls, leading into the darkness. There were at least a dozen on either side.

"The writings didn't mention them."

"What did it mention?" asked Big Al.

"The Dragmha, but you already knew that."

"Is that what those bones are?" cackled Nina. "Someone already killed it."

Before anyone could stop her, she leapt upon the disc and scurried over to the bones. She held one up like a sword.

"See. The boney bastard had the good sense to die before we got here."

Big Al looked to her youngest sister.

"Halley?"

"The dead are all around us."

Big Al sighed and followed her sister onto the disc.

"Come on, Greta, let's get this stupid thing and get out of here," said Archer, following.

Remi was planning on staying on the ledge, but Halley didn't move either. She didn't like being near the Veil-touched Scythe. There was something brutally supernatural about her that transcended the normal oddness she was used to in the hospital.

The gap between the ledge and the disc was only five feet. Not too far for an easy jump, but wide enough to make her nervous. The stone shifted slightly upon impact. She looked into the darkness to see the chains swaying and moved away from the edge.

Remi approached the fallen Dragmha. She had a feeling that if she'd touched the wrong runes, or they'd forced their way into the chamber, it would have been waiting for them fully formed. Or perhaps it'd fallen into disrepair during the long centuries.

"I've got it!"

Nina was standing in the alcove with the Horn hoisted above her head. She looked small compared to the artifact, but she was having no problem lifting it.

The relief that the bones didn't form into an ancient dragon upon the taking of the Horn lasted until Big Al turned around and looked directly at Remi.

"It's time, Halley."

Everyone in the chamber knew what it meant. Her parents spun on their heels.

"We made a deal," said her father.

"Now that we have the Horn, it wouldn't be prudent to let her live."

Remi spun when she heard Halley land on the stone. She glowed with eldritch lights as she gathered power around her body. The disc left little room to escape, so Remi moved to the opposite side of the bones.

"We agreed to help because you said you wouldn't hurt her," said Greta.

"And now that deal has changed," said Big Al, cracking her knuckles as she approached them. "We still want to meet your friends. The ones who sent you after the Horn. We think we could be of great value to them. But Remi, she can't leave the Veil alive."

Her parents glanced between themselves. Neither of them made a motion towards her.

"You're just going to let them kill me?"

Greta spread her arms.

"What can we do? We're thieves, not mages."

A bottomless pit formed in Remi's stomach. How could she have not seen how little they truly cared for her? She'd only been a tool. Not a daughter. Not a child. Just another member of their team and completely expendable.

Remi gathered elemental energies around her fists as she backed away from Halley, but the disc provided nowhere to escape.

"Ho!"

The new voice startled all of them.

In the mouth of one of the tunnels stood her friends. Damon looked halfway transformed.

"You're not touching Remi."

Big Al growled, pulled an elixir out of a hidden pocket, and downed it in one go. Then she smashed a fist into her open hand as her eyes glowed with menace.

"Kill them. Kill them all!"

THIRTY-FOUR

Lily twisted her ankle when she landed on the stone disc, but the adrenaline from the battle and the enchantments she'd placed on herself before they entered the final tunnel quickly erased the pain.

Damon had hit beside her, fully in werewolf form, a raging furry missile launched at Big Al, but the eldest Scythe threw him over her head in a judo-like throw.

"Protect her parents," she shouted to Neko.

A whirl of movement had Lily flinching away only to find a short blade in her shoulder, a few inches from her heart where it would have hit had she not moved. She yanked it out and tossed it over the side as Nina came sprinting towards her with more blades flying.

A force shield deflected most of the assault, but one slipped through, slicing her across the thigh. It shouldn't have been possible, but then she saw liquid dribbling out of the end of the Horn in the alcove and realized that she'd conjured a liquid that had made her more formidable.

On the far side of the disc, Remi was matched in a battle of Veil-powers with Halley, which wasn't going well for her friend. It looked like the northern lights had descended onto the battlefield, whipping between the two mages like unruly waves in a storm.

Lily almost tried to pull from Medb and the delay nearly cost her. She switched to a limb-lock curse that sent Nina into convulsions and ran over to Remi's side.

An elemental force blast should have knocked Halley over the side, but she shrugged off the impact and continued her assault on Remi.

"Watch out!"

The warning from Archer saved Lily. She threw herself to the ground as three more blades went sailing past her head.

"How many blades does she have?"

Nina stalked forward with two more in her fists.

The entire disc shook as Big Al drove Damon into one of the massive iron chains, tipping it slightly, which made a few large bones at the center slide towards Nina, but the nimble woman leapt over them and kept running.

Lily kept up her shield until the last moment and then she ducked under the blades and tackled Nina around the midsection. Landing heavily on Nina should have knocked the wind from her lungs, but she was still fighting. Lily tried to defibrillate her, but she kept blocking her hands.

A knee to the stomach and Lily found herself flung onto her back, landing hard enough to bring spots to her vision. Nina was on her in a flash, one blade dangerously close to her throat and the other already in her shoulder. Lily was holding them back but the other woman had leverage.

"Augh!"

The tip of the blade piercing her shoulder, already wounded from before, was making it harder to hold on.

She tried to knee her, but Nina blocked it with her own, leaving Lily with the impression that the end of the battle was near. With her hands tied up keeping Nina from stabbing her, there was no way to use her magic, and the enchantments she'd applied earlier weren't enough against her supernatural strength.

"I can't wait to drink from the Horn again," said Nina, her eyes lit with inner fire. "You can't imagine how good I feel right now. It's like I was gifted the powers of the gods."

One blade was a quarter inch into her shoulder while the other had nicked the catch in her throat.

A great ripping filled the air, shaking the disc hard enough that their struggle was paused. Lily spared a glance to see that Halley's magics had ripped one of the chains from its anchor. As the iron flew into the air, the disc shifted precipitously.

"Don't worry, witch. You won't be alive much longer to worry."

Out of the corner of her eye, Lily saw a section of bones sliding towards them. She braced herself at the impact, which sent them both flying towards the edge, but Nina never stopped trying to stab her, which meant Lily couldn't try to stop their movement. The edge approached quickly and only at the last moment did Nina relent.

As Nina released her grip and prepared to stab the stone with a blade to stop her slide, Lily pressed her hands against Nina's chest and blasted her with a force bolt, sending her flinging into the air.

One of the blades slipped out and Lily quickly grabbed it, slamming it into the stone. The anchor stopped her momentum, but not before the lower half of her body slipped over the edge. A hand grasped at her leg, but Lily kicked her off and Nina's cry was quickly swallowed by the darkness.

Holding on by the tip of the blade in the stone left Lily feeling like she was destined to follow Nina shortly. She tried to struggle back onto the disc, but it was tilted at an angle and there was nothing to grab for purchase.

A second shaking impact broke loose more bones from the center, and they headed directly towards her. She thought there was nothing to do until Neko came bounding over the bones and grabbed her arm with his mouth, yanking her upward. She scrambled forward and then at the last moment, rolled out of the way and grabbed onto Neko's leg to keep from sliding off.

The disc was shaking more wildly as the battle between Halley and Remi was in full force. Between them, eldritch energies and incorporeal beings were flung in both directions. Dark green flashes of light like the sparks of a thunderstorm imprinted on her gaze.

Earlier in the fight, it'd appeared that Remi was outmatched, but it appeared her friend had found a reserve and was holding her own. Remi sent a whirlwind of ghostly energies at Halley, then leapt over the gap to reach the alcove with the Horn, giving her the advantage of stability.

To her right, Damon and Big Al were brawling. It looked like a heavyweight fight with both of them covered in blood and sweat. Lily headed in that direction, determined to eliminate another Scythe Sister to swing the odds in their favor.

Halfway across, another ear-rending snap startled Lily. The chain on the opposite side as the one that had already broken flung into the air, leaving the disc tethered on two points. The structure wobbled, sending the enormous Dragmha bones spinning either way.

The next few seconds were pure chaos. Damon used his claws to hold onto the stone, and managed to knock Big Al away, but she somehow latched onto the edge, which swung the momentum. Like a giant seesaw, the disc tipped, and the remaining bones came flying at the three of them.

Lily leapt over one huge thigh bone, rolled out of the way of a section of interlocking wing bones, and jabbed the tip of the blade into the stone, halting her slide as the rest of the Dragmha went toward the edge.

Big Al, for all her strength, could do nothing as the wave of bones hit her, and they descended into the darkness.

Lily worried that she might slip, but Damon bounded across the stone and grabbed her, using his claws to hold them fast.

But now that the bones and Big Al were no longer weighing their side, the disc shifted back the opposite way, where the trio of Halley, Greta, and Archer were fighting not to fall off.

The youngest Scythe was holding herself in place using swirling ghost energies. It looked like a pair of apparitions had a hold of her arms. Remi's parents, on the other hand, had suction devices keeping them in place.

The two sides rocked back and forth until finding an uneasy equilibrium with Neko at the fulcrum and Remi safely in the alcove with the Horn. The precarious position was further compromised when the groan of the chains holding more weight than they were designed for announced that they had to get off the disc or follow the others into the abyss.

THIRTY-FIVE

The second chain snap was like a cannon blast. Remi put a hand to her chest thinking she'd been hit when she realized it had just been the sound. She watched in horror as the disc shook, nearly sending her friends and parents over the edge, but miraculously they managed to hold on.

The last two chains creaked and groaned, announcing they had little time left before the entire structure collapsed. Remi was looking around for something to throw across the gap when she heard a warning.

Halley levitated across the disc, held in the air by ghostly hands. The scene transfixed Remi until a blast of incorporeal energy came whipping forward like a solar flare. Remi barely deflected it with a water shield.

The youngest Scythe rose high with her arms raised, preparing to bring down powerful energies.

Hungry, injured, and exhausted, Remi wasn't sure she could withstand the attack. The battle had taken all her reserves and her opponent had a better grasp on accessing the Veil energies.

Remi...

The voice startled her. She knew it was the Stranger, but what did he want?

Was it the Horn? Was it the tomb?

Then she realized what was different about this place. It wasn't quite the Veil. Not entirely. If it had been, their magics would have drawn the hounds and other beings, but once they'd passed the outer barrier, those dangers had fallen away.

But what if…?

Remi drew on her remaining reserves and before Halley could blast her into oblivion conjured a barrier at the entrance of the alcove. The translucent wall barely was in existence before pale tendrils slammed against it.

"Just hold for a little bit."

The ritual words came easily to her lips. She'd practiced them with Dr. Morsdux in the Hospice Ward. But this time, she was performing the ritual without the protective wards. She hoped her assumptions about this between-realm would work.

Halley pounded the barrier with incorporeal magics. The wards would fail soon. Remi had to hurry.

She opened a portal to the Veil and as soon as she could see the featureless gray landscape, she sent the last of her faez into the realm. It was more than chum. It was a full-fledged banquet. She just hoped something was near enough to take the bait.

A wave of eldritch energies disintegrated the barrier, leaving Remi exposed, but she kept up the chanting.

The howl nearly stopped her heart.

It was like hearing metal imploding in the depths of the ocean. Groaning, rending sounds that made her bones shake.

Not only was something near, but it was one of the hounds. It'd probably stayed near the tomb, hoping to catch them on the way out.

An enormous shadow forced its way through the portal. It was like a black hole being given birth.

The nature of the hound made it impossible to see the details. It wasn't a hound by the standards of her world, but a force of hunger—and it wanted the living.

For a split second, Remi thought the hound was going to turn on her, but then Halley made herself a brighter candle. She sent a blast of energy at the hound, but since it was a creature of the Veil, it swallowed the attack as if it were drinking from a hose.

The hound surged forward, a blob of impenetrable darkness overtaking Halley. She was there one moment and gone the next. Not even a scream, or cry.

Then the hound began to turn.

Remi backed against the Horn. She felt like she was staring into the void.

Then the hound rotated its head.

Remi thought she heard a voice in the distance. The hound bounded away towards the tunnels, disappearing in a blink.

Relief started to set in, but she wasn't done yet.

The chains were swaying and groaning. Dust fell from the ceiling that was too high to see.

Her friends were on one side and her parents on the other. They were balancing the disc with their weight, but neither could move, or it would tip and everyone would die.

"Nobody move! I'll figure out how to get you off."

"There's rope behind you in Nina's pack," yelled her father.

It was at least a hundred-foot rope. Enough to reach one side or another. She tied a knot at the end for catching and the other half around the stone altar.

"Throw us the rope, kiddo," said her father. "We're your parents."

Throwing the rope to one side would doom the other. Her friends stared back as they balanced with their arms out.

"What about your suction cups?"

"They won't hold if the whole thing tips over. The stone isn't smooth enough," said Greta.

A rumble, followed by more dust streaming from above, made the disc wobble.

"Hurry, it's going to fall soon," said Greta, staring into the shadows of the ceiling.

Remi looked from her friends and back to her parents.

"How can I choose?" she whispered to herself.

"Honey, please, throw us the rope. I know this is hard, but the answer is clear. We're your parents. The ones who brought you into existence. You have to choose us," said Greta.

"Whatever you decide," said Lily with her hand on Neko's back. "We understand."

Remi started swinging the rope around, preparing to throw the end towards her mother, but she let the tip fall instead.

"Why did you lie to me?"

"We'd never lie to you, sweetie," said Greta.

"You lied about the C-section. You never had one, because I was born in the Fae."

They stiffened at her words and glanced at each other. She saw the worry in their eyes and it made her realize she'd been wrong about her assumptions. She wasn't their child at all. It explained why she looked nothing like them. They'd always said they'd gone into the Fae in search of treasure, a powerful magic that would help them reach the Horn.

"It was me. You stole me from the Fae. I was the powerful magic.

You stole me because I could lead you to the Horn."

"We've always done right by you, kiddo," said Archer. "We treated you as if you were our real child. Which makes you our child. Right?"

"My very existence was built on lies. No wonder you were okay with me spending a year in jail and then you didn't pick me up. No real parent would ever do that. If I were one, I wouldn't. I wouldn't forget them. Or let anyone get in my way of returning."

"That's not true. We wanted to pick you up," said Greta, clasping her hands together in prayer. "We're your parents, even if we're not the ones who birthed you."

The disc rumbled again, followed by deep groans in the iron chains.

"Then tell me who they are."

"I...we..."

Disgusted by their bevy of lies, Remi threw the rope to Damon and Lily. It fell short, but Neko lunged forward and grabbed it. Lily climbed on Damon's hairy back.

"As soon as you start moving, the entire thing is going to tip, so be fast."

"I was planning on it."

"Remi, no! Please! We love you! We cared for you all your life!" yelled Greta as she dropped to her knees.

Remi wrapped the rope around her arms and prepared to haul her friends to safety.

"You never loved me. I was just a tool for you, one that you were ready to discard once you had the Horn. Merely a bauble. The same way I saw the pendant. A means to an end. I should have seen it years ago, but now my eyes are open. Goodbye, Greta and Archer. I'm sorry. I'm sorry I couldn't save you too."

Their pleading words morphed into screams as the disc shifted when Damon and Neko ran forward.

For a moment, Remi worried they weren't going to make it as the disc shifted wildly. Then they both leaped, clearing the gap, and the entire structure slammed to one side and the chains snapped at the base. The disc plummeted into the darkness without a single scream.

THIRTY-SIX

He caught Remi before she fell. As soon as the disc had disappeared into the abyss, her knees had lost their rigidity. Damon cradled her in his arms as she stared at the ceiling, her face wracked with pain.

"It was an impossible choice. No one should ever have to do that."

But deep within he was relieved. Damon had been sure that she would pick her parents—until they weren't her parents.

The truth was hard to fathom.

They'd already known she'd been born in the Fae, but now she didn't know who her parents were. They could be anyone.

And none of that explained why she had the powers of the Veil. Fae and Veil. A strange combination.

"Remi..."

He caressed a strand of hair away from her face. Brown eyes shifted until they locked gazes.

"Is that even my name?"

"It can be if you want, or you can change it. It's up to you."

Her expression broke, squeezing back tears until a sob slipped out, followed by shaking. Damon held her to his chest as his body shifted back into his human form. He held her until she'd finished crying.

"There were good times," she said, wiping away tears with the meat of her palm. "They weren't all bad."

Lily spat on the stone.

"Hate me if you want for saying this, but they were shite parents. They used you and then planned on discarding you when they didn't need you anymore. That's not what family is. They don't abandon you when things get rough."

Damon shook his head. "Lily..."

"No, she's right," said Remi, crouching on her heels. "I was a prisoner and didn't even know it. They gaslighted me into believing their bullshit behavior was love. *We're just showing you how the real world works.* Isn't that a bunch of crap. I was barely above a set of lock picks. A tool that had a singular purpose. You're right, Lily. They were willing to discard me as soon as I was no longer useful. Trade my life for their own safety, but dammit, why do I hate myself so much right now?"

"If you didn't, I'd be worried about you. Even if they're not your parents, it was a hard choice. They were still people—stupid, greedy, feckin' eejits, but people nonetheless. And they paid the price for their choices. That's not on you."

Remi paced away with her hands on the back of her head. Then she spun on her heel.

"I don't regret it. Not one bit. I know it was the right choice, but blood and bone, it hurts. It hurts more than anything that's ever happened to me. It's like my soul has been scooped out and dumped into a pile of hot ashes."

"Time will heal it, even if it doesn't seem like it now," said Damon. "I thought our world had ended when the clan died. But we move on."

Remi speared him in her gaze.

"What if I can't?"

"You're too strong not to."

Lily rapped her knuckles on the Horn.

"Not to diminish the gravity of your decision, but we're faced with an equally shite one now. How in the fook do we get out of this tomb? And even if we do, how do we manage not to get eaten by that black blob of hunger that got Halley?"

"I sent the hound from the tomb."

Damon turned to find the Stranger in the alcove. He smelled like old bones. Shadows haunted his expression.

"How did you get here?"

The Stranger knocked black hair out of his eyes and glanced over the edge into the void.

"I made this tomb centuries ago. It is mine to come and go as I please."

"Are you here to stop us from taking the Horn?"

"I am forbidden from directly interfering."

Lily snorted with derision.

"He doesn't need to stop us. We're stuck here. He only needs to watch us die of hunger and add our bones to this lovely place."

"It would bring me great sorrow to see you perish."

Damon believed the Stranger, even if he didn't know why. Not that he thought the Stranger couldn't lie.

"What are your plans with the Horn?"

Lily stepped forward.

"We told you already. We have to take it. Too many lives are in the balance."

"The Horn is too powerful. It always ends in tragedy."

"If my family dies, then worse things will happen in our world. We've been protecting the isles for centuries. If Medb falls then who will hold the shield?" asked Lily.

"We'll do everything we can to protect it," said Damon.

"Your sense of justice is strong, but you're insignificant when it comes to the beings that want the Horn. They'll easily cast you aside and take it."

"Then help us protect it," said Damon. "You're powerful and you seem to be able to visit Golden Willow. Remi told us as much."

"I cannot."

"Then what is your purpose if you can't?" he asked.

The Stranger smirked beneath the shadows.

"A servant. No more. I gave up my life a long time ago to serve the Lady of this realm." He stilled with thought, a thousand painful memories passing across his black eyes, before he seemed to remember others were watching. "The Horn won't help you in the way you think it will. It can't fix Medb, or the corruption. The rot is too deep. You have to find the source and cut it out, before it's too late."

"We're taking the Horn," said Remi.

The Stranger's response was both disappointed and elated, which confused Damon given the circumstances.

"I believe you when you say it's dangerous and that we won't be able to protect it and all that. But look what we've done so far. We're not incapable. And I get it, there are always more powerful beings out there. But that's no reason not to try. If we don't do something, then we're doomed to fail. Better to try the Horn. Try something. Try anything. Otherwise, I'd never be able to forgive myself. Otherwise, their sacrifice would be for nothing," said Remi as she strode to the Stranger.

Damon wanted to argue with her that theirs wasn't a sacrifice, but a naked grab for power, but he knew it wasn't the time. Despite what they'd done to her, they still existed as pseudo parents in her mind. She wanted to believe they had meaning. He would too if he were in her shoes.

The Stranger stared back at Remi, thousands of thoughts swirling across his black eyes.

"If you take the Horn, you'll know no rest. They'll come after you, try to destroy you or anyone you love in an attempt to acquire it. Are you sure you want to sentence your friends and family, the hospital, the other patients to that fate? Are you willing to pay the price, even if it means the destruction of everyone you know and love?"

"I am."

The Stranger stilled until Damon wondered if he would ever answer, but then he lifted his chin ever so imperceptibly. He stepped to the side as the air shimmered with unseen force. Damon didn't know what it was until he saw the garden behind the Mists.

"You may pass."

Damon hesitated until Remi nodded towards the Horn. He grabbed it in both arms. It was lighter than expected.

"Wait," said Lily, holding her hand out. "That's the Mists. Won't Lady Nimueh know what we've brought back?"

"She's not at the Mists and her sight is elsewhere. But it's the most convenient way back that won't cause more problems. Hurry, before I change my mind."

Lily nodded and hurried through the portal. Damon followed, but paused at the threshold before going over. Remi had approached the Stranger.

"Why are you doing this? Why are you helping us?"

"The portal is closing."

Damon held his hand out and Remi hurried over. They stepped into the garden behind the Mists together as the Stranger watched them from the empty tomb.

THIRTY-SEVEN

It was evening at Golden Willow. The hospital created a dome of light which felt like a sanctuary to Lily after all they'd been through. An ambulance passed them on the way to the ER, the driver's eyes wide when he saw them.

"I think we'll be getting a reception when we arrive," said Lily, tugging on the dirty clothes that had gotten them strange looks on the train.

Damon ran his hands through his messy hair.

"Are we sure the Horn is going to be okay at the clinic?"

"Dr. Marcie owes us, and she wants more help for her patients. Besides, she doesn't know what we hid there," said Remi.

"She won't be curious?" asked Damon.

"Did we have any better options?" asked Lily, who'd been in a foul mood since she tried to get the Horn to produce a cure for her family but came away empty.

Damon frowned.

When they stepped under the overhang, Remi glanced to the ceiling.

"I never thought I'd see this place again."

"Nor I," said Lily.

The chaos of the emergency room was both too much and strangely comforting.

"It's like coming back to my grandmother's house during the holidays," said Lily.

Boon appeared in the entryway with a clipboard under his arm and confusion on his brow.

"What happened to you three? We thought Broomfield secretly had you killed."

"It'd take a lot more than that asshole to take us down," said Lily, scowling.

"Well, I'm so glad to see you. This place hasn't been the same since you left."

"Since we left? We've only been gone a—"

Heavy footsteps startled Boon to head the opposite direction.

"I'll catch up with you later."

From around the corner at a brisk pace, Dr. Broomfield marched up to them in his white coat. His tight Afro had more steel gray than when they'd left.

"Where have you been? The hospital had to put out a missing persons report. You can't just leave the school and expect to waltz back and resume your studies. You should have just—"

His tirade was interrupted when Dr. Fairlight came hurrying around the corner. Her dirty-blonde hair was pulled back in a ponytail while the bags under her eyes had grown two sizes.

"Oh, thank Merlin. You're safe."

The Chief of Staff hugged them each in turn, then stood back with her arms crossed and her palm cupped under her chin.

"What happened? Where have you been these last months?"

Remi coughed.

"Months? It's only been a week, maybe a little longer."

The realization set in that their trip through the Fae had been time stretched. Lily was aware that it happened at times. Going to the Fae might take longer than their experience would suggest, but this was more than usual. She suspected that Kabo had something to do with their experience.

"It wasn't our intent," said Damon.

"Where have you been?" asked Dr. Fairlight.

Dr. Broomfield forced his way back into the conversation.

"What does it matter? They've been absent for months, a complete dereliction of duty. They put their patients' lives at risk. They should be immediately expelled from the hospital and the Hall."

"I cannot speak for Patron Jenner as the Hall is his to manage, but I would like to hear their reasons for being absent before I make any decisions."

"Well, I can speak for the patron. It will be my expectation that they will be expelled unless there is a reasonable explanation for this behavior. Which I seriously doubt is possible."

Dr. Fairlight turned.

"Damon, Lily, Remi, do you have an explanation?"

Lily was about to throw herself on the sword and blame her ties to the Fae, when Damon dug into his pocket and held out a handful of reddish-orange flowers that she remembered from the swamp.

"What is this?" asked Dr. Broomfield.

"Floremus, or death blooms."

"Where did you get those? They only grow in the Fae," said Dr. Fairlight.

Damon nodded.

"I've been working on Dr. Broomfield's alchemical challenge and I ran across some old literature from Roman times that suggested they used a flower that looked like old wounds to mix with the iron grass. There were suggestions that the flower came from the Fae, and after cross-referencing other readings, I thought it might be the floremus, or death blooms, from the lands of Autumn. I enlisted my friends to help me with what I thought would be a short trip, but things went astray and it took longer than we originally thought. Much longer. From our perspective, we were only gone a week."

Dr. Broomfield was focused on the crumpled flower in Damon's hands.

"Floremus? You think it'll fix the iron grass in the solution?"

"I'm almost positive. We wouldn't have risked a trip to the Fae if I didn't think it was."

Dr. Fairlight looked to Lily, who nodded, even though it was a total fabrication. She wondered if the plant would do anything with the iron grass, but then again, she'd never known Damon to lie and he had been working on the alchemy project in his spare time.

"How do I know this isn't a sad attempt to get out of your punishment?" asked Dr. Broomfield.

"You can test our clothes. This is mud from the Autumn Fae," said Remi.

"You won't have to do that. We can do a dye test right away," said Damon, heading towards the specialty alchemy lab that had been set up for Dr. Broomfield.

When they arrived, white-coated lab technicians were busy working their stations. Everyone stiffened at Dr. Broomfield's appearance. Damon went straight for an empty station.

"Could I get some iron grass extract?" asked Damon.

A beaker of the pale green liquid was set on the counter. Damon dug into the supply closet and produced a dark bottle with a rubber stopper. Then he took a quarter of the flower material and put it in a blender, which turned it into an orange goo once he ran the machine.

"If I add the floremus to the iron grass then it should excite the faez receptors, which should turn the entire mixture printer blue with the dye."

The other lab technicians slowed their work as they watched to see what was going to happen.

Lily held her breath as Damon poured the orange goo into the iron grass extract. He gave the mixture a few swirls with a glass mixer before reaching for the dye, but Dr. Broomfield put his hand over top.

"If this doesn't work, then I don't see why you should be a part of Aura Healers. While your intentions were noble, the fact that you were gone for nearly two months is inexcusable. Healers of your potential should be more aware of risks, even to themselves. Or at the very least, do more diligent research and check with their superiors before attempting such a foolish endeavor."

Dr. Fairlight cleared her throat. "Marcus...are you being too harsh?"

"It's my decision."

"Put the dye in. If it works as Damon suggested, then I think we'll owe them an apology," said Dr. Fairlight.

Lily held her breath when Damon squeezed three drops of amber liquid into the beaker. The drops disappeared into the mixture.

"What is it supposed to do?" asked Remi.

Damon peered into the glass.

"It should turn the surface pink."

Dr. Broomfield tilted his head.

"To think, you wasted two months and impacted countless people for a foolish endeavor. And to think I believed you were one of the strongest students in the hospital. But this egregious lapse of judgement proves I was incorrect."

Damon tapped on the glass.

"I was sure it was going to work. Maybe the flowers were too old. Maybe they need to be fresher. We could go back. Get new ones. I bet it would work then."

Dr. Fairlight put a hand on his shoulder.

"I'm sorry, Damon. I can do nothing about Hall matters."

Lily leaned close to the glass, putting her forehead against it. The surface was slightly warm.

"Is it an exothermic or endothermic reaction?" she asked.

Damon shifted his mouth to the side in thought.

"Exo."

She grabbed the glass and gave it a quick three swirls. As soon as the beaker hit the table, pink coloration bloomed within the center of the liquid.

"Blood and bone, it worked," said Damon.

Before anyone else could speak, applause broke out in the laboratory. The technicians were all cheering.

"The floremus won't be easy to get," said Dr. Broomfield as he scowled at the pink color. "But I suppose a difficult solution is better than none."

He held out his hand to Damon.

"My apologies, Damon Wolfhard. You've found a solution to the iron grass problem. In the most irresponsible way possible, but you did manage it."

"That's wonderful news," said Dr. Fairlight, throwing her arms around each of their shoulders in turn. "I guess you get to stay. Right, Marcus?"

He was focused on the beaker. Something about the way Dr. Broomfield stared hungrily at the changed liquid put a stone in Damon's gut.

"Huh? Yes, of course. They earned it."

"What will you do now?" asked Dr. Fairlight.

Lily was certain that the question was about the mixture, but Damon stretched his arms.

"I'm ravenous. I'd like to eat everything in the cafeteria, then take the longest, hottest shower known to man and wolf alike. Then sleep."

Dr. Broomfield checked his watch.

"You can eat and shower. You stink like a chicken coop, but I expect you back on shift in two hours. You have a lot of hours to catch up. All three of you. I wouldn't plan on getting any sleep through the summer."

It could have been worse, so they nodded and left Dr. Broomfield staring at the pinkish liquid with equal excitement and hunger.

"I hate that we did something for that asshole," said Remi in the hallway.

"Me too. I hope that doesn't come back to bite us later."

But thoughts of the alchemical mixture quickly disappeared as they reached the cafeteria and set their sights on eating gut-bursting amounts of hospital food.

THIRTY-EIGHT

Remi finished the death rites for Mr. Brown in the corner room. He thanked her for the ritual and clicked on the TV to continue watching *The Magelings* as he had before they'd come in.

"That was excellent, Miss Wilde. You've come into your own with the death magics," said Dr. Morsdux.

She squeezed her lips white while shaking her head.

"I've been back for three days and you haven't said a word about my unexcused absence. I missed the end for Miss Baker, Mr. Uvalde, and at least three others. I promised them I'd be there at the end and I wasn't."

Dr. Morsdux put a bony hand on her shoulder.

"I know you had your reasons."

Remi turned on him.

"How can you be so unconcerned about my behavior? I was gone for nearly two months!"

"Of course I was disappointed when you weren't here and so were the patients. I won't lie to you and tell you that they were pleased about your absence. But I won't treat you like a child, or like Dr. Broomfield."

"You heard about that?"

"Even before you came back, he was vocal about what he intended to do."

"I wasn't expecting you to banish me from the ward, but I was expecting you to get mad, or punish me."

Dr. Morsdux stared at her before turning.

"Come with me."

She followed him down to the lower floors, eventually ending up in the chapel while a service was going on. Two women in the pews in front were wailing while the other attendees sat quietly with their heads bowed. After they watched for a few minutes, Dr. Morsdux pulled her into the hallway.

"I don't understand. Was I supposed to see something?"

"It's not what you see, but what I see. In you. You're grieving. I don't know what happened on this trip to the Fae, but it ended badly, despite your success in finding the death blooms."

The memory of her once-parents disappearing into the void without a sound replayed in her mind for the thousandth time. She kept thinking of ways she could have saved them in that moment, but it didn't matter. They were dead. Even if they hadn't really been her parents, they were all she knew.

"It was a rough ending to the trip."

"Did it happen in the Veil?"

She lifted her head.

"How did you know I was in the Veil?"

The corner of his wrinkled lips curled upward.

"I can see it in you. There's something else too. You wield the Veil magics more easily now. They seem natural as if you've made peace with their strangeness."

"I wish I knew why that was."

"Did you see the Stranger?"

Remi sighed, but it did nothing to release the tension in her chest.

"He helped us on our journey."

"That's most unusual."

"Yeah, well, just about everything on our journey was unusual. I scarcely believe it myself now that I'm back here. It feels like a dream."

"A good or bad dream?"

"A dream that revealed truths I wasn't ready for."

"I see."

"I doubt it."

Dr. Morsdux clasped his hands in front.

"If you'd like to take some time off, I would approve it. I know that wouldn't relieve you from the duties that Dr. Broomfield has saddled you with, but maybe it would give you a chance to grieve."

"No," she said right away. "I think being in the ward and helping people on their final journey would comfort me more than having to contend with what happened."

"I see."

"Are your parents dead?"

Dr. Morsdux tilted his head.

"They have been for a decade now. Why do you ask?"

"Were they good people? Do you miss them?"

He opened and closed his mouth like a dying fish before finally answering.

"They were people like any other. A mix of good and bad, most of the bad stuff being artifacts of their time. They had unfortunate views about the nature of magic and people. They were also stern and somewhat emotionless, which made my youth a difficult time."

A grin ghosted to her lips at the thought of Dr. Morsdux thinking someone else was emotionless.

"Yes," he continued. "I was quite different back then. I would sneak out of the house to go to wild parties in Paris. Dance all night and sleep until noon the next day. I attended secret plays and played trumpet in a jazz band."

"I would have never guessed it."

"We hold multitudes, each of us. It's the one thing I've learned in my time in the ward. That no matter our actions in life, we go out the same way, scared and alone. And we can never truly understand what went on in someone else's life. Even if it appears bad on the surface. There are few true villains in this world. Mostly it's people struggling to make sense of it all."

Remi sighed again, this time feeling the vise loosening around her chest.

"Thank you, Dr. Morsdux. That was important to hear."

"I'm pleased."

"I'm ready to get back to work. If that's okay with you."

They walked in silence for most of the way back to the ward. When they were waiting for the elevator, he turned his head slightly.

"Whatever happened to the three sisters? Do we need to worry about them any longer?"

Remi smirked.

"No. We don't have to worry about them any longer. They got what they deserved."

The elevator dinged and the doors opened, revealing a mostly full car with room enough for two more.

"That's good news."

"It is."

He held the door open, but she shook him off.

"Go ahead. I'm going to take the stairs up. I need a moment to clear my head."

As soon as the door closed, her body shook with uncontrollable tears. She sobbed openly, then before anyone saw her, briskly strode to the stairs. Once she was in the echoing concrete stairwell, she leaned against the wall and let it all out. She wasn't sure how long she remained there, but when she was finished she felt like she'd run a marathon.

When she returned to the Hospice Ward, Remi grabbed a few tissues from a wall unit and cleaned up her face, before striding through the swinging doors.

THIRTY-NINE

Lily cradled the cheap beer between two hands, staring at the illusionary display over the Glitterdome as she enjoyed the peace and quiet of the hospital roof. Some band was having a concert, but she'd been working so many double shifts she barely knew what day it was, let alone the latest city events.

"Got room for one more?" asked Remi.

Lily reached between her legs to pull a beer from her cooler and handed it over.

"It tastes like warm piss, and my sisters would hex me for even being seen with it, but I have another shift in two hours so I didn't want to get battered."

Remi cracked the top of her can and after a swallow scowled at the drink.

"I've had worse." She raised her drink towards the center of the city.

"I see the Manics are in town."

"Any good?"

"Every year kids end up with early-stage faez madness trying to keep up with their antics."

From a distance, the illusions were difficult to make out except that it appeared the band was fighting something large and hairy.

"Doing okay?" asked Lily.

Remi crinkled the can as she stared at the rooftop.

"It's background noise that's always there when I slow down for a moment. I keep replaying that decision. Should I have tried to throw both ends of the rope to either side? Was there a way to keep the disc from falling? Two people died because of me."

"Two people?"

"They weren't my parents."

"But for a long time, you thought they were. That's a bloody head scrambler if you ask me."

Remi leaned her head against Lily's shoulder.

"Any idea who the lucky people might be?" asked Lily.

"My real parents? Not a clue."

"Going to try to find out who they are?"

Remi snorted.

"Would have to have free time for that. Dr. Broomfield is determined to make us so miserable we quit."

"He's a right bastard, he is."

"How's your family?" asked Remi, leaning away.

"Same. I mean, getting worse, but that hasn't changed. Bloody fooking Horn was a lie. Any liquid you want?"

"I know, I know."

"Don't look at me like that. I know everyone warned us that it wouldn't work for that. But I had to try. I had to know if the bloody Horn of Bran

Galed could fix them."

"You had to try..."

"Now what?" asked Lily.

"I wish I knew. We can't use it for anything important or bring attention to the fact that we have it. But I hate leaving it at its hiding place, even if I know that's the safest thing."

Lily nodded, thinking about Dr. Marcie's clinic. She'd agreed to hide the artifact without knowing a single thing about it, why it was important, or how much danger it would put them in.

"I came to the Halls because I thought it would help me fix the corruption, but I'm no fooking closer than I was when I first arrived. I'm a bloody failure."

"That's not true."

"No, it is. I don't get points for trying. And I'll never forgive myself if all my family dies and I'm left alive."

"They could leave Medb."

"Never happen. Not in a million years. It'd mean they wouldn't be witches. Wouldn't be themselves. It'd kill Medb too. Right away to have that much backlash. I know they've talked about letting a few of the young ones leave, but the rest, I think they'll go down with the bloody ship."

Remi took a long swig, then crumpled the can and tossed it behind them to clatter across the roof.

"Ick. That was gross. Wish we had time for the smoke bar."

"I'd take a whiskey neat in my room if I could."

"I'm worried about next year," said Remi.

"Me too."

Remi shook her head.

"I can feel it. Like a thunderstorm brewing in the distance, and your skin feels electric. I worry about what it means when it gets here."

"Is this some sort of Veil premonition?"

"No. Just logic. The moment we brought the Horn back, we put a lot of awful futures into play. I fear we should have listened to the Stranger."

"He was a strange chap."

"I kinda liked him."

Lily smirked.

"You would."

Remi elbowed her.

"Not like that. But, I don't know, I sensed his melancholy. It's the same thing I feel in the Hospice Ward. Duty, sadness, pride, the elation of helping someone at their worst moments. It's messed up, but I always strangely like it."

"I'm glad you've found something for you."

Remi rotated on the top of the picnic table.

"I won't rest until we've fixed the corruption. I can't let that happen to you, or your family. Not to mention, I think it'd screw up the realms too."

"I appreciate that, Remi," said Lily with a heavy heart. "But I knew that already."

Dual buzzes from their phones had them both groaning. Lily refused to look, but Remi checked her phone.

"Broomfield."

"Another meeting to tell the lot of us how stupid we are."

"And how lazy."

"And lucky we are to have him!"

"And that if we don't shape up, we'll be shipping out!"

Lily drop-kicked her can against the metal HVAC unit and pulled a stick of gum out of her white coat.

"Want half?"

"Better not smell like beer. Again."

Lily chuckled under her breath.

"Hey, you know what?" asked Remi.

Lily raised an eyebrow.

"Only one more year under that bastard."

"One more year. Doesn't sound so bad."

"Yeah, if we can survive it."

Lily paused with her hand on the door. She checked over her shoulder at the sound of two howlers headed their way.

"I believe we'll survive. But will everyone else?"

§ § §

This ends the fourth book of the Aura Healers Hall series. Stayed tuned for the fifth and final book:

THE DEATHLESS KING

Special Thanks

From the ashes of failure, new growth can form.

As my newsletter readers know, this series started off as something entirely different. I wrote a book that once I got to the end I realized was neither a Hundred Halls story, nor was good enough to publish. Yet, without it, this series wouldn't exist in the wonderful form that it does. For that I have to thank my best friend and wife of twenty-seven years, Rachel, for her excellent advice as we discusssed what I should do with that failed book on the way to see Phish in Denver for four days. That conversation helped me find clarity of where I'd gone wrong as well as how to start over with fresh eyes.

I must also thank my team who help make each novel as best as it can be: Sasha Almazan & Gene Mollica from GS Covers, Tamara Blain from A Closer Look Editing, the beta reader team (Tina Rak, Andie Alessandra Cáomhanach, Lana Turner, Phyllis Simpson, and Melanie Coupland), as well as my writing group that we affectionately call the Murder Cabin (Andrea Stewart, Anthea Lawson/Sharp, Annie Bellet, Megan O'Keefe, Marina J. Lostetter, Jamie Thornton, and Tina Gower). Additionally, the Vanguard plays defense for little errors that sneak through the cracks, and for this book, I have Leslie King, Debbie Davis, Phyllis Simpson, and Brian Busby to thank!

ABOUT THE AUTHOR

Thomas K. Carpenter resides in Colorado with his wife Rachel. When he's not busy writing his next book, he's hiking, skiing, and getting beat by his wife at cards. He keeps a regular blog at www.thomaskcarpenter.com and you can follow him on twitter @thomaskcarpente. If you want to learn when his next novel will be hitting the shelves and get free stories and occasional other goodies, please sign up for his mailing list by going to: http://tinyurl.com/thomaskcarpenter. Your email address will never be shared and you can unsubscribe at any time.

www.ingramcontent.com/pod-product-compliance
Lightning Source LLC
Chambersburg PA
CBHW030423310726
48979CB00009B/1592/J

* 9 7 8 1 9 5 8 4 9 8 2 6 2 *